Face to face with the fey folk!

We locked eyes. I knew, instinctively, that I should look away, pretend not to see him, just go about my business, but the rational part of my mind still had a fingertip hold on my body. Mind told body: Stay put. The creature doesn't exist. The market doesn't exist. You're imagining things. You're high.

But I wasn't high. I'd been wasted too many times not to recognize the effects. This time I was stone cold sober and gaping like an idiot as some sort of monstrosity—Bogie? Goblin? Kobold?—crept towards me.

Step, lurch, step. He took awkward strides across the street, the effort to walk upright with a bent spine belying the power in his legs. Step, lurch, step. An ungainly gait, but closing the distance faster than I would have liked.

I was still trying to convince myself that it was the single most lucid and horrific hallucination I had ever seen when the creature revealed surprisingly white and pointed teeth in a wide grin and leapt at me. The rational part of my mind went gibbering off into the darkness and my fight or flight reflex jammed a triple load of adrenaline into my system.

I bolted. . . .

Also by Adam Stemple

• • •

Pay the Piper (with Jane Yolen)

SINGER OF SOULS

• • •

ADAM STEMPLE

A TOM DOHERTY ASSOCIATES BOOK
NEW YORK

SINGER OF SOULS

Edited by Patrick Nielsen Hayden

A Tor Book
Published by Tom Doherty Associates, LLC
175 Fifth Avenue
New York, NY 10010

www.tor.com

ISBN-13: 978-0-765-35027-5
ISBN-10: 0-765-35027-0

First edition: August 2005
First mass market edition: October 2006

Printed in the United States of America

0 9 8 7 6 5 4 3 2 1

FOR MS. JANE HYATT YOLEN,
WITHOUT WHOM NONE OF THIS
WOULD HAVE BEEN POSSIBLE

Surely Elisha's servant having his eyes opened, as in 2 Kings 6:17, and seeing the mountains full of horses and chariots of the Heavenly Host shows that there is a Sight beyond ordinary, acquirable even on Earth, by infusing some quality in the eye. That Intelligences traverse daily among us on Earth, directing, warning, or encamping about the faithful, though unknown and unseen to most men that live.

—Robert Kirk, *The Secret Commonwealth,* c. 1690

Singer of Souls

• • • one • • •

I held the needle in my hand and flicked it idly with my right index finger.

January twentieth, I thought. *Only took twenty days to break my one New Year's resolution.*

"Doc?"

Doc. Not my real name, or my job. But ever since I'd spent one night, twisted out of my gourd, speaking entirely in rhyme, I had been known as Dr. Seuss. Doc for short.

I looked around the cramped apartment. Winter coats and unwashed roommates were draped over every available surface not already covered in beer cans or dishes. Nicky, one of two ex-girlfriends in the room, lit a cigarette, adding to the gray-brown cloud that clung to the ceiling.

"I cooked you up a nice one, Doc," she said, her voice already tobacco-rough despite being just out of her teens.

It's not too late, I thought, watching the liquid in the needle quiver each time I flicked it. I was through the hard part, the physical symptoms of withdrawal fading, and only the mental addiction to go. I had beat it; I had won. But here I was, three weeks of Hell about to go to waste because I couldn't say no to a pretty face and a simple, "You want a taste?"

Handling withdrawal had been easy. I didn't even remember the first few days—though apparently I did a lot of screaming and smashed a fair number of things—but I came through with no new scars and all my most worthy possessions intact. Which is to say, I didn't break my guitar. The stomach cramps that followed were painful, but not deadly, and the shakes and hallucinations were a lot like dropping acid outside in the cold Minnesota winter, a not-uncommon occurrence. The puking was a bit more troubling, but I'd thrown up at least as much drinking cheap tequila or Southern Comfort. Even the explosive diarrhea, once I learned to catch it in time, just meant an extra minute or two on the can. I brought a book or a crossword puzzle with me and waited it out.

I couldn't wait this one out.

I put my hand over Nicky's as she tied me off, then looked around at my motley collection of friends.

"I love you guys," I said, and received many a woozy smile and a few blank stares in return. And I did love the whole dirty, pierced lot of them. Pulling Nicky's hand off my arm, I continued, "But I won't see any of you ever again."

If I did, they'd be the death of me.

My hand shook as I dropped the needle in her open palm.

Nicky shrugged and sat down in my chair, tugging at the one long forelock on her otherwise closely shorn skull. She waved for the tube around my arm, and began prepping herself. She'd take my load.

When I came out of my room a short time later carrying a small bag and my guitar, I didn't expect much of a send-off. I wasn't disappointed. Counting two waves and one, "Later, man," I was out the door, down the two flights of stairs, and on the street, homeless for the first time in six years.

I had learned early on that it's one thing to be a junkie, it's another to be a *homeless* junkie. No matter how strung out I got, I always had enough money stashed away to pay rent. "Roof money," I called it.

The Christmas season had been good to me. I'd staked out a particularly busy spot in the rat's warren of downtown skyways and bribed the beat cop with donuts every morning so he wouldn't move me on. The coins had flown into my open guitar case in great numbers and I had nearly seven hundred dollars of "roof money" hidden about my person when I left the apartment. Now I needed somewhere to spend it.

I walked east on Lake Street, past two gas stations perched on opposite sides of the street. They were locked in mortal mercantile combat, the slings and arrows—LOWEST PRICES! BEST GAS! FREE CARWASH!—they hurled across the four-lane DMZ almost making me duck my head. I smiled at the outlandish characters perched in the window display of a purple brick-fronted bookstore. I'd passed many an afternoon there, reading in the easy chair set out for potential customers. Never following through on the implied contract to buy, I just read novel after novel until the counter girl threw me out—sometimes pissed off, sometimes with a "See ya tomorrow or the next day, Doc." I passed a tattoo parlor and a hemp store and a shop that sold stripper's clothing (what there was of that particular product) before finally turning right onto Lyndale Avenue. It was cold, Minneapolis cold, and by the time I reached Twin Town Guitars on the corner of Thirty-fourth Street, I was shivering with it.

"Hey, Zee," I said as I entered.

Zack Johannson, the owner of Twin Town Guitars, was mantling a '79 Strat with its guts splayed out. Older—in his thirties—he was married, with a new baby. A retired musician, he was an addict like me. Only his addiction was gear: exotic, expensive, hard-to-find guitar gear. It was going to be tough for him to get rich owning a music store; he was a dealer who kept dipping into his own stash.

"Doc! The Lowden need some love?" He glanced up from his work only long enough for identification. The smell of solder was in the air.

My guitar did need a little attention. Dress the frets, maybe shave the bridge down a little.

"Nope."

"Picks? Strings?"

I shook my head. "Nah. I need to ask you a favor."

"Sure. What's up?" He grinned. "Doc."

"Haven't heard that one before," I said dryly before grinning back. "I need a place to stay for a couple of days. Just lost my apartment."

Zack unbent from over the Strat. He put his hands on his hips and twisted from side to side until his back gave several audible cracks.

"No can do," he said. "The wife would never go for it."

"I really need your help on this one, Zack." I needed to stay with someone who wasn't going to offer me dope every other day.

"Don't you have any family you could stay with?"

"No." I couldn't go back to my parents' house—I'd left that bridge a smoking ruin—and as for my brother and sister, youthful sibling rivalry had blossomed into full-blown resentment and bitterness. There'd be no help there.

Wait a minute. A thought hit me hard enough to stop my whining to Zack. *Maybe it was time to implement The Plan.*

When I was thirteen years old, we'd flown to Edinburgh, Scotland, to see my maternal grandmother. Grandma McLaren, short and matronly but tough as a Franklin Avenue crack dealer, with a voice that could still make my mother jump. The trip ended badly, as all our family outings inevitably did, but I distinctly recalled Grandma McLaren saying, "If any of you kids ever want to visit, you're welcome to stay here as long as you like."

Something about that had stuck with me, and I'd always thought that if I could get clean, maybe get a little money saved, I'd take her up on that.

Maybe I could get to Scotland, stay at Grandma McLaren's, in a place where I didn't know anyone. And where no one knew me. A place where I wouldn't know where to score even if my will failed me again.

A pipe dream, whispered a dark voice inside me. *Forget The Plan. Forget Zack. Go back to your apartment.*

I could almost feel the needle in my skin.

Yeah, I thought. *It was a nice walk in the cold, but now it's time to go back home. A pipe dream.*

Or was it? Grandma McLaren, the little I remembered of her, hadn't struck me as someone who would make an offer like that lightly. *I am clean—or mostly, anyway—and I've got a little money saved.*

I clamped down on the nay-saying voices and ticked off the things I would need. *Passport, plane ticket, Grandma McLaren's address . . .*

"Zack, can I borrow your credit card?"

"No fucking way."

I dug into pockets and socks and chained wallet, spilling my roof money out onto the counter.

"Here, Zack. Take it." His eyes bulged to see me with that much cash. "I just need your card to get a plane ticket. I try to pay cash and they're going to get the guy with the longest fingers at the airport to give me the twice-over."

"A plane ticket?" Zack ran a hand through his hair. It had been cobalt blue the last time I'd been in. He must have dyed it back to normal after his kid was born. "You going somewhere?"

"Scotland," I nodded. "Visit my grandmother."

"Scotland, eh?" Zack began scooping the crumpled bills into his free hand and stuffing them into his pockets. "You got a passport?"

I shook my head. "Going downtown to get one today." I smiled inwardly. *I was really going to do it!*

"It'll be a while till it gets here," Zack said.

"Really? How long?"

"Couple of weeks, maybe?"

You won't last three days, said the voice. *Go home.*

"Shit."

"What are you going to do till then?"

"That's why I need a place to—"

"Can't do it, Doc." He began pulling bills back out of his pocket. Spreading them flat on the counter. "Here, take your money back."

A bell hanging over the front door jangled loudly, signaling a potential customer had just entered. Zack and I turned to see a teenager with a junior rock mullet and an Audioslave concert tee saunter into the store.

"Hey," he squeaked. "You guys give lessons here?"

"Guitar?" said Zack. He didn't need to ask. This kid had "Aspiring Rock God" tattooed all over his face.

"Yeah," the kid said.

Before Zack could answer, I said, "Sure we do, Boss. In the basement. Head on down—I'll be with you in a second."

"Doc," Zack warned.

"I don't have an ax." The kid scratched his belly, gazing wide-eyed up at the rows of guitars that lined the walls. "Yet."

"Don't worry about that," I said. "I'll bring one down for you to play."

"Doc . . ."

"You like Gibsons, Boss?"

The kid nodded. "Hell, yeah."

"Hey, Doc." Zack was beginning to sound angry.

"I'll bring you a Les Paul," I said, still ignoring Zack. "Head on down." The kid wandered downstairs and I finally turned, holding my hand up to Zack before he could speak again. "Zack, let me do this," I pleaded. "I've been playing music since I was five. I even went to school for it. Probably have a degree somewhere I could show you."

"Doc—"

"I can do this. I don't even want to get paid!"

Zack blinked. "I'm listening."

"Okay, here it is. I work for you. Lessons, repairs, sales. Anything. You let me stay here in the store. In the basement. I've seen the cot down there."

Zack nodded. "Yeah."

"And when my passport comes, I'm gone."

I could see him weighing the wisdom of letting a junkie stay in his store after hours.

He won't go for it, said the voice, ever the pessimist. *He isn't that stupid.*

But the voice sounded doubtful. Zack had known me since before I was the Aspiring Rock God's age. Since before I used. He'd give me this one chance. And if I blew it, he'd never talk to me again. Never let me in the store. And he knew I loved the store.

"Okay," he said. "It's a deal." He pushed the pile of now neatly folded bills toward me. "You better take your money till you get your tickets, so you have something to live on."

Yeah, said the voice, desperately. *Without money, you can't—*

That's right, I silenced the voice. *I can't.*

"Tell you what, Zack," I said, sending the cash back across the counter to him. "Why don't you hold on to it? And up my pay to room and board."

I could see it dawning on him, what I was trying to do. He suddenly realized the danger the money represented to a recovering junkie with time on his hands.

"Yeah. I guess I'd better hold on to the money." He pulled it toward him, then looked up. "How much board?"

"Two burgers and a six-pack a day oughtta do it."

"Okay," he said. "But you're sharing the beer."

"Pleasure doing business with you, Zee." I shook his hand, then headed down to the basement to give my first lesson.

I SETTLED INTO my first regular job easily. I was a musician, after all, and spending my time surrounded by the tools of my trade—playing them, fixing them, talking them up to potential buyers—was not a bad way to go. And during the day, the busywork and out-of-tune students kept my demons at bay. But each night, I lay on my tiny cot, staring wide-eyed into the near dark until the cords and wires that hung from the walls began to twist and move in the moonlight. LEDs and power strips glowed like eye-shine round a campfire and whenever I finally drifted off to sleep, I inevitably came awake with a start minutes later.

You could get up, said the voice. *You could walk ten blocks. You could knock on the door of your old apartment and shoot yourself into a peaceful slumber within the hour.*

I lay still and waited for morning to come.

MY PASSPORT ARRIVED after ten days.

"A good likeness, Doc," Zack said, peering over my shoulder.

It was a chiaroscuro image, all white face and black hair, sharp lines of cheekbones and nose. Like a fossil of someone I used to see in the mirror. I wished he was wrong.

It turned out I couldn't fly direct to Edinburgh on the money I had. I could only get a ticket to Glasgow and then take a train cross-country. But even to Glasgow, the plane ticket cost nearly all my ready cash. I didn't have enough left for a train ticket. Once I changed my remaining dollars into pounds, I suspected I wouldn't even have enough for a candy bar.

No problem. From what I remembered of my last visit to Grandma McLaren's, Scotland was littered with hitchhikers. And it must be safer there than in this country, because my grandmother, all five foot one of her, had continually picked up German teenagers even rattier-looking than me without hesitation.

So, it was to be my thumb for transportation and my guitar for working capital. Wouldn't be the first time.

As a last favor, Zack gave me a ride to the airport. We banged fists at the curb.

"Good luck, Doc," he said. "Have a good trip."

"Thanks, Zee. Thanks for everything."

I checked my guitar, suffered through one perfunctory search and two thorough ones, and boarded the plane. As soon as we were off the ground, I spent the little cash I had on three miniature bottles of Jack Daniel's, trying to drink myself to sleep. But it wasn't what I wanted, or it just wasn't enough, and I succeeded only in souring my stomach, which made the airplane food seem even less appealing. I refused every meal the attendants offered on the long transatlantic crossing.

I ARRIVED IN Glasgow, hung over and tired. And hungry. Once on the ground, my appetite recovered with a vengeance, and not even the gigantic plaid decals peeling off the airport windows could put me off my feed. I was hungry enough to eat the proverbial horse. I was even hungry enough to eat one of the airplane meals, but I had missed my last opportunity somewhere over Iceland.

Stone broke and starving, it seemed everyone I saw was eating. An attractive older woman pulled granola bars and juice boxes from a backpack her husband wore, producing them with a magician's flourish to the delight of her children. A man in a suit ate from a package of pretzels stolen from the beverage cart. Why hadn't I thought of that? Even the customs official made me wait while he finished off some sort of pastry. He licked his fingers clean and motioned me forward.

"Name?" he asked.

"Douglas Stewart."

"Well, that's a fine Scottish name."

"So they tell me."

"Purpose of your visit?"

To get clean. "Visit my grandmother."

"That the address you have listed here?" He pointed to the customs form I had filled out.

I nodded. I hoped it was, anyway. It had cost me a half-hour of tense long-distance conversation with my sister to get it.

The customs official plucked another pastry out of a bag on his desk and took a bite off the corner. I tried not to salivate as the spicy-sweet smell hit me right in my empty stomach.

"You don't look too good, son," he said, taking in my dirty clothes and dearth of luggage. He brushed his hand twice across his uniform front and sent a shower of puffy flakes to the floor. "Not good at all."

Uh oh, I thought. *Don't panic.* I shrugged. "Long flight."

"No," he said, his eyes starting to go all cop-flat. "It's not just that."

I'm strung out, broke, starving, and I'm about to enter your country for an indefinite amount of time without a work visa. Okay, so I couldn't say that. But I had to tell him something. And in my experience, a half truth always works better than a whole lie.

"Tell you the truth," I lied, "I'm hung over and starving." I pointed at the pastry in his hand. "And you are absolutely torturing me with that . . . that . . . what is that?" It appeared to have a hot dog or something inside the puff pastry. "A meat donut?"

He laughed at that. "That, my young American friend, is what we in Scotland call a 'sausage roll.' "

"A sausage roll?"

He nodded.

"I'll have to get me one of them."

"Good plan." My condition was apparently explained to his liking because he popped the rest of the sausage roll in his mouth and ran his finger down my paperwork. "How are you getting to Edinburgh?" he asked, his voice muffled by dough and meat.

"I'll take the train," I lied again. "Right after I have a sausage roll or three."

He laughed and stamped my forms. "On you go, then."

OUTSIDE, IT WAS cloudy but still bright and, at what felt like thirty degrees, quite warm for someone used to Minnesota winters. I stuck out my thumb when I had walked a fair distance from the airport and was picked up by an elderly couple within minutes.

"Wa ya gang?" the old man asked. It took me a few seconds to decipher his thick Glaswegian accent. *Where are you going?*

"Edinburgh," I replied.

"Good. Ye dinnae wanna spend any more time in Glasgow then ye have to."

"Why not? Nothing to see here?"

"Och, aye, there is."

"What's that, then?"

The old man winked at me in the rearview mirror. "Edinburgh."

He guffawed and slapped his knee while his wife sighed loudly, as if she had heard the same joke a thousand times before.

I laughed, too, and, encouraged, he began spinning a yarn involving himself, an Irish merchant marine, and a three-legged cat, but I was too tired and hungry to give it my full attention. I leaned my head against the window and watched the world speed by on the wrong side of the road, Glasgow's tenements and factories slowly turning into rolling hills dotted with stone farmhouses. The old man's swift guttural words soon became a meaningless lullaby and I drifted off to sleep.

I SWAM UP out of my strung-out slumber with difficulty. Nicky was tying me off again, but this time she used a guitar string. It cut into my flesh and, unlike in most dreams, I could feel the pain quite vividly. I tried to speak, but she covered my mouth with a third hand and said, "I'm cooking you up a nice one, Doc," before sticking a foot in my chest and heaving back on the string with all her might. I could smell her breath, spicy-sweet and earthy, like sex and a sausage roll.

"Och," she said in a thick Glaswegian accent. "Wake up."

I blinked twice. Once in my dream and once as I woke up. The old man was suspended in midair over me. *No, wait.* The world spun and righted itself and I realized I had fallen to the side as I slept. I now looked at the old man as he leaned in over me through the open back door. My arm was painfully asleep and I was still starving.

But I was in Edinburgh.

"Wow," I said, and rubbed my eye with the arm that still had feeling left in it. "I didn't realize you would take me all the way here. Thanks."

"Well, it wasnae far out of our way. Now, I hate long good-byes," he said, and dragged me bodily out of the car by my lifeless arm. "So awa with ye."

I just barely cleared my guitar and bag from the trunk before the couple's car was in motion and I was left on the street.

Edinburgh was stone. Gray stone, brown stone, red stone, stone blackened with age, stained with smoke, shaped by wind and water. There were stone buildings, stone walls, stone bridges. Arches, pillars, crenelations—all of stone.

Turning slowly, I tried to get my bearings. It had been nine years since I'd been here and I was just barely a teenager then. But some things still looked familiar. There was a black tower—made of stone—just across the street from me, like something out of a demented fairy tale. I had a hazy memory of climbing up its cramped stairs and getting stuck, backpack to the wall and head sticking out a window that overlooked a three-story drop. Claustrophobia and vertigo at the same time.

I found a road sign stuck high up on the wall of a building: PRINCES STREET. I let my gaze travel the length of the busy shop-lined road, past the black tower again—*Walter Scott Memorial!* I remembered—and all the way to the huge castle that perched on top of the hill like a dragon on its cache of gold. That didn't help me figure out where I was; Edinburgh Castle could be seen from just about anywhere in town. But at the bottom of the hill, I noticed train tracks running toward me before disappearing under a bridge directly to my left.

I did a left-face a sergeant major would be proud of and quick-marched until I could see where the tracks went: Waverly Station. I was a hundred yards from cab stands and phone booths. All I had to do was cross the street.

I stepped off the curb and narrowly avoided certain death in the form of a speeding Mini. The driver slammed on his brakes and I could see his mouth form the words "bloody tourist" as I leapt back onto the sidewalk.

Oh yeah, I thought. *Look to the right first in this country.*

I played it safe and looked both ways repeatedly till I spotted a break in traffic, then crossed the street with my head still on a swivel—right, left, right, left—finally reaching the other side without any further threat to life or limb. Traveling down the long ramp into the train station, I thought maybe I had got it wrong and I was heading into a subway system. But I could still see sky when I hit bottom. I thought of the street above me; the castle even farther up the hill. Pictured the multiple bridges I'd seen spanning train tracks and park trails and streets and even other bridges, till the city looked like an Escher woodcut.

Edinburgh is stone, I said to myself. *And multileveled.*

I found the phones and read the instructions printed on them carefully before attempting my call. Grandma McLaren answered on the fourth ring, accepting the charges from her, I hoped, favorite grandson.

"Young Dougie," she said, pronouncing it "Doogie." "So nice of you to call. How are you?" Her accent was a strange amalgam of the many places she had lived when she was younger: Scotland, Ireland, England, the U.S.

"I'm good, Grandma," I replied. "But I'm here." I hadn't called to inform her I was coming. Easier to get forgiveness than permission, I'd figured.

"Here? In Scotland?"

"In Edinburgh. At the train station."

"Well, grab a cab and come visit."

"Um . . ." I had no money for a cab.

"Wait," she said, "I need to get some groceries, anyway. And a strapping young lad to carry them is just what the doctor ordered. I'll come fetch you."

She arrived in under fifteen minutes, driving a Peugeot that looked old but meticulously cared for. Much like herself.

"Grandma!" I yelled to her as she pulled to the curb. She scanned right past me and then swung her head back in surprise. I guess I was a little different from the thirteen-year-old she'd last seen. I'm not real sure what I looked like back then, but it probably wasn't tattooed, tall, and rail-thin, with a wardrobe that ran mainly to hand-painted black leather and combat boots. She leaned over and unlocked the passenger door. When I had folded myself into the car, she eyed me carefully, up and down. It was as if she could read the nine years of my life since she had seen me last and wasn't too impressed with the result.

"You," she said, "look like shit."

I nodded. I felt like shit, too, but didn't bother mentioning that.

"You aren't here on vacation, are you?"

I shook my head.

"I assume you wish to stay with me for a wee bit, then?" she asked. She didn't look too thrilled at the prospect. "Till you get yourself back together?"

I nodded again.

"I have only three rules," she said, holding up three wrinkled fingers. "But if you break any of them I will throw you out on your ear."

Another nod. Quite the conversationalist.

"One," she said. "Don't ever offer me money. You don't pay me rent. You are family, so you are my guest. For as long as you need." She dropped one finger, leaving her hand in a peace sign configuration. "Two. Don't ask me for money and don't steal from me. Or anyone else for that matter. If you can't support yourself honestly while living rent free then you're no good to anyone." I waited for her to drop her middle finger but she dropped her index finger instead. "Three," she said, shaking her hand at me, her middle finger proudly extended. "Don't fuck with me. I've buried three husbands and I'll bury you, too, if need be. We clear?"

"Crystal, Grandma."

She started the car. "You're probably starving after your flight." She patted me on the knee like I was thirteen once more. "Let me buy you a sausage roll."

I loved Grandma McLaren.

MAYBE IT WAS the two sausage rolls Grandma McLaren bought for me finally settling my growling stomach, or maybe I was just done in by jet lag, but I was asleep about two minutes after entering her house. One second I was being enveloped by her ancient but very fluffy couch while she puttered in the kitchen making tea, and the next thing I knew it was dark out and Grandma McLaren was shaking me gently and telling me my room was ready.

"You should try to get some proper rest in a bed. Turn your internal clock around." She led me up a short set of carpeted stairs and into a den that had been hastily converted into a guest room by the addition of an air mattress and a travel alarm clock.

"Now, don't let me see you again till the sun is up," Grandma McLaren said, clucking and shooing me into the room. I barely managed to get my boots off before collapsing onto the bed for ten hours of dreamless sleep.

• • • TWO • • •

The morning sun set up shop in an east-facing window and began prying my eyelids open at roughly a quarter past obscenely early. When I could no longer ignore it, I stumbled downstairs hoping Grandma McLaren had coffee in the house. The stairs dumped me into a foyer that provided a good view of the entire house: a living room with a decent-sized TV, completely inadequate stereo system, and the aforementioned man-eating fluffy couch; a minuscule dining room with a four-top wooden table and chair set housing a dried flower centerpiece; a plain interior door leading to Grandma McLaren's bedroom; and, straight ahead, a tidy kitchen with actual tile flooring, a half-fridge that looked incapable of holding more than two pounds of food, and an AGA cooker—a Swedish contraption, ridiculously popular in Britain, that turned perfectly good gas into "nondrying radiant heat."

As I got to the kitchen, Grandma McLaren was just pulling a steaming kettle off the AGA to fill a press pot of ground coffee beans that sat on the counter by her left hand.

I loved Grandma McLaren.

"Morning, Dougie!" she exclaimed, far too cheerfully for so early in the day.

I grunted what I hoped was "good morning" in reply, but I knew I would be incapable of intelligible speech until I had a cup of coffee in me. Heroin I could quit; they'd have to pry my coffee cup from my cold dead fingers.

Grandma McLaren smiled knowingly and said nothing more until I had drunk a cup and a half of the bitter black gold.

"So what's on the docket for today?" she asked. We were sitting in the dining room, my chair scraping the wall and my feet nearly poking out the other side of the table. Plates with a single egg, a stewed tomato, sausage, and cold toast sat in front of each of us. "A little sightseeing? Maybe bum around the Old Town? See a show?"

I laughed and narrowly avoided choking on a bite of sausage. We both knew she was setting me up. "Thought I would get to work, Grandma."

She nodded. "Good answer. Newspaper's on the stoop. Plenty of jobs to be had."

"Don't need one."

She looked up from her breakfast and raised one eyebrow at me. "You didn't impress me as a young man who had arranged himself employment before this trip. Am I wrong?"

I shook my head. Here came the hard sell. It was tough trying to convince someone—especially a family member—that playing your guitar on the streets was a viable occupation. But the truth was, I was good at what I did. I understood the business of panhandling. I knew which corners made money. I knew how to talk store owners into letting me play and not moving me on. I could spot a cop before he spotted me, and I could always tell which ones would take money to let me stay and which ones would be offended by the suggestion.

And, most important, I had a hook.

See, it's not enough to just sit out there playing your guitar with your case open. Might as well join the guys with their hands out asking for spare change. Pool your money at the end of the day and maybe buy a six-pack. No, you need something to bring people in, make them *give* you money.

I knew a guy, every morning he would hit the street with a pocket full of quarters. He would line them up to spell out a capital *B*, a capital *E*, and half of another *E*. Then he would whip out a sign that said HELP ME FINISH MY BEER and just wait for the money to roll in. Soon as he got close to finishing the word and nobody was looking, he'd scoop half the change into his pocket. He had no discernible talent or skills. Yet he made a ton of money.

A hook.

I had come up with my hook the same night I got my nickname. I figured that if I could speak in rhyme, then with a little extra effort I could sing the words as well. Which meant, with one more additional push, I could play chords to back my singing. Instant songs.

The rhyming came easy. Coming up with unique and listenable melodies was more difficult. Discovering chords to match both was nearly impossible. But I am an obsessive person by nature, and I had a lot of time on my hands. I spent weeks practicing, trying to come up with spontaneous melodies and chord progressions. I don't know whether it was my natural ear or the music theory that had been drummed into me since childhood, but before long I could sing a unique couplet about any subject given to me, with no pause except the deep breath needed to begin singing. String a few couplets together and I'd have a verse. From there, the songs practically wrote themselves.

I tried to avoid doggerel. *Baby* and *maybe* had no place in my songs. I scoffed at false rhymes like *time* and *mind* and tried to avoid stock chord progressions like the twelve-bar blues or the fifties doo-wop song. I used my voice to its best advantage. I had an arresting tenor with just enough whiskey grit in it to not sound feminine, and I knew which notes to go for and which to leave behind. When my hook was ready, I took it to the streets.

It turned out to be a dynamic act. I sang about the news or the weather or just riffed on people who were walking by, writing songs about the way they walked or what they were wearing or where I thought they were going. Singing about the people garnered the most attention. Crowds were drawn and my take went up. But there was still something missing. Something to not only draw the people to me, but draw the money out of their pockets as well.

And then I had it. I was too scattershot, too random to really make people pay attention. I was losing money by singing about people who would never give me a nickel while other, more generous souls walked clean by. What I needed to figure out was who would pay and who wouldn't, and I needed to sing directly to the less miserly.

So I came up with a novel idea. For one dollar, I would ask my mark a few questions about himself and then sing a short, unique, and—if I say so myself—quite catchy song about him. For five, I would record the song on a stolen tape deck I had bought for twenty dollars and give the mark the cassette.

The money rolled in like I had a straight job at a law firm. It seemed my hook tapped into a deep-seated need of the human race. There is nobody on this earth who doesn't, deep down, feel that they are worthy of notice. That they have done deeds worth recording. That sagas should be written about their exploits.

That songs should be sung about them.

Not that any of this mattered. To most people I was still just a bum on the street corner looking for handouts.

"No," I said to Grandma McLaren, trying to lean back and look nonchalant. There was no room for my chair to lean, however, and I succeeded only in banging the back of my head against the wall.

Smooth.

"I didn't arrange a job," I continued, rubbing the back of my head. "But I know I can make money with my guitar."

"Where?" She leaned forward, pinning me with her eyes.

I sighed. *Here goes nothing.* "On the street." I prepared to launch into a well-practiced though unfailingly futile attempt to make my chosen profession sound both glamorous and lucrative. To my surprise, a broad smile spread across Grandma McLaren's face.

"You're a busker!" she cried out happily.

"A what-er?" Obviously, this was not the reaction I was expecting.

"A busker. Edinburgh is a great city for busking." She was visibly bouncing in her chair. "Oh! I can take you to all the best places to play."

"A busker? That what they call it here?"

"Certainly. They have another name for it in the States?"

"Yeah. A misdemeanor."

"Well, that's a shame." Grandma McLaren peered out the window at the bright low sun. "A bit early to make any money, I think. But we can scout some locations and you can get set up for later. What do you say?"

"I'd say you're a remarkable woman, Grandma," I said, and she laughed.

"Now, tell me something I *don't* know."

THE ROYAL MILE starts with the name Canongate at one of the Queen's Scottish residences, Holyrood Palace, and runs a cobblestoned mile uphill, morphing into High Street at some indeterminate point in the middle, then Lawnmarket for a moment, and finally the self-explanatory Castlehill, before spilling into the esplanade of the centerpiece of the Old Town: Edinburgh Castle. Plaid-filled souvenir shops butt against staid historic houses; dark pubs sidle up to government buildings; whisky and cigars are peddled right next to strict Protestant churches. And at the top of the hill, the castle stands guard, still aiming its ancient guns down the length of the road, waiting for the English to reappear on the horizon.

As we drove the Royal Mile toward the castle, the potential for busking was obvious. Even early in the morning, in the dead of winter, the area had tourists to spare, all looking for some place to spend their vacation money. A few hardy bagpipers had already started marching back and forth, staking their claim to a particularly nice corner or storefront, and their instrument cases clanked with heavy gold-colored pound coins. It couldn't all be seed money.

"This is amazing, Grandma."

"Just wait till the Fringe."

"What's the Fringe?" We reached the end of Castlehill—from there, it was foot traffic only on the esplanade. Grandma McLaren spun the Peugeot in a tight U-turn.

"The Fringe Festival," she said, shooting across traffic to take a right. "Acts from all over the world come to Edinburgh to perform. Music, theater, dance—you name it. And half of them play right on the street to advertise for their shows." She took another right, this one more dramatic than the first, almost heading us back the way we'd just come. "International stars performing right next to the everyday buskers." She laughed. "I sound like a Fringe brochure. But it's really quite a scene."

We swept left and the street suddenly opened up. Pubs, restaurants, and hotels all fought for attention, their stone walls painted bright reds and greens. Holding her hand out like a *Price is Right* model, Grandma McLaren indicated our new surroundings.

"Grassmarket," she said. I looked back over my shoulder. Suddenly, the castle seemed a thousand feet above us.

Multileveled, I thought.

"This is where they held the public hangings," Grandma McLaren said.

"Not anymore, though?" I asked.

"No, not anymore," Grandma McLaren chuckled. "Though there's some in government who'd bring them back if they could."

The tourist flavor slowed as Grassmarket turned into West Port and then Fountainbridge. *Do any of these streets hold the same name for more than three blocks?* The stones faded back into muted grays and earthy brown as the tartans and St. Andrew's crosses that hung in the windows became signs for printing shops, laundry services, plumbing supplies. Grandma McLaren frowned and took a few quick lefts to head us back toward the Old Town.

"Well," I said, "it's nice to get a feel for the city. And later I'll probably pick a better spot. But, for now, there's really only one place to start."

"The train station," stated Grandma McLaren.

"Got it in one." There may be more profitable spots, but for pure volume of people, you can't beat a public transportation facility. The people there may not be happy—which is not really conducive to procuring money from them—but they're there. Grandma McLaren dropped me off at Waverly Station with a promise to return later and take me out for a late lunch.

"Sausage rolls!" she said, by way of farewell, and sped off.

I stood on the opposite side of Waverly Bridge from where I had been dropped off just yesterday. The morning sun that had seemed so bright a few hours earlier had failed to break through the tough Scottish cloud cover, and it appeared as though the lazy orb was going to call it a day and go back home for a hot toddy and a nap. The temperature was probably in the upper thirties but the wind howling across the exposed bridge lowered that number by at least half.

People here probably think it's cold, I thought. *I bet it's fifty degrees colder in Minnesota right now.* I hitched my collar up a little and bent my chin into my chest before heading across.

I assumed there was no busking allowed in the station proper. Otherwise I would have seen a hundred people with upside-down hats and open guitar cases in the protected area when I phoned Grandma McLaren yesterday. No matter, there were a number of promising spots where the foot traffic bottlenecked, spitting people out into the city in bunches. I propped my guitar case open a short distance from one such exit and set to work. Since I had left all my gear back in Minneapolis—sign, tape deck, cassettes—all this entailed was strapping on my guitar and flipping my case open in front of me.

Missing all my gear was another reason to start at the train station. People weren't looking to stop for anything here, so my normal hook was less useful, but they might throw a few coins in while passing. Wishing I had some seed money to toss in the case, I set up a slow blues riff in E. And began.

I sit beside the old men
On the front porch corner store
As they talk in circles, wholly
About the weather on the shore.

I was almost speaking the words. It was a warm-up I liked to do. Keep the music and melody real simple and freeform the lyrics.

I wouldn't talk about the people passing by yet. I just wanted to get the juices flowing. I'd do more targeted stuff later.

For it'll be here in the morning
Or I'll meet it near the bay
Where the painted eyes of Sheba
Saw your brother's feet of clay.
And I'll roll up in a hard top
With a fifth of Irish Cream
And the rain will come down sideways,
The wind six points abaft the beam.

Yes! Ever since reading a Patrick O'Brian novel I'd been trying to work "six points abaft the beam" into a song. This time I think it finally worked. I modulated to G and eased up on the reins of the tempo a touch.

Now the weather's coming quickly
But the dawn won't come at all
For the sun's been drowned in Babylon
When the rain refused to fall.
Like the hammer on both barrels
You can hear the click, then fire,
The moment before creation
When you could look on God's desire.

The tempo had the bit in its teeth now and I modulated again. I was in A now, the blues riff become a fast shuffle.

A muzzle flash in darkness,
Madness, divine or not.

The bullet is my universe,
A sin, a deed, a thought.

I punctuated the last three nouns with sharp cuts on the guitar and looked around. A few people had stopped to listen despite the cold and wind. Time to wrap it up and get to work.

Still, I sit beside the old men
On the front porch corner store
And they talk in circles, holy,
About the weather on the shore.

A coin hit the bottom of my guitar case with a velvety thump. Then another.

By the time Grandma McLaren returned, I had nearly ten pounds in change that I happily spent on lunch for the two of us. We sat in a Fisher and Donaldson's near her house munching on sausage rolls and mince pies.

"So," said Grandma McLaren, teacup in hand, pinky out like a proper lady. "What do you think of Scotland so far, Dougie?"

"I like it, Grandma. I like it a lot." I washed the last crumbs of a sausage roll down with a sip of tea and grabbed for another. Winking at Grandma McLaren over the top of my new pastry, I said, "I just hope Scotland likes me, too."

She smiled at that before peering into my eyes seriously for a few moments.

When she didn't speak again I said, "What? Something in my teeth?" and bared them for inspection.

She gave a low chuckle, then turned serious again. "Dougie?"

"Yes, Grandma?"

"I think you're going to be all right."

I looked at her there, a little old lady in a crisp blue dress, drinking tea and eating pastries. And I wondered what she could possibly see in me that would make her think that I would ever be all right.

I'll probably be back on the junk in a week and stealing her silver to pay for it.

But I didn't want to argue with her, so I just nodded mutely, and we sat in companionable silence while the sun made an early day of it, diving back into the hills before it was even four o'clock.

• • • Three • • •

The change of seasons came to Edinburgh without fanfare. One day the rain stopped insinuating that it could turn into snow at any moment if we didn't behave and just poured down mutely.

Must be spring.

The winter had been profitable. After a few days at the train station, I'd traveled south to a prime spot about halfway up High Street in front of a souvenir shop. Each time I'd played, I slipped a few pounds to the owner, a tall Pakistani with a tartan turban to match his kilt, and he saved my spot for me, moving on any other buskers who tried to work my corner. I re-equipped myself with a portion of my profits and now had a sign, a tape deck (used, not stolen this time), and a large supply of blank tapes, guitar strings, and picks.

I stayed clean.

Part of staying clean was keeping to myself. I spent most of my free time either alone or with Grandma McLaren and was brusque with anyone who showed an interest in me beyond giving me a pound for a song. I considered shaving my head in a tonsure so my look would more closely match my monastic existence, but

I thought better of it and tried to grow a beard instead. When I became tired of Grandma McLaren's snickers, I shaved off the few pitiful hairs.

One morning, I stepped out of the shower and made a horrific discovery: I was getting fat! The combination of staying clean and eating three full meals every day—plus a high tea of cookies and half sandwiches, as well as the occasional midnight snack—had given me a little potbelly.

I didn't want to go back on the junk, nor did I want to quit eating. Especially sausage rolls! I was going to have to start exercising. I began turning down Grandma McLaren's offers of rides to work and walked the mile and a half there and back. Three hilly miles a day carrying guitar and gear was enough to stem the tide, and by the time summer rolled around I was in the best shape I had been in for a long time. My fish-white Minnesota pallor had even turned a light brown.

"How did I get a tan in Scotland, Grandma?" We were sitting in the living room eating scones slathered in clotted cream and strawberry jam, and washing them down with tea I dumped sugar into until it rivaled the scones for sweetness.

"Well, Dougie," she answered, "You've discovered the secret of eastern Scotland: the weather is quite nice in the summer." She looked suspiciously around the living room and then spoke in a conspiratorial whisper. "Don't tell anyone, though."

I nodded. "Wouldn't want everyone moving here."

"Especially Americans."

ON DAYS I didn't work, I still took the walk into the city, visiting the museums or the historic houses, or just spending the afternoon reading in one of the many pubs on High Street. I even hopped in an ersatz whisky barrel for the bizarre, Coney Island–like ride through the Scotch Whisky Heritage Centre.

I steered a different course each morning, exploring the smaller streets and alleyways and their unique shops and gardens. One that I never took more than once was a short curved street called Cockburn Street. The south end was lined with head shops, sex shops, tattoo and piercing parlors, and a variety of other retail establishments that suggested a thriving drug culture. It looked a lot like Minneapolis's West Lake Street. I knew if I spent a minute or two talking with some of the proprietors, I could be shooting up in a back room within a half hour.

I climbed back down the aptly named Fleshmarket Stairs and found a different route to work.

BY THE TIME summer began drawing to a close, I felt I was beginning to know the city fairly well. Not just the names of the streets, the right pub for a pint of eighty, or the bakery that made the best sausage roll; but the city's melody, her song. She was a European tango, measured and refined, yet played on bagpipe and fiddle, her air of sophistication unable to hide the stink of sheep byres and whisky barrels. I loved it. I thought I might try to write a song for her.

Then the Fringe arrived and the place went insane.

The Edinburgh International Festival had been launched shortly after World War II as a way to reunite a shattered and distrustful Europe through the shared culture of the arts. Or so said one of the many pamphlets pressed into my hands as I walked to work. The finest international musicians, actors, artists, and performers of the day were invited and, for a week, Edinburgh was the cultural center of the western world.

The Fringe Festival was started by a pack of Scots who weren't invited.

"A whole city to perform in," Grandma McLaren said. "And

Herr Bing tells us there's no room at the inn." She snorted. "Well, we came anyway, didn't we?"

"You were there, Grandma?"

"Oh aye, my mother was one of the 'Festival Adjuncts,' as we called ourselves that first year. Showed up like the wicked witch at Sleeping Beauty's christening, we did. About as popular, too."

She told me that the Fringe's gate-crashing spirit created a tradition that eventually came to overshadow the main festival. While the International Festival had a committee that selected what it considered the finest hundred or so acts in the world and invited them to perform, there was no such selection process for the Fringe. No one was invited; no one got paid. Yet ten thousand performers and nearly a million observers now descended upon the city for three weeks every August.

Mayhem.

I KNEW THE Fringe was coming but I was not fully prepared for the transformation the city would undergo. Nearly two hundred pubs, libraries, houses, gymnasiums, courtyards, alleys, or any place that could fit a stage and more than twenty people in it suddenly became a Fringe venue. One year, an enterprising soul even turned his car into a venue, entertaining four people at a time. Everyone—actors, musicians, singers, dancers, jugglers, mimes, comedians, and a Fellini-esque cast of thousands—took to the streets to advertise their shows and try to make a few extra bucks. Half of the Royal Mile was closed to motorized vehicles to make room for the sheer volume of busking.

My spot was taken. I confronted the shop owner about our deal but he just shrugged.

"It's the Fringe," he said, adjusting his turban. It was Royal Stewart today. "Permits and pols on High Street for a bloody month." He pointed at the girl in my spot who was gamely playing a fiddle two sizes too small for her. "She has a permit. Do you?"

I didn't have a permit. Hadn't needed one till the Fringe. Still, I wasn't overly concerned. Pushing my way through the crowd that morning, I had spotted a long promenade near the National Gallery with an impromptu arts-and-crafts market lining its east side. There were rugged stalls featuring tie-dyed or batiked fabrics, handmade jewelry laid out on blankets and folding tables, watercolors of Edinburgh taped to a railing, booths advertising henna tattoos, face painting, hair braiding. There was also an unending stream of pedestrian traffic jostling their way toward the epicenter of Fringe activity, the Royal Mile.

The west side of the promenade had been unaccountably wide open and I thought I'd set up shop there. But when I arrived, I decided there must be a good reason for the lack of people on that side. I squeezed into the southeast corner instead, between a long set of stone stairs called the Playfair Steps and a bony girl in a paisley peasant skirt selling crystal necklaces. I salved any hard feelings she may have had about my infringing on her space by doing a little musical hawking for her wares:

Come see the jewel, the jewel of the fair;
The line of her face, the curve of her hair.
In all of Scotland, no fairer is found;
And to think she sells jewelry for under ten pounds!

There was more where that came from. Horrible, mawkish stuff, but she smiled and waved me in beside her when I had finished.

"How come no one ever sets up over there?" I asked the girl, pointing at the other side of the street. "It's wide open." I pulled out my tape deck and sign.

"Em," she said in a soft Edinburgh lilt. "The people from the museum kick you out if you try."

Our neighbor on the right, a long-haired man selling tie-dyed shirts, piped up. "The pols cruise by every hour or so to check on it."

"It's some kind of horse trail, like. You know, for the carriages," added another voice from further down.

"It's an overflow lot for when Parliament is in session."

"Gotta keep it clear for bicycles."

"Taxicabs."

"Emergency vehicles."

The list went on. It seemed everyone had an excuse for not setting up a booth on the west side. They all sounded like good reasons to me. Shrugging my shoulders, I propped my sign against my tape deck and got to work.

And went on to make the most money that I ever had in a single day.

I loved the Fringe.

I WORKED TWELVE hours a day for the next three days. Grandma McLaren tried to convince me to go to one of the multitude of shows but, while they certainly looked interesting—who wouldn't want to see the entirety of *Henry V* performed by a single man in a trenchcoat?—there was just too much money to be made. I had earned nearly a thousand pounds already. My coat pockets were stuffed with coins and I had a roll of bills hidden underneath my air mattress. If I could keep up this pace throughout the Fringe, I might not have to work all winter.

It was a little overcast on the morning of the fourth day of the Fringe, and the bony girl at the crystal necklaces booth smiled at me as I arrived. Her name was Sandra; she was born in Inverness but grew up in Edinburgh, and she liked the band Phish. Today, I thought she might finally invite me to a "party" she had been hinting about. And I didn't need an engraved invitation to tell me what kind of party it would be. The look in her eyes and the little marks on her arms told me all I needed.

I was going to have to find a new place to play.

Around noontime I began a song for a man from West Virginia, here with his son tracing their Scotch-Irish roots. The father was a coal miner, the son a recent high school graduate. They were exact opposites of each other: the father, crooked and white-haired, his face scarred, his teeth mostly gone; the son straight and tall, with a shock of hair so black his father could have just pulled it from the ground. I was going to do something authentically country—backwoods-marry-yer-cousin-don't-have-no-dang-teeth country—for the father when I realized that though the man wanted the song about him, it was the son I had to impress if they were going to buy a five-pound tape and not just take the one-pound listen. With that in mind, I started with something more modern country, a flashy "chicken-picking" intro where I hit downstrokes with the pick and plucked up with the free fingers of my right hand.

I been in the mines, digging hard
Since I was ten years old.
Naught down there but coal and rock
I never did hit gold.
My boy, he'll have a different life,
Won't have to live what I been through.
Break your nails on cold hard stone
Doing what I do.

I had them. The old man was nearly in tears and the boy was beaming at me and his father in turn. I scanned the crowd as I shifted up to the relative major for a chorus.

Buried alive!
It's how I spend my day.
Buried alive!
It's how I earn my pay.

A woman who looked to be in her late twenties was making her way through the thick crowd surrounding me. I didn't see her saying "excuse me" or shoving anyone in the back, but she slipped to the front seemingly without touching a soul. The people parted before her like the Red Sea would have if it had been only Moses making the crossing and not all the Jews in Egypt. Having been to my share of concerts where I had tried to get to the front row, I was quite impressed by this trick.

The way she walked—smooth measured steps, her upper body rigid, chin held high—triggered a memory, but I couldn't quite place it.

Buried alive!
And I know
When I die, I'll go to heaven
'Cause I spent my life below.

I sang another verse about the son going to college and getting a good job before making enough to come back and bury his dad in the unforgiving ground, then a few reprises of the chorus before stopping the tape and asking, "Would you like a copy?"

It was a rhetorical question; the father had been reaching for his billfold before the last chorus ended.

The woman stood in front of me now, wearing a long, hunter-green linen dress—half summer-casual, half wedding formal—and I adjusted my age estimate sharply downward. She was maybe out of high school, but couldn't have been for long.

Suddenly, it came to me who she reminded me of.

"Lady Di!" I blurted.

She raised an eyebrow at me. She looked nothing like the late Princess Diana. She was tall for a woman—I could see over her head, but not easily—with a youthful, athletic body. Her black hair was long and lightly curled, held back loosely with a silver wire clasp. Her chill blue eyes fit her pale complexion, if not her hair, and she had a nose marginally too long and hooked for magazine work. Yet together with her thin red lips and arching cheekbones she was quite beautiful. Beautiful, but not very inviting.

A regal bearing.

On the day Lady Diana died, they kept showing stock footage of her wedding day as part of the news. The queen had been hunched and bowed under voluminous cloaks; Prince Charles's Howdy Doody ears and Ichabod Crane physique had made him look like a demented Muppet. Neither looked particularly royal. But it struck me that, unlike the rest, the young Diana had carried herself like a fairy-tale princess. A regal bearing. That's what this woman had.

"You got a dubber on that machine?" the West Virginian father asked. "I'd like me a few more copies for my family."

I nodded and started a copy running, but as the machine did its work, I turned and asked the woman, "You looking to get a song written about you, young lady?"

She smiled at the "young lady" and thought for a few moments before answering.

"Yes," she finally said. "But not here." Her voice sounded too old for her appearance: not unpleasant, just . . . weathered.

I mentally edged her age up a few years before abandoning the exercise. *She's somewhere between seventeen and forty,* I thought and left it at that.

"We will meet somewhere later?" she asked.

Maybe I was imagining the question mark. Upon reflection, it sounded more like an order. Or an imperial edict.

"Twenty pounds for a private session," I said. Always looking to make an extra buck.

"Twenty pounds and you will sing me?" That was an odd way to state it. But I was noticing a trace of an accent I couldn't place. Maybe eastern European, maybe Irish, maybe . . . I put her nationality in a box with her age.

"And five more for a tape."

"I do not wish to haggle," she said. "It is agreed. The Meadows at an hour before sunset?"

"Sure. What time would that be?"

She just looked at me. "It is agreed," she repeated and held my gaze until I nodded again. Then she disappeared into the crowd.

She's a strange one, I thought. *But an hour before sunset's probably eight-thirty or so. I usually break for dinner around then, anyway.* Tonight, I'd break a little early, grab a sandwich for the walk to the Meadows, and make twenty-five quid on my dinner hour.

THE MEADOWS WAS the name of a sprawling park a half mile south of the Royal Mile. Even during the Fringe, it was spacious and out of the way enough that the crowds were kept to a minimum. You could sit there in the middle of the city and be, for all practical purposes, alone.

It took me ten minutes to walk there, and I was just brushing the last crumbs of a cheese toastie off the twisting serpent logo on my Headstones tee shirt as I arrived.

Maybe eight-thirty, I thought. *Hopefully, an hour till sunset.*

She was standing at the head of the long walking path down to the Meadows, underneath a tall column topped with a stone figure of a unicorn and Scotland's motto in Latin: NEMO ME IMPUNE LACESSIT. Beckoning me to follow, she turned without speaking and began walking. I followed her, admiring her form as we traveled, first downhill through the trees on a wide paved path, then out into the sun and along the northern edge, before cutting down Coronation Path and settling in an isolated spot in the southwest corner. She spread a blanket and sat cross-legged on it. I put my case on the ground and shrugged out of my pack-o-gear.

"What's your name?" I asked. She shook her head.

"No," she said. "That is not how we will do it."

I shrugged. "It's your money, but if I don't know anything about you, it's going to be hard to, as you say, 'sing you.'"

"Trust me," she said.

I didn't. But I couldn't see what harm would come from spending a few minutes in a park with a beautiful, albeit crazy, foreign girl. I sat down on the blanket across from her.

"Look at me," she continued. This wasn't a tough assignment because she was, admittedly, quite attractive. "And when you are ready, begin."

Usually, I make an honest attempt to understand what makes a person tick before singing their song. I like to ask them about their jobs, their hobbies, what's important to them personally or politically. Find a center, something to draw on. Have it really be *their* song. I guess that's why my act was so successful: people could tell I was making an honest attempt to write a song specifically for them. Not too big an attempt, mind you—I had to get my buck (or quid) and move on to the next person—but an honest one, nonetheless.

But without being allowed to question the woman, I didn't see how I could do a full treatment. I could sing about what she looked like—her eyes, her bearing—and, I suppose, mention her accent. But after that the gravy train ground to a sharp halt.

I stared at her openly for a minute and decided that I would sit for a few minutes more, then sing some crap about a pretty girl in a park, take my money, and get back to work.

But a few minutes passed. And then a few more. And I was still sitting, still staring, my eyes now locked with hers. I couldn't move. I couldn't speak. My vision had narrowed until everything that wasn't her was blurry, then insignificant, then not there at all. I tried to break her gaze but I couldn't. I wasn't paralyzed; I had just lost all interest in moving. After another minute she finally nodded and said, "You're ready."

And I was. Though I didn't recall picking up my guitar or putting my fingers on the strings, I found myself strumming a chord. It was an E minor 9 in second position, three strings fingered and three ringing open. A sweet sounding chord with just a hint of dissonance in the middle, where the ninth sat a mere half step away from the second. The sound of the notes broke something loose and I was able to speak again.

"What's your name?" I asked again.

"You tell me," she replied.

I let the open strings ring and began a descending run in E Dorian, high on the neck of my guitar, left hand pressing into the cutaway. The raised sixth softened the funereal effect of the minor key as I alternated seconds and thirds the length of the B string. When I ran out of neck, I went back and played it again. I sang the run the third time—no words yet—just humming nonsense syllables, and I harmonized with myself on the high E string, extending the run all the way down, down, down, skipping strings and alternating intervals until I eventually splashed down into a loud jangling D chord. I paused a beat, maybe two, then quietly strummed the sweet starting chord again. And began to sing.

It was incredible. I had made a living singing *about* people. This time I was skipping the "about." I was, as she had said, "singing her." It was as if I were defining her: every note, every word, was perfect in its depiction of her. There was only one problem.

I was forgetting everything as I was doing it.

I couldn't remember the chord preceding the one I was fingering. Each note of the melody floated free in its own space, unconnected to anything that came before. The lyrics disappeared, each word leaving an empty space in my brain as it flew out of me. And into her. I could see the woman listening intently, her lips parted, her breathing shallow, excited. She, at least, was catching every word, every note, every nuance.

The song ended. On a G major 7.

No, wait! I looked down at my fingers. They were resting on a thirteenth as well. You barely heard it amidst the lushness of the rest of the chord.

I smiled. Those were the exact same notes I had started the song with—I could remember that much at least—but they formed a different chord.

Music is a funny business.

I looked up at her, sitting cross-legged on the blanket two feet from me. I looked at her and, for that single moment, I *knew* her. I had sung her, I had played her, and now I knew her. Her loves, her hates, her past, her present. Her myriad possible futures.

"Aine," I breathed. Her name.

She gave me a curt nod. The *knowing* passed, and she was once again just a girl in the park, with me as ignorant of her nature as I'd been ten minutes before. I remembered her name, though.

"Twenty pounds, correct?"

I thought about it. I had never experienced anything like that before. It was the best high I had ever felt, knowing someone that deeply, that . . . musically. Even if I couldn't remember what I had played.

"Fine," she said, taking my hesitation for bargaining. "Twenty-five, though there is no tape."

She was right. I had forgotten to turn on the tape deck.

"No," I decided. "No charge." It was too profound an experience to turn into something mercenary. It wasn't like I was losing money; this was my dinner break, after all.

"You are refusing payment?" Aine hissed, her face suddenly bright red and her lips getting even thinner. She was obviously furious at the concept. Not exactly the response I was expecting.

"Um . . . yes." I was confused.

"We had an agreement."

"Consider it a gift."

This infuriated her even more. "A gift?" she screeched. A blackbird, which had ventured close in hopes that we had crumbs, spooked at the sound, its wings pumping furiously as it flew off to safety. Aine began muttering, half to herself. "Payment I could make, but a gift? A gift requires something of equal value be given in return."

"Well," I said, not really following her line of reasoning, just trying to bring the conversation to a close. "Let's just say you owe me one and call it a day."

Aine laughed then, not trying to hide the fact that she was laughing *at* me. It was not a pretty sound, a little too much scorn in it. If I hadn't still been warm in the afterglow of *knowing*, I don't think I would have liked her much.

"That is too expensive," she said. "And you could not find me to collect anyway." She thought a moment. "You could not find me . . . ," she repeated softly, then stood and reached into the folds of her green dress. "You have given me an idea, singer." It didn't appear that she could stash anything in there, but she came out with a small vial. Filled with white powder.

"No," I stated as firmly as I could. My left hand started to twitch.

"Yes," she said, and grinned. It was not a pleasant grin. "This will open up a whole new world."

"I'm familiar with that world."

"I doubt that."

I stood to leave, whipping my pack onto my back and grabbing my guitar. But before I could turn away, Aine tossed me the vial.

I let it bounce off my chest. Or I had planned to.

My left hand had other ideas and snatched the vial nimbly from the air before stuffing it deep into my jeans pocket.

"I do not think that anyone could argue that these gifts exchanged were not of equal value." Aine sounded as if she were reciting from a contract.

"I won't do it," I told her, and she nodded.

"Keep telling yourself that."

I had no answer for that so I just turned and walked away, guitar in one hand, gear strapped to my back, my traitorous left hand in my pocket, caressing the vial.

• • • FOUR • • •

I went directly to Grandma McLaren's from the Meadows, intending to throw the vial away as soon as I got there. I was distracted from my task by a sketch comedy show on BBC2, then went to bed, solemnly swearing to toss it first thing tomorrow. The next day, my morning rituals completed, the vial was still in my pocket. It wormed its way into my hand at the breakfast table. I went to the kitchen to throw it away. Came back with a glass of milk. And the vial back in my pocket. By the time I left for work, I'd come to believe that I was physically incapable of throwing it away.

No problem, I foolishly thought, *I just won't ever use it. Ever.*

I lasted three days.

The presence of the vial was too much for me. It made me crazy, ate at me, wore me down. Two more days of thinking about it there in my pocket, waiting for me, calling to me, singing me its siren song, was more than I could take. By the time the third day rolled around, I'd made a beautiful junkie's rationalization. Some time during my long sleepless night, I'd decided that the only way to get rid of the vial was to do it. Yeah, do it. Bang it. Shoot the whole load. Then it'd be gone and I could get on with my straight life.

But how? I considered asking Sandra, the crafts market girl, for a hand, but she might have some of her own she wanted to share and the whole purpose of this was just to do what was in the vial and be done with it forever.

Again.

WHEN I BROKE for dinner that evening, I took the short walk to Cockburn Street, leaving guitar and gear with Sandra, and started asking around.

I'd been wrong about the area; I didn't score in a half hour. It took a full forty-five minutes to find what I needed. But before it was dark, I was sitting on the can in the reeking back bathroom of Wee Willy's Fun Shoppe with a hypo sold to me by a fat biker who went by the name "Wet Dog." I tapped the powder out onto a little piece of tin foil and cooked it up with a Zippo bearing the Scottish flag. The result went through a cotton ball into the needle, the needle went into my arm, and . . .

Nothing.

Absolutely nothing. I waited for a rush, a tickle, a taste. Anything.

I felt nothing.

I leaned my head back and laughed out loud. Three days of anguish so I could shoot a load of baby laxative or Similac or some such thing. I chuckled and choked and coughed and banged my head against the stall until the noise finally attracted Wet Dog's attention and he sent back three buddies to "throw that daftie junkie out in the street." They followed his directions literally and I hit the pavement all elbows and knees, but still laughing, only stumbling to my feet and moving on when the three large men threatened to put the boots to me.

I walked down the Fleshmarket Stairs, turning my head to catch the evening wind full in the face when I reached the bottom. There was a bit of a chill to it, a little reminder that the North Sea was just around the bend and, despite it still being summer, fall was on its way with winter not long behind.

I felt free. Aine may have been ripped off when she purchased that stuff, but she had given me a greater gift than she had intended. I had faltered and fallen. I had gone all the way down. *But I hadn't had to pay the price.*

And now that I knew the way, I was certain I could avoid ever going down that road again. For the first time that year, I felt fully free of the tidal pull heroin had always had on my soul.

I ARRIVED AT my spot on the promenade, feeling fresh and clear and ready to take on the world. I'd only been gone an hour or so but the west side, which had been empty all week, was now filled to capacity.

Strange, but the only real wonder was that it had taken so long for people to fill up such prime real estate, museum people or police be damned. As I strapped on my guitar, I was thinking there was still time to make some money. *Or I could just give away songs all night.* I chuckled at the thought, scanning the crowd, trying to guess who would be my next customer.

The evening sun slanted hard over my shoulder, casting crazy shadows across the promenade. A young man dressed in an anachronistic waistcoat and breeches strolled by. He stepped past me, one foot, then another, then a third and a fourth.

I froze.

He had just turned into a horse!

Now, I had taken my fair share of drugs but never, even on the freakiest acid trip, had I ever seen anything like that. One second, I was looking at an oddly dressed young gentleman browsing the booths and stalls across from me; the next, he was galloping off on four long black legs and disappearing up the stone steps toward the Royal Mile.

I shook my head to clear it. *I did not just see that!*

Maybe the stuff Aine gave me wasn't baby laxative after all. Maybe it was something I was unfamiliar with—something with no other effects except for ultrarealistic hallucinations.

And here comes another one.

I was staring across the way. What I had thought were people along the west side of the promenade, now appeared to be strange alien creatures. Names, half-remembered from bedtime stories by Celtic grandmothers on both sides, popped into my head unbidden: *luchorpans, pookas, pixies.*

Faeries.

And they were shopping.

The booth right across from me was an ornate oaken structure festooned with a variety of animal skulls, few of which were immediately recognizable. It was managed by a warty old woman who puffed a meerschaum pipe, the glowing embers reflecting in her dark eyes each time she inhaled. Next to her stood a plain but well-put-together booth selling shoes of all shapes and sizes. It appeared unattended until I spied a dwarfish figure dressed in homespun green leaning out a window carved low into the frontispiece. He was yelling at the knees of his next neighbor down, a hulking greasy-haired creature who, judging by the look of his booth, specialized in dead, rotting things. And plenty of them.

My mouth hanging open, I gazed past the booth of dead things at the line of fey merchants that stretched the length of the promenade, mirroring the human activity on the east side. Where hand-painted signs advertised henna for 50p or tie-dyed shirts for ten pounds on the east, embroidered flags or glowing eldritch symbols advertised God knew what goods or services on the west. Where pretty young girls with dirty faces and peasant skirts sold baubles on the east, well . . . often enough it was pretty young things in peasant skirts selling baubles on the west, as well. But their faces were cleaner and their ears were pointed, and their baubles floated and hummed and glowed.

I shook my head again, rubbed my eyes. But the creatures remained.

This is not fucking cool.

Just then, a hunched humanoid, gray and leprous, turned from examining some crystal jewelry that was laid out on a floating table. He caught me staring at him. I couldn't help myself. Even in that fantastic and often grotesque lot he was impressive in his ugliness. His face was covered with a volcanic landscape of pustules and sores, creating an oozing, seeping backdrop for normal human features drawn skew—a nose here, an eye or two there—as if a drunken Picasso had played God on his birthday. The creature's crooked spine was lined with stiff, boarlike bristles, and he would have stood maybe four feet tall if he'd been able to straighten up. I could count every vertebrae and bristle because he wore nothing but a stained leather loincloth; his thick muscular legs sprouted from beneath it, an odd counterpoint to his sunken chest and thin arms.

We locked eyes. I knew, instinctively, that I should look away, pretend not to see him, just go about my business, but the rational part of my mind still had a fingertip hold on my body. Mind told body: *Stay put. The creature doesn't exist. The market doesn't exist. You're imagining things. You're high.*

But I wasn't high. I'd been wasted too many times not to recognize the effects. This time I was stone cold sober and gaping like an idiot as some sort of monstrosity—*Bogie? Goblin? Kobold?*—crept toward me.

Step, lurch, step. He took awkward strides across the street, the effort to walk upright with a bent spine belying the power in his legs. *Step, lurch, step.* An ungainly gait, but closing the distance faster than I would have liked.

I was still trying to convince myself that it was the single most lucid and horrific hallucination I had ever seen when the creature revealed surprisingly white and pointed teeth in a wide grin and leapt at me. The rational part of my mind went gibbering off into the darkness, and my fight-or-flight reflex jammed a triple load of adrenaline into my system.

I bolted.

I felt a rush of wind that smelled of rotten eggs and fish guts as the creature flew past me. He landed in the spot I had vacated a moment before, and then I was on the stone stairs, whipping my guitar off over my head as I took the steps three at a time. I hit Bank Street at a full sprint and the crowds of people moved out of my way, maybe thinking I was late for a gig, this crazy Yank racing through the streets with his guitar in hand. I had no thought to where I was going or what I would do when I got there. I was in a full blind panic and was just trying for speed, speed, more speed.

And escape. There was an opening in a fence and I shot through, tripping, twisting, launching myself up stairs and across landings, hoping to get out of sight before my pursuer turned one of the corners or reached the top of the stairs. I saw a placard reading, FREEDOME IS A . . . , but I never learned what *freedome* was, because I was past the sign and off the stairs and into a stone-floored courtyard. The one exit was straight ahead: a covered alleyway, maybe two people wide. More words were scrawled into the flagstones now, all in broad Scots, unreadable at my speed, and I entered the alley at a dead run, the German tourists already inside pressing to one side as I came on. I burst out the other end almost immediately, and the pavement turned to cobblestones, almost tripping me up. The Royal Mile. A left, a right, and I was across the street and back on the sidewalk, still at a full sprint. Fringe traffic was heavy and yet there was always a space here, an opening there, and I shot through the crowd without slowing.

Risking a look back, I saw the creature keeping pace easily, hunched over, using his knuckles to gallop on all fours. People were moving out of his way, too, a trick I realized I had seen before: Aine moving to the front of the crowd while I played.

I was running downhill now, nearly falling forward, still going as fast as I could but starting to think a little, too, as the raging panic faded.

He'll catch me soon, I realized with preternatural calm.

The creature looked to be running effortlessly, while I had developed a painful stitch in my side and was beginning to tire. I was glad that I had not yet let go of my guitar. It was all I had for a weapon. I was deciding whether to die tired or turn and fight while I still had some energy left, when I spotted an unassuming stone church just ahead on the right.

Sanctuary! The word leapt into my mind. *If this isn't all some drug-induced dream, and that really is a creature out of Faerie chasing me, then maybe it will be unable to stand on holy ground.* It was a much better hope than fending the monster off with the Lowden F35 Cutaway I held in my right hand. I went for the church like a tired horse spotting the barn.

The creature must have sensed my newfound purpose because his easy gallop suddenly became huge leaps and bounds that ate up the yards between us at an alarmingly fast rate. I made a leap of my own over the short wall surrounding the churchyard and charged through the front door ten feet in front of the creature. Then I turned and slammed the door in his deformed face, the boom of its closing echoing throughout the empty chamber.

Pressing my forehead into the cool wood of the door, I breathed heavily and quickly came to two realizations. One, the creature hadn't been trying to catch me. Not until I made for the church, anyway. The speed with which he'd moved then meant he could have been on me at any time during our half-mile sprint. No, not trying to catch me, he'd been herding me, moving people magically out of *my* way as well as his, driving me somewhere. Probably someplace nice and quiet and secluded so he could kill me. Like this church. If my holy-ground theory was wrong, I was screwed.

The second thing I realized was that the church wasn't empty.

"Why the haste?" asked the sole other occupant of the church in a booming voice. He was a giant of a man, with broad peasant features and thick calloused hands to match. He wore a priest's long cassock and a black eye-patch over his left eye. A huge iron cross hung from his neck on a thickly braided chain.

Fixing me curiously with his uncovered eye he asked, "Is the Devil himself after ye?" His words bounced off the walls of the church, chasing after the fading echoes of the slamming door.

I didn't answer. I was too out of breath and fully occupied trying to lock the ancient door. My hand didn't seem to be working right—shaking too hard—and I fumbled and pawed at the latch. I tried my other hand, but it didn't seem able to let go of my guitar. Staring at my useless hands, I pressed my foot—at least my feet still worked—against the door to hold it closed.

The priest reached over my shoulder, pushed me aside with one of his big mitts, and shot the bolt home. I searched for additional dead bolts or a chain or maybe a thick wooden crossbeam I could throw across it like in those old Robin Hood movies. There was nothing more—just the one thin metal bar separating me from slavering, pus-covered death.

I finally found my voice. "Sanctuary," I rasped.

The priest laughed then, a deep rumbling affair that matched his voice, and said, "Of course, of course, that's what we're here for. Father Croser at your service, my son." He stuck out his hand and I shook it automatically, my hand working fine now that the door was latched. Tugging me away from the door, he guided me to a nearby pew. It was like being pulled by a tame elephant: gentle but irresistible. I sat down hard and tried to catch my breath.

The church wasn't large by Edinburgh standards, only a dozen pews on each side, but still impressive due to a vaulted ceiling and the massive stained-glass windows depicting the miracles of Christ. Behind the altar, in the same style as the windows but obviously more modern, was a mural of Jesus, red blood seeping from beneath his crown of thorns and from the holes in his hands and feet, and spurting from the fresh spear wound in his side onto the faces of the Roman soldiers below.

"Now, how can I help you, my son?" Father Croser said.

"Thank you, Father." My breath was coming more or less normally, now. "But I don't think you can help me with this."

He bent down, looked me right in the eyes. Well, in one eye. "Don't be too hasty in your judgment, lad. In earthly matters, true, the church can be of little use. Especially when your conduit for divine assistance is a poor country priest like myself, who knows nothing of power or politics or the sinfulness that this modern-day Gomorrah is rife with." His voice grew even more stentorian, and I could picture him leaning out over the pulpit, playing to the back rows of his tiny church, imploring the sinners to *repent! repent!* or suffer the consequences. "But if your problem is more spiritual, or even demonic, in nature, then, my son, you have come directly to the right place. For that is the church's, and my own, area of expertise."

"Demonic?"

"Especially demonic."

Well, if he wanted demonic . . .

"Is there a window we could look out?" I asked.

He nodded. "My office. Come with me."

Leaving my guitar on the pew, I followed Father Croser down

the aisle to the front of the church and through a door to the left of the pulpit. It led to a short hall, through another door, and into an old-fashioned office. A giant desk, meticulously tidy, dominated most of the room, with a table, two chairs, and a bookshelf, all antiques, taking up the remaining space. In the west wall was an iron-banded door, and high in the east, a tiny window paned with leaded glass. I dragged a chair under the window and hopped up. The old glass was cloudy with dirt and I rubbed at it with my sleeve until I could see through it. Between the evening gloom and the dirty glass it was hard to tell, but I was pretty sure there was nothing moving out there. Maybe Ol' Bristleback had gone back to the market to finish his shopping.

Maybe he had gone for reinforcements.

I heard a scraping and creaking and Father Croser stepped onto the other chair beside me. He squinted through the window for a moment then pulled hard on the rusty latch holding it closed. After a brief battle, the latch gave up the ghost, coming completely off in Father Croser's hand, and he pushed the window open, swinging it out and up with a screech of long unused hinges.

The creature reappeared around the corner, twenty yards away, one visible ear cocked forward, searching for the source of the sound.

"There, Father!" I whispered and pointed. "Do you see it?" The creature had slowed now and was snuffling along the side of the church. *What's the freakish thing doing?*

Father Croser peered through the open window. "No, my son," he said. In full booming voice. The creature's ear cocked in our direction and his head twisted until both his eyes pointed up at us. And the open window.

"Then you can't help me. Close the window."

"Now, I told you not to be hasty, lad."

The boar-man was looking for another way in.

"Close the window, Father!"

"Now, now . . ."

And we had given him one!

"Father, the window!" I screamed at him, but strangely, he was lifting his eye-patch off his eye.

Gathering his legs beneath him, the creature prepared for a mighty leap. Having seen those legs in action, I had no doubt that he could reach the open window. Whether he could fit through was another question entirely, but not one I wanted to field test. I grabbed the window to close it but some sort of nineteenth-century technology held it locked in an open position. Father Croser closed his right eye tight; his now-uncovered left eye appeared undamaged.

The creature sprang, massive frog legs catapulting him up to the window.

I tried to leap back—too slow—and one of the creature's claws tangled in my hair while his other paw grasped the sill. Cackling, he yanked hard.

He's not looking for a way in, I thought, *but a way to drag me out!*

My head banged on the upper sill, and I flung my arms to the side, barely keeping myself inside. Wondering what Father Croser would make of my spastic behavior, I pulled back, my hair and shoulder sockets screaming in protest. I could hear the creature scrabbling for purchase on the stone wall with his toes.

With those legs, if he gets some leverage—

I didn't finish the thought. I didn't have to. Father Croser suddenly exclaimed, "There you are!" and grabbed the creature's head in his huge hands, popping it through the window with a grunt and a heave. The creature's momentum was too much for our precarious perch, and the chairs toppled, sending us all to the church floor. Father Croser recovered first, having broken his fall on my ribs, and leapt to his feet in a swirl of black robes. Like a startled crab—but far less graceful—I scrabbled backward. The creature arose and shot a quick glare at the priest before turning and coming for me.

Big mistake. As soon as the creature turned away, Father Croser pulled a long black knife from somewhere deep in his robes. With surprising swiftness for a man his size, he jumped forward and, with two quick strokes, sliced the thick tendons at the back of the creature's legs. Blood—red blood, as red as any earthborn creature's—sprayed across the floor of the office and the creature collapsed onto its face, hamstrung.

"Well, well," Father Croser said, "A demon in the house of the Lord."

The creature made two attempts to stand on his crippled legs, then gave up and began dragging himself toward me by his hands. Father Croser stopped this meager progress by stepping in front of the creature and kicking it full in the face. He was three feet from where I had come to rest, my crab-flight stopped by the office wall.

"You can see it?" Father Croser asked, and I nodded. "Out of one eye or both?"

"Both."

"How did you come by the gift of sight?"

Good question. It had to be from the vial. The vial that Aine had given me. Aine who could magically move crowds of people out of her way. Just like the creature dying on the church floor had been able to do.

"I got it from one of them." *Aine was one of them.* It was unnatural that Aine should be related to a creature as loathsome as the boar-man, but that was the only logical explanation I could think of. "From one of them," I repeated.

I was about to ask him where he got *his* sight, but I was interrupted by the bloody creature flipping onto his back and hissing at us. Father Croser leaned in closer to it.

"You have something to say, demon?" he asked cheerfully.

The creature began chanting in a buzzing, droning voice, like a cloud of insects descending on a field.

May the life you save end your own,
May the souls you save not atone,
For what you—

There might have been more coming, but the rest died in a giant slash Father Croser opened in the creature's throat. The creature itself followed suit moments later, gurgling his last breath into the blood staining the hardwood floor. Father Croser stared at his handiwork for a moment. Then he turned to me.

Pulling his black patch down, but onto his right eye this time, he said, "Let's have a drink, shall we?"

"You put your . . . ," I began, half-pointing at the eye-patch, then stopping when he raised his eyebrows inquisitively at me. *The guy just saved my life. He can put his patch on whichever eye he likes.* "Yeah. I could use a drink."

"Good on ye."

Father Croser fetched a long key from a desk drawer and unlocked the iron-banded door. It opened to reveal a set of dangerous-looking stairs that Father Croser dragged the dead creature's body down. Its head made a hollow thumping sound as it bounced rhythmically off the stone steps. Returning several minutes later with an open bottle of red wine and two glasses, Father Croser plopped them on the table and said, "Sit. Drink." I went to the front of the church and retrieved my guitar while he went back downstairs, this time for a mop, a bucket, and a bottle of cleaning solution. Then I followed Father Croser's directions, sitting and drinking while he worked at the bloodstained floorboards.

Sploosh, splot, splash.

The dark stain spread farther and farther as he scrubbed; the old mop was well past its prime and failed to absorb much of the dark, sticky blood.

"So," he called. His back was to me and I couldn't see his expression. "Do ye wish to be saved, my son?"

"Father," I laughed. "I think you *did* just save me."

He didn't join me in laughter. "Have ye taken Communion? Tasted the blood and the body of Christ?" He stopped mopping and fixed me sternly with his uncovered eye. "Do ye wish to be saved?"

"I've never done any of that." I took a sip of wine. Wondered if it was good or not. "Not my thing."

"Not your thing?" His one eye flashed with something like anger, but when he spoke it was in a calm, conversational tone. "Nae bother, then." He turned back to his mopping. *Sploosh, splot, splash.* "Tell me a wee story, then. Tell me how you come to see these demons."

"Like I said, Father." I gulped down two fingers of wine. "It was one of them."

"But why would one of them give you this gift?"

"Don't know. I sang a song for a good-looking girl in the park. And she must have been one of them, because . . ." *I suppose I shouldn't tell a priest it was shooting up that had done it.* "Because she gave me the sight as payment."

"Payment?"

"For the song, I guess."

Sploosh, splot, splash. "Hrmph."

Putting the wine glass to my lips, I asked, "And how did you get your sight, Father?"

"Why, from God, of course." He looked to the heavens and tapped on the cheekbone underneath his left eye. "My own mother, God rest her, anointed my eye in this very church when I was a boy. Saw my first demon in August of '93 and have destroyed no less than twenty-two of them since that day." *Sploosh, splot, splash.* "My mistake, twenty-three."

I took another taste of wine. I was almost through with my first glass and already feeling its calming effects. The room was growing distant, as if I were shrinking into my own head, and Father Croser's idiolect—part soothing country priest, part ravening fire and brimstone—was fading into the background with it. I reached for the bottle. It was farther away than I'd thought. Noting that my hands had finally stopped shaking, I refilled my glass.

"In the fight against Lucifer," Father Croser continued, "I have faced many different forms of demon. They have fought me with claws and teeth." *Sploosh.* "With spells and philters." *Splot.* "I have been injured a dozen times and cursed twice that." *Splash.* "They have tried to tempt me with riches, power, carnal pleasures." He shot me a triumphant smile. "I have defeated them at every turn."

I tipped my newly filled glass to him in a silent toast, then drained a decent amount.

Feeling good. Wonder when the priest will join me for a sip.

"Now, you," Father Croser turned and rested his elbow on the top of his mop, looking me in the eye. "You are the first person I have met who shares my gift." He turned his back and took up mopping again.

Sploosh, splot, splash.

"At first, I thought that you, like myself, were also touched by God. 'And Jehovah opened the eyes of the young man; and he saw; and, behold, the mountain was full of horses and chariots of fire.' "

Sounded like a Bible quote, but I wasn't familiar with it. Not that I was familiar with much of anything in the Bible. Not my thing. I lifted my glass again. Couldn't quite get it to my lips, though.

"However if, as you say, you were changed by one of *them*—a succubus by the sound of it—then your gift is sullied, your sight an offense unto God."

No, I tried to say, *it's not my fault.* But my lips just flapped meaninglessly and I mumbled something incoherent. I was wasted.

Off of a glass and a half of wine?

"An offense unto God!" Father Croser suddenly boomed out, as he turned to face me again. He searched my eyes—I could barely keep them open—and he must have seen something he liked because he nodded and turned back to his mopping.

Sploosh, splot, splash. The sound was mesmerizing, hypnotic. I blinked once, long and slow.

"And if thine eye offends thee . . ."

I knew the end to that one. *Pluck it out.*

"But don't worry, I am not an animal. You won't feel a thing. There's enough Roofies in that wine for a dozen university lads to gain unlawful carnal knowledge. You should be sleeping like a baby in just a minute."

Ahh, Roofies. The date-rape drug. That would explain it. But I didn't think rape was what Father Croser had in mind. I shook my head trying to clear it; it made my brain rattle off the sides of my skull. The room swam crazily.

Sploosh, splot, splash.

"You won't even remember what happened tomorrow," He peered over his shoulder at where I was slumped in his chair. "And the demon sight will be gone." I let my eyes close to just slits, and he sighed and went back to work on the floor. "Along with your eyes."

Just keep on mopping, motherfucker.

I knew a guy, a three-bag-a-day user, who ended up in the hospital with a burst appendix. He went under easy enough, but woke up in the middle of the operation, screaming bloody murder with his guts wide open and a team of doctors going ghost-white behind their surgical masks. It's called *cross-tolerance*: you do enough heroin and nothing works quite right on you anymore.

I may have been gone, twisted, blasted, fucked up beyond all belief—but I wasn't sleepy.

I timed the swaying of the room like a ship in high seas, and pushed myself to my feet on the upswell.

"I ain't sleepy," I mumbled to the priest's back, as he mopped—*sploosh, splot, splash.* I lurched to one side and kept myself upright by grabbing on to something.

My guitar! It fit my hand like a kid leather glove. I had played that guitar for hundreds of hours in similar sobriety-challenged states. I could play a decent melody long after I had drugged myself past the ability to walk, stand, or even speak. Just feeling it in my hand made my vision clear the tiniest bit. Hefting the guitar upside down by its neck, I held it in a two-handed baseball grip.

"Just go to sleep, my son. It will all be over soon," Father Croser said, his back to me, rubbing hard at a particularly recalcitrant blood spatter.

I lurched the three steps to him, guitar held back over my head. The floor was slick and wet from blood and soap, but I was weight forward, my feet following my body on despite the treacherous footing.

He must have heard or sensed me coming because he spun—*Damn, he's quick!*—and, dropping the mop, reached into his robes for his knife. His left foot slipped on a wet spot and he was forced to catch his balance with a brief wave of his free hand. With one hand deep in his robes and the other flailing to keep himself upright, his broad face was an easy target for a huge arcing swing. I put my hips, shoulders, and arms into it, and my guitar, my baby, my Lowden F35 Cutaway with the extra pickguard and the hipshot tuner, shattered on the bridge of Father Croser's nose.

He fell to the floor, the back of his skull hitting a ringing tone off one of the door's iron bands halfway down. Then I, too, lost my balance and only kept myself from falling by stomping hard on his midsection.

"I said I ain't sleepy, motherfucker!" I yelled into his bleeding, unconscious face, and I stomped again, hard, on his rib cage.

I kept kicking until I felt something crack and give, then stumbled to the office door, muttering a string of profanities under my breath. Down the long hall and into the church proper, I thought, *If I don't go to hell for beating up a priest, I might go for this string of expletives in a church.*

I left bloody footprints the length of the aisle as I made for the exit. Fumbled for the latch on the front door again, finally got it open, pitched out onto the stone walkway. Blinking in the streetlight's glare, I realized I still held two feet of shattered mahogany and dangling bronze strings in my right hand—all that was left of my beloved guitar. I tossed it into the bushes by the front door and made for Grandma McLaren's.

• • • Five • • •

My traveling bag—fully packed—hit the mattress next to me, jolting me awake. My eyes were blurred, my mouth dry, and the morning sun streaming through my window immediately set my head pounding.

"You're packed," said Grandma McLaren. The words were barely audible, so clenched were her teeth. "Get out." She spun smartly and marched downstairs.

I lay still for a few minutes trying to get my bearings.

Well, I thought, swinging my legs over the side of the air mattress, *I should probably be going, anyway. Maybe someplace where crazed elves and mad priests won't try to kill me.* I let that thought swim around with the hazy memories of the previous night. Tried to chase both away with a saner thought: *Maybe none of it happened. Maybe . . .*

I stood up to get dressed but discovered that I was already fully clothed. Hadn't even gotten my boots off before collapsing into bed last night. They were still covered with blood.

Faery blood? Father Croser's?

Heaving my bag over my shoulder, I headed downstairs. I was going to walk out the front door. Walk right out and not look back. Buy a new guitar, maybe get a Eurail pass and head to Amsterdam or Paris or some such place. Forget about Grandma McLaren, Edinburgh, and whatever insanity I had experienced last night.

But halfway down the stairs, I heard Grandma McLaren running the coffee grinder. It reminded me of my first morning here, waking up to her fixing me coffee. Something about that mechanical whirr drove nails through my feet and I stood glued to the stairs, a flood of memories like fast-dissolving movie scenes shooting through my head:

Grandma McLaren bouncing in her chair. "You're a busker!"

Fade . . .

Dusting pastry flakes off our shirtfronts in unison after sausage rolls at Fisher and Donaldson's.

Fade . . .

Late-night comedy on the BBC, Grandma McLaren laughing uproariously at a political reference that I had missed altogether.

The coffee grinder went silent, but the visions continued:

Grandma McLaren, after perhaps one too many glasses of wine, telling me, "My third husband blew himself up with a bomb meant for Parliament. Thought he was Guy Fawkes, he did."

Fade . . .

"I once spent eight days in a Turkish prison. My second husband's fault."

Fade . . .

The coffee grinder's insistent whine dragging me awake, the prospect of fresh java, a home-cooked meal, and pleasant conversation swiftly stifling the horror of the early hour.

I couldn't take another step toward the door. This wasn't a stop on the road, a place to crash while I straightened up. This was a home. My home.

My sanctuary.

I caught up with Grandma McLaren in the kitchen. She was bringing water to a boil, one long fingernail clicking rapidly on the side of the stove.

"Grandma," I said. No answer. "Grandma."

She spoke without turning. "I've said my piece."

I nodded, though she couldn't see the gesture. "I know. And I'll leave if you want me to. But I'd like to tell you what happened first."

"Yes," she said, leaving off her tapping and finally turning to face me. "Tell me what happened. Tell me why you thought you could come into my house high on . . . whatever you were high on."

"Wine."

"Bull. Shit. Wine." She spat the syllables at me.

"Wine was all I meant to drink, Grandma." I stood up straighter and tried to keep the pleading tone out of my voice. "Someone spiked my drink."

The kettle whistled. Grandma McLaren turned back to the stove and poured it into the press-pot. The grounds swirled up and stained the water black.

"Why should I believe you?"

Why should she? "Because I have no reason to lie to you."

And I hadn't lied to her. Not yet. I spun her gently around and looked into her face, my hands still on her shoulders. It was a long way down.

"Grandma," I said. "You know what I am. I won't hide things from you—I don't think I could. If I fuck up, you'll know. Besides, if I can't get through this here, with you, then I don't think I could get through it anywhere. And I might as well go back to Minneapolis and die with my junkie friends."

She spent what must have been a full minute just looking into my eyes, not speaking, searching for something.

Screw it, I thought. *I won't lie to her.* At that moment, if she had asked me for details, I would have told her everything, though I wasn't even sure I believed it myself. And then, I assumed, I'd have been thrown into an insane asylum.

"All right," she finally said. "I have a fourth rule I never mentioned." She turned back to the counter and pressed down on the coffee plunger, crushing the grounds to the bottom. "The fourth rule is this: Everyone gets one chance to screw up. And, if you're telling me the truth—"

"I am."

She held up one finger, not interested in my response. "And if you're telling me the truth, then someone else spent your one chance for you." She waved her finger at me before I could speak again. "It doesn't matter. It's time to move on. Now, did you sort out the person who drugged you?"

I looked down at the brown stains on my boots and nodded.

She followed my gaze. "You in any trouble?"

"Maybe. But not the kind you think." Father Croser didn't strike me as someone who would run to the police.

"I can think of a lot of different kinds of trouble, Dougie."

"Fair enough. But this is kind of . . . complicated."

She snorted. "Dougie, I am well aware of the kind of world we live in and—"

"No, no," I interrupted. "It's not—" I stopped and collected myself. "It's not that I think you wouldn't understand. It's just that I seem to have gotten myself into something big and complex and dangerous and I don't want to drag anyone else—especially you—into it."

She stared at me for a moment, her face softening. "Maybe you should leave town."

"No." I shook my head. "No. I can work it out so I can stay. I know I can."

"How?"

"That I don't know." *How could I stay in a town where a psychotic priest and possibly a ravening horde of monsters were trying to kill me?* I felt like I was close to an answer. If I could just get my head to stop pounding.

Grandma McLaren handed me a cup of coffee. "Drink up. You look like shit."

I didn't need anyone to tell me that. I always looked like shit.

I always looked like shit . . .

A thought was beginning to form. A person more optimistic than me might even have called it a plan.

"Grandma, do you have any hair dye in the house?"

"What are you saying?"

"Nothing, Grandma, nothing. Just . . . that isn't your real hair color, is it?"

"Why, of course it is!" She looked shocked at the accusation. Then a sly grin crept up and stole the disbelief from her features. "Which isn't to say it doesn't need a bit of help now and again."

I CUT MY hair, bleached the black out, and then dyed it a dull brown. It was a rough-looking job, but I figured I could get it cleaned up professionally in town. I discarded everything in my wardrobe that didn't cover any tattoos Father Croser might have seen and put on my one pair of unripped jeans and a long-sleeved black cotton tee shirt. I checked myself in the mirror. I looked like a different person. I doubted my own mother would recognize me, let alone a crazy priest who had met me only once—even as memorable as that one meeting had been.

I was going to have to do something about the bloodstained boots, however.

"The new look going to keep you out of trouble, Dougie?" Grandma McLaren asked, as I came down the stairs.

"Part of it."

"Hrmph."

"I figured out a way to keep my drinks from getting spiked, though."

"Oh, aye?"

"Yeah. I'll just quit drinking."

"Just like that?"

"Sure, why not?"

"Well, good then. It never made much sense to me. You drinking. Can't toss the devil out with one hand and invite him in with the other."

GRANDMA MCLAREN TOOK me shopping. We drove down the hill toward town and I peered south across Princes Street Gardens to the promenade where my busking spot was. I'd hoped to see it half-empty, like it had been before my day in the park with Aine. But booths still crammed the west side, with pennants and banners and strange lights flying over them, attracting shoppers who, even from this distance, didn't look human at all.

"You okay, Dougie?"

I swallowed hard, having trouble speaking. "I . . . um . . ."

Faeries. Fucking hell.

"Dougie?"

Right, I thought, giving my head a shake. *That's it, then.* The faery market, the boar-man, Father Croser . . . all real. I might be crazy, but I sure as shit wasn't high.

"I'm okay, Grandma." I wasn't. But maybe I would be soon.

We traveled up and down Princes Street, popping in and out of the myriad clothing stores. I bought a whole new wardrobe: button-down shirts, dress pants, brown shoes, and brand-name sneakers. And no fewer than four pairs of large, mirrored sunglasses.

We passed Father Croser's church on the way to the music store. There were no police cars parked outside.

I probably hadn't killed him then, I thought. *More's the pity.* Though for a moment I did wonder if he was still lying there, undiscovered.

I spent the rest of the stake I'd earned at the Fringe on a Gibson Super 200 Cutaway, big, fat, and loud. We had shopped right through lunch, and for the first time since I came to Edinburgh I was once again stone broke and starving. Grandma McLaren treated me to sausage rolls and an Irn Bru—the world's most disgusting soft drink—and then to a professional, if dirt cheap, haircut.

I decided to put off going back to work until the next day, returning home—*home!*—where Grandma McLaren and I talked and swilled Irn Bru until the cloying bubble-gum flavor began to grow on me. Much as I imagined a fungus would.

THE NEXT MORNING, I walked to work as usual, but with my eyes skittering back and forth behind a pair of mirrored shades, trying to distinguish faeries from Fringe performers and street people. It was not an easy task. Was that a homeless person muttering to himself as he walked, or was there another set of eyes peering out of his long coat? Was that an actor in period dress hustling to an early show, or had he been wearing that medieval doublet since the time it was in style?

I kept my head down and talked to no one, not even daring to meet anyone's gaze, despite my reflective glasses.

Looking down on the promenade from Princes Street, I considered the sprawl of the twin markets. The human merchants—tattooed, pierced, and dressed in outlandish clothes—looked like midwestern aldermen compared to the shuffling, flying, hopping, slithering mass of insanity that comprised the faery side.

I reconsidered my plan.

I shouldn't go back there. What if the other faeries had seen me run? What if the boar-man had signaled something to them before he came after me? And then an even more frightening thought: *What if Father Croser comes shopping?*

But my busking spot was at the far end, just a short hop to the Playfair Steps and out of sight. Little chance any faeries besides the one chasing me had noticed my mad flight of the other day. And Father Croser only knew me as a breathless punker who had charged into his church seeking sanctuary. No reason to think he would look for me here. And even if he did, I didn't believe he would recognize me in my new outfit.

I haven't spent a week establishing myself on this prime piece of Fringe real estate to get chased off by the first mad priest or homicidal faery that came around.

I took a deep breath and marched down to set up.

"Spot's taken, sir," Sandra said.

"Oh, really?"

"Aye. Sorry, but you'll have to move on."

"Sandra, it's me."

"Who?"

I pulled my glasses down a little and looked at her over the rims. "Douglas," I suggested.

"Jesus!"

I laughed. "No, Douglas."

She eyed me slowly, up and down. "Jesus," she said again.

I put my guitar case down and flipped it open. "Thanks for saving my spot."

"No bother," she answered. Then, "Hey!" She dug around beneath her table of wares. "I held on to your gear for you." She pulled out my pack-o-gear. "I think it's all in there. When you didn't come back I . . ."

"Thanks," I beamed at her. "That'll save me some trouble."

"No bother," she said again, then stopped and looked hard at me once more. "Em, where'd you run off to the other day, anyway?" she asked, still not sounding certain that it was me.

I tried to think of something that would kill the line of questioning before it even got started. Rubbing my stomach, I said, "Diarrhea."

She made a sour face. "And the new look?"

Across the way, a tall elf in a long green surcoat haggled with the pipe-smoking old woman over the price of a horned skull. The little shoemaker was nowhere to be seen, but I could hear a pounding I guessed was made by a hammer on a cobbler's bench. The troll at the dead-thing booth seemed to have given up on sales and was eating his merchandise.

It was tough concentrating on what she was saying, like trying to watch TV while talking on the phone.

"What?" I said.

"The new look?"

A small faery man, thickly covered in coarse black hair and nothing else, raced up the promenade, whooping and ripping the bottoms out of shopping bags. A group of creatures, similar-looking but dressed in gray breeches and tunics, applauded his antics and snickered at the humans as they gathered their fallen purchases. The elf in green took one look over his shoulder at the commotion and shook his head disapprovingly.

I shrugged. "Just time for a change, I guess."

I pulled the Gibson out of its case and strapped it on. It was a good, serviceable instrument. Yet it wasn't the Lowden, and I experienced a moment of overwhelming sadness for my old guitar. I thought of all the miles we'd covered, all the songs we'd played, all the melodies unwritten that would now never grace its strings. I tried to shake the feeling off, telling myself that all the strings were in the same order on the Gibson, all the frets the same interval apart.

It isn't the Lowden, I told myself. *But it is a guitar, and I'm a guitarist. So . . .*

I strummed a chord. Not as subtle as the Lowden had been, but it had a gutty low end that I liked. Sounded earthy, masculine. I picked several intricate runs, high and low, testing each string alone and in combination.

Could probably go with a lighter gauge of strings than I'd used on the Lowden, I thought, *and not sacrifice any bass or volume.*

I hunched over the guitar, my chin nearly touching the top of it, and watched my fingers fly over the mahogany fingerboard, testing by touch and sight and hearing the limits of my new ax. Not wanting to leave my other senses out, I breathed in deeply, inhaling the new wood smell of it.

I drew the line at actually licking it.

After five minutes of putting it through its paces, I deemed its performance satisfactory and looked up from my hands.

I had drawn a little crowd.

And not just humans. The snickering faeries in their gray garb were sitting cross-legged in front of me. Quiet now, their eyes were closed as they swayed back and forth, waiting for the last chord to die. The elf in green, a horned skull now in hand, was leaning against the old woman's booth with a pleased smile on his face. Another elf, this one in a gray surcoat, stood behind the snickering faeries. He had a small stringed instrument strapped to his back and he gave me a nod of respect, one musician to another.

I nearly responded with a nod of my own, but caught myself in time and merely kept scanning the crowd. With relief, my gaze fell on someone I knew was human: a young woman I had written a song for some weeks ago, though I couldn't remember her name or what her song had been about.

"You there!" I called to her. *Now what was her name? Cassie . . . Carol . . . Caligula . . . Collusion . . .* "Colleen!" *That's it.* "Another song for you?"

She smiled and shook her head. "Just listening today, I'm afraid. But here's some cash anyway." And matching word to deed, she dropped a few coins into my case.

"Even better! Money for nothing, I say. I— And you, sir, how about a song for you?" I called to a man in an enormous Stetson. I didn't know much about them yet, but I was willing to bet no denizen of Faerie would ever wear a cowboy hat.

"Whatcha mean?"

I pulled out my sign and launched into my spiel. Pretty soon, the two elves moved off. The pack of hairy men stayed. After playing a song for the man in the hat, I wrote another for an old woman with bifocals and a cane. I played two songs for a young couple whose shopping bags had mysteriously burst, the hairy men giggling uncontrollably the entire time. The little troublemakers eventually left and a group of tiny winged faeries flew into the space they vacated. They flitted around my head while I made a tape for an attractive girl in a business suit. Then they danced with each other in midair while I made a tape for the girl's even prettier, but not quite as well-dressed, friend. The two girls chatted me up for a bit before leaving and, if I hadn't been so distracted by the flittering fey, I might have realized they were waiting for me to ask one of them out.

I wrote song after song and made tape after tape until the money was threatening to overflow my case. Around lunchtime, I told Sandra, "I'll buy if you fly," and she ran to get cheese toasties from a nearby pub. I choked mine down in less than a minute and got back to work. I didn't stop again, or even slow down, until well after the sun had set.

Despite knowing I was being watched by a pack of potentially murderous faeries, or perhaps because of it, I had worked the crowd like a ringmaster. The fear of making a wrong move had kept me sharp and alert, and I didn't think there was a human who walked by me that day who hadn't, at the very least, dropped a coin or two in my case.

Or maybe the faery dust had something to do with it.

I was cramming the last of the pound coins into my overstuffed pockets and wondering whether to have my shades on or off for the dark walk home, when I felt a tap on my shoulder, startling me. Change scattered on the pavement as I spun and raised my hands in a defensive posture that was half Bruce Lee, half Three Stooges. I must have looked like an idiot.

"Douglas?"

It was Sandra. Now I felt like an idiot, too.

"Um . . . yes?" My hands seemed frozen in front of my face. I stuffed them into my pockets and then immediately pulled them out again to gather coins from the pavement.

"How about one for me?" She had a five-pound note in her hand and she inclined her head toward my guitar case.

"Put your money away and help me grab this change. I'll do you one for free."

Her leg brushed against mine as she knelt to help me scoop the coins up. I didn't think it was an accident.

"There," she said when we had finished. "Now what?"

"Now we sit."

We sat cross-legged on the ground, my back to the faery market this time. I could just make out the lights of the train station through my sunglasses. Sandra was looking up at me with a familiar expression on her face. It was a junkie's look, a sad-happy affair that seemed to say: The world sucked but you were only ever one hit away from happiness.

"What now?" she asked. "Want to know more about me?"

"Shhh."

I took off my sunglasses and examined the lines on her face. Too many of them for someone who was probably as young as me. She leaned forward a little and put her hand on my knee, giving me a nervous smile.

"Sandra . . . ," I began.

"Yes?"

She really was a nice girl. But I couldn't get involved with another user.

"A haiku," I said.

She blinked as I picked a few odd intervals on the middle strings of the Gibson, grabbing them in a strong vibrato that rattled the pitches back and forth. It sounded foreign, alien.

Only bone remains
And hoofprints on too-thin arms
There's no song for you.

She stared at me. Slowly took her hand off my leg.

"You asshole," she said.

I nodded in agreement.

"You arrogant, fucking asshole. You think you're all that and a bag of chips? What makes you so different?" She was standing now and I looked up at her with difficulty. "New clothes? A new haircut? You're the same as me!"

"I know."

She looked like she was about to say something more, but she clamped her lips tight and stomped off instead. My fingers played the short song again of their own volition. Without the vibrato, it sounded sweet, like a lullaby. My knee was still warm where her hand had been.

I stood, packed up my gear, and walked home, never turning back to look at the faery market.

GRANDMA MCLAREN WAS still up when I got home, which wasn't unusual. What *was* strange was that she had cooked me dinner.

"I thought you might be hungry after spending all day trying to solve your 'problem.' " She raised her eyebrows inquisitively. "Are you near a solution?"

"I think so," I replied, eyeing the heaping plate of gammon steak and potatoes before me on the dining room table. A plate with quarter portions of the same sat in front of Grandma McLaren. She'd not make me eat alone, it seemed. "If I can get through the next few days, I think it'll be clear sailing."

"That's brilliant, then. Care to talk about it yet?"

I shook my head as I stabbed a piece of ham. "Not yet." I couldn't talk about it. Not ever. *Or maybe I could.* "Grandma, do you believe in the supernatural?"

She smiled. "Changing the subject?"

"Sure, why not?" I said, trying to return her grin while chewing.

"Well, what are we talking about here? Ghosts?"

"Ghosts, goblins . . ." I paused. "Faeries. All of it."

"Oh." She tilted her head and looked upward, thinking. When she spoke, it was more to the ceiling than me. "Your grandfather died in Korea," she said. "In the war."

"I know." I followed her gaze, eyeing the old paint, peeling slightly with age. "My mother told me."

I looked back down at Grandma McLaren and now she was staring straight at me, her eyes bright.

"I saw his ghost the night he died," she said.

"Really?"

Nodding, she said, "Oh, aye. Your mother was just a baby. And a colicky one at that. I remember, it was late at night. I was standing in the middle of our little flat, rocking her, both of us crying our eyes out. Then something odd happened."

"You saw him?"

"Well, not immediately. First off, the baby stopped crying. Felt like she'd been crying for days. And then she said her very first word." Grandma McLaren shifted some food from side to side on her plate. "Can you guess what it was?"

"Nope."

"Why, it was 'Daddy,' of course. Even though she'd never seen him. And then I felt Donald," Grandma McLaren pointed her empty fork at me, "your grandfather, there with me."

"Felt him how?"

"It's hard to explain. Have you ever lived with someone so long that when you come home, you can tell if they're in the house already? Not because you see their coat on a chair or their shoes in the hall, but just because you *know* they're there?"

I shook my head. "No. Never lived with anyone that long. Not even my parents."

Grandma McLaren peered at me. "No, I suppose not. Well, anyway, I could feel him there in the room with me. I called to him, 'Donald?' And then I heard his voice in my head."

"What did he say?"

"He said, 'Dinnae worry, Lizzie. I'll be hame soon.' " She sighed. "And he wasn't lying. They shipped his body back six days later."

She pushed her untouched plate toward the center of the table. For a moment, she looked frail and old. Then she gave herself a shake and smiled up at me.

"So, I suppose I believe in ghosts," she said. "Or something like them. But as to the rest of it: faeries, pixies, bogies and boggarts, spriggans and spunkies . . ." She covered her left eye with one hand

and fluttered the other hand in front of her chest. "The Fachan." She chuckled. "No, I don't believe in them. Probably because I've never seen one."

"You sure seem to know a lot about them."

"Oh, aye, Dougie. I'm an old Scottish woman. We're required by law to know those kinds of things."

"Tell me about them, then." I thought of the snickering men I had seen that morning. "Are bogies little hairy troublemakers?"

"Aye. Sounds about right."

"Any difference between them and boggarts?"

"Not much. They're both bad little bastards."

They hadn't seemed that bad. Just . . . "Mischievous bad? Or evil bad?"

Grandma McLaren thought a moment, tapping a finger on her cheek. "They run the gamut, I suppose. Some are no more than petty thieves and pranksters. Some are murderers and worse."

"What about spriggans and spunkies?"

"Shipwreckers and kidnappers."

I covered one eye with my hand like Grandma McLaren had. "The Fachan?"

"One eye, one ear, one leg, and one hand that comes straight out of his chest. Mean bugger. Carries a big club in his one hand and uses it on anyone who gets near him."

"Don't you know of any *nice* faeries, Grandma?"

"In Scotland?" She snorted. "They didn't pluck the term 'dour Scot' out of thin air, Dougie. There's not a Scottish fairy tale that doesn't end without someone getting hanged or burned at the stake or thrown down a well. And the faeries themselves? They're all the wandering spirits of unbaptised children or murdered relatives, and even the good ones will turn on you in a second if you break one of their unwritten rules." She lowered her eyebrows, scowling at me. "But don't you have bigger worries than pookas and piskies? Or the Fachan wanting a piece of your liver for supper?"

Not really, no. I shrugged. "It's something that's interested me lately."

"Well, go to the bookstore. Or the library. They'll know more about it than me."

"Not much more, it seems," I said, smiling.

"Perhaps," Grandma McLaren sighed. "But they won't tire as easily." She pushed herself up and away from the table. "I'm away to bed. You'll clear up for me tonight?"

"Of course, Grandma. I'll see you in the morning."

Given my illegal immigrant status, I didn't think trying to get a library card was such a great idea. But the bookstore sounded good. Ignoring the faeries had worked so far, but it certainly wouldn't hurt if I knew more about them.

THE NEXT MORNING found me ensconced in a corner of the James Thin bookstore at South Bridge. There was a remarkable amount of material on faeries to be found. I read through a short treatise by a seventeenth-century Aberfoyle minister that treated faeries as established fact, before skimming a recent "encyclopedia" of faeries that was more interested in them as a cultural phenomenon. An 1880 collection presented faery stories from around the world, while a self-styled *Witch's Guide to Faery Folk* gave hints on how to contact them.

Contact? That was one thing I *didn't* need help with.

After paging through another dozen or so volumes, I began to realize that while there were some inconsistencies from one book to the next, the inconsistencies were more remarkable for their rarity. I could sense a consonance, an underlying theme, that ran throughout all the legends and tales.

It's as if the stories are based on real creatures and events, I thought, and surprised myself with a slightly maniacal giggle. I glanced around to see if anyone had noticed and spotted a bald man, a pin on his shirt identifying him as bookstore staff, staring at me pointedly. I'd seen that look before. It said, "You've been here for hours and haven't bought so much as a bookmark." I was about to get kicked out.

Not today. This time, I had cash on me. I surprised the bald man by waving him over.

"Can I help ye?" he asked, not bothering to keep the suspicion out of his voice.

"Yes, you could. Could you give me a hand bringing these to the front?"

"You're buying them?"

"Every last one."

It took us two trips to haul the books to the register, and twice as many bags to hold them all. Deciding to continue splurging, I ordered a taxi to take me to Grandma McLaren's, tipping the driver well when he helped me to the front door with my loot. I climbed the stairs and dumped the bags out onto the air mattress before hopping onto it myself. I picked up one of the books at random and dove in.

"**COMING DOWN TO** dinner, Dougie?" Grandma McLaren called up the stairs.

I blinked and rubbed my eyes. *Is it really dinnertime?* Around me, the pile of books had grown to include reams of notes, hand-drawn charts, maps, sketches. I was halfway to completing my very own field guide to Scottish Faeries. All I needed now was John Audubon to "collect" a few and paint their portraits.

I could probably get Father Croser to fill the first part of that order. I shuddered at the thought.

"Just a minute, Grandma."

"I'm starting to not believe you."

"Hrmm?"

"You've been saying that for nearly an hour."

Whoops. "Ummm. But I mean it this time."

"Oh, aye. I'm sure you do."

I dug out of my piles of research and started tromping down the stairs. I could finish after dinner.

Or, I thought, looking out the front window and gauging how much sunlight was left in the day, *maybe I need to do a little more live observation.*

"Grandma?" I called. "You mind putting mine in the fridge? I have to run out for a bit."

As I scampered out the door, I could hear her calling to my back, "Aye, you meant it that time for sure."

But it sounded like she was smiling.

I HIT PRINCES Street Gardens cocksure in my new knowledge. The bright August sun beat down on me and I cursed the need to wear my tattoo-concealing long sleeves. Striding manfully into the chaos of the faerie market, I began naming faeries to myself as I watched them through my mirrored shades.

There, by the henna booth, a pack of bogies, like I'd seen yesterday. Strolling past them, browsing, a young couple with webbed fingers that they twined together, sealskins draped over their backs: selkies. A hobgoblin, warty and short, bought potions from a remarkably human-looking elf. Large black dogs wove through the crowd, narrowly avoiding tripping the tall faeries or trampling their smaller brethren.

I continued on. Knowing the names and attributes of the faeries lent me a kind of strength, and I walked with my head held high, my chest puffed out.

A urisk, half man and half goat, leered at a young tourist in tight shorts and a halter top, while the prim glaistig with him stomped her cloven hooves and shook a finger in his face. A squat brownie swung a broom wildly at a swarm of formless glowing spunkies buzzing around the sweets she was selling. A troop of robin-sized pixies were using the distraction to mount a raid on the brownie's wares, tossing tiny grappling hooks to the counter and hoisting themselves hand-over-hand toward the piles of pastries heaped there.

It was hard not to just stop and stare. I was glad for my dark glasses, and I reached up and touched them, reassuring myself that they were still in place.

As I neared the far end of the promenade, I noticed that the little shoemaker—a leprechaun, over from Ireland, perhaps—was doing a brisk business today. A line of red-capped dunters waited impatiently while the Nuckelavee, a skinless, man-eating centaur, got his hooves shod. The troll at the dead-things booth eyed the queue of diminutive fiends hungrily, whether wanting them for customers or hors d'oeuvres, I couldn't tell. And at the skull shop, in a heated discussion with the witch who ran it, was the Fachan.

He was huge—well over seven feet tall—and balanced his bulk all on one precarious and surprisingly dainty foot. His single eye was bloodshot and baleful, and it took up most of his face, leaving barely enough room for a pinched mouth, a vestigial nose, and an ear that swept behind his head like a bird's crest. Even more avian was the short shock of blue feathers clinging to his thin stretch of forehead. A long, muscular arm shot straight out from his chest, ending in a hand that clutched a giant horseman's flail. He was shaking this ominous weapon directly in the face of the old woman.

"Gi' us mair'n bawbees for it, ye grippie auld spaewife!" he roared down at her, spittle flying. I wondered what the hell he had just said.

The old woman shook her head and blew out a smoke ring that enveloped the Fachan's head.

"Three is what I offer," she said, her voice rasping like worn sandpaper. "Three is what I will give."

Ah. They're bargaining.

The Fachan snorted and sputtered, his limited features reddening. Suddenly, he swung his arm up and his weapon's many tails snaked back over his head. I thought he was going to remove the old woman's head with it, but instead, he gave his wrist a sharp twitch, and the weapon wrapped itself neatly around his neck. He let the pommel bounce on his chest and reached into a pouch at his side.

"How's about another wee deek, then?" he asked the witch, his roar turned now into an ingratiating whine. "Aye, mebbe another leuk'll pry a bit mair clink frae yer pootch."

And with that, he pulled a skull out of his pouch and plunked it down in front of the old woman. Bits of flesh and short black hair still clung to it and though I couldn't tell what sex it had once been, it was undoubtedly human.

You're an idiot, I told myself.

Anonymity and a pair of sunglasses weren't going to be enough to keep me safe. I should have known that. After Grandma McLaren's warnings and all the accounts I had read—not to mention my own run-in with the boar-man—I should have damn well known that. These weren't benign nineteenth-century Cottingham faeries playing with little girls in the woods; these were dangerous magical creatures whose motivations and capabilities I could only guess at. Instead of spending the day trying to identify as many faeries as I could, I should have concentrated on what—if any—protections were available to mortals who dealt with the fey.

I would have castigated myself further but I had a bigger, more pressing problem.

I had gasped.

When the Fachan had smashed the skull down on the counter, sending flecks of rotten flesh flying, I had gasped like a fourteen-year-old girl at a rock concert. Apparently, without my work to distract me, I had let my defenses drop, and gotten too involved in the scene I was observing.

And now the Fachan had turned and was fixing me with his single malignant eye.

• • • six • • •

Shit, I thought. *Not again.*

The Fachan was staring at me and reaching for his flail, and I just stood stock still, panicked into immobility, waiting for death.

Do something! Anything!

The Fachan slipped his flail off his shoulder and swished it through the air once. He was fifteen feet away but seemed closer. His eye began to fill my vision, and I could hear a hint of strange martial music in my head. I could almost pick out a melody. Something I could sing out loud . . .

"Douglas!" yelled someone from behind the Fachan.

Sandra. She was coming down the Playfair Steps, a cheese toastie in her hand, still gloriously angry from yesterday.

"Hey, Sandra. You surprised me there," I called back, all the time telling myself: *That's why I gasped, that's why I gasped.*

"Yeah, well, I've got a wee surprise for you, too, asshole." She went on, but I wasn't listening anymore. I was walking straight toward her. And toward the Fachan.

"Yeah, Sandra, yeah." *Sandra surprised me. So I gasped.*

I was just a few strides away from him. He was swinging his flail back and forth, and tracking me with his eye. From this distance I could see the yellowish veins in his arm, bulging with each stroke of his weapon.

Another step, and I could see that his eye was incongruously hazel. He stopped the flail on the upstroke as I came beside him and the tails rattled and clanked as they settled. I could smell him, now: musty caves and old blood.

"Sandra, listen now," I said, and I was by him, trying not to shiver noticeably as I nearly brushed against him.

"No, you listen, Douglas." And she slapped me hard across the cheek. Even with the noise of the crowded market, the sharp crack echoed off the steps. A few people stopped and stared. I felt a welt raising on my cheek. She hauled back for another swing but I was ready this time and caught her hand in midair.

"Sandra, now just hold on . . . ," I began, but before I could say more, she dropped her cheese toastie, clenched her free hand in a tight little fist, and punched me right in my solar plexus.

I folded like a piece of origami.

I could hear the Fachan cackling with glee behind me. "Och," he said to the old woman. "I'll take the three for ma heid, afore the lassie sells ye his for twa!"

"You're a right bastard," Sandra said. I was doubled over and she was speaking directly into my ear.

"Erg." I struggled to catch my breath. "I know."

She shook her hand loose and bent to pick up her cheese toastie. Changing her mind when she saw how dirty it had become, she let it lie and, tossing her hair behind her, marched stiffly to her booth. There she sat primly on her stool and very pointedly did not look in my direction.

I stayed hunched over for another minute or so before I had recovered enough to unfold myself. Ignoring the snickers of the onlookers—faeries and humans both—I mustered what dignity I could and walked back the way I came. I would deal with Sandra tomorrow, when I got back to work. Right now, I needed protection.

I MADE IT to Grandma McLaren's, ate a quick dinner, and hit the books. There was, once again, a lot of information to digest, even having narrowed my subject matter down to just protection. Bread, bells, scissors, certain plants, religious artifacts or activities, a father's clothes or your own turned inside out, even salt—all were said to be proof against faeries. But not all the faeries, all the time. I needed something that would work against the multitude of faeries I was likely to run into at the market. I read and reread, cross-referenced and read again. Eventually, I decided that there was one thing that all the books could agree on, one thing that was one hundred percent guaranteed to be anathema to any faery denizen: iron.

Cold, hard iron. And if they were afraid of iron, I figured they ought to be terrified of steel. I resolved to pick up supplies in the morning and finally went to sleep.

THE STREETS IN the Old Town are packed full with souvenir shops. Scottish souvenir shops. "Tartan Tat," the locals call it. And once past the plaid scarves, Nessie dolls, and minibagpipers that played "Scotland the Brave" when you pressed their bellies, I found that the Scots sell a lot of knives. From six-foot-long Claymores to tiny letter openers, you could outfit a small army from the stores on High Street alone.

While the bigger swords would have made me feel the safest, I presumed that I would have trouble walking the streets with one. With that in mind, I purchased a six-inch clasp knife that fit comfortably in my palm along with, in a nod to my Scottish heritage, a *sgian dubh,* the piper's traditional "black" knife. It was designed for concealment, and the whole thing—thin wedge-shaped blade, leather-wrapped pommel—couldn't have been more than four inches long. Looked deadly enough, though. In the bathroom of Deacon Brodie's Tavern, I put the clasp knife in my front right trouser pocket and tucked the *sgian dubh* in its small sheath into my left sock. I checked myself out in the mirror: *No knives visible. Good to go.*

Now armed, I went in search of the biggest hunk of metal I could comfortably wear around my neck. I found it in the form of a Celtic cross on a thick leather band. I cut the band shorter so it wouldn't bang against my guitar when I played. The solid weight of it was reassuring, as was the smooth leather of the *sgian dubh*'s sheath against my calf and the feel of the clasp knife when I put my hand in my pocket.

I was ready.

IT WAS MIDMORNING when I pushed my way through the people milling about on the promenade. Surreptitiously, I scanned the faerie side through my dark glasses.

No sign of the Fachan this time; it looked like Elven Day at the fair. Groups of well-dressed elves milled about, drinking from long-stemmed crystal goblets and doffing their velvet hats politely to one another. They seemed grouped by color, both of skin and clothing: pale elves wearing green and white steering clear of their swarthier brethren who preferred blacks and grays. If there was some mention of this kind of cliquishness in my books, I'd missed it. I'd been completely absorbed with classifying the faeries and then equally obsessed with protecting myself from them. I was wondering if the groupings were familial, political, or entirely of my own imagining, when my line of thought and my feet both came to an abrupt stop.

Someone was in my spot.

There, tucked into the southeast corner, where I'd been spending the Fringe, was a squat young man hawking poorly constructed dreamcatchers on a ragged blanket. Sandra was at his side, bubbling happily, touching his arm as she laughed.

No. I don't think so.

Three long strides and I stood before them.

"Introduce me to your friend, Sandra."

She opened her mouth to say something snide, but the look on my face must have stopped her.

"Douglas, this is Tommy. From California."

"Hey, man," he said in a bland West Coast accent. "Really cool to meet you." He stared up at me, waiting for me to respond, his big blue eyes devoid of malice. Or intelligence.

I could just walk away, I thought. *Things will be uncomfortable here with Sandra, anyway. I could find a spot farther away from the faery market, make a little less money, be a lot more safe.*

I put my guitar and my pack-o-gear next to him on the blanket.

"Can I talk to you a second, Tommy? Privately?"

He nodded and we moved a few steps away.

"What's up, buddy?" he asked.

"Listen, you might not have known it. But you're in my spot."

"Hey, it's cool. We can share it or—"

I put my hand on his shoulder to stop him. Shook my head. "You're going to have to move on."

"Hold on a second, man—"

I gave his shoulder a little squeeze. He tried to shake it loose but I had been playing guitar for as long as I remember. Makes for strong hands.

"Move on," I said, leaning down and speaking directly into his ear. And then, quite calmly added, "Or I'll tear off your motherfucking arm and rape you with it."

I was right in his face and I looked over my glasses to make sure he could see my eyes. I made them go flat, lifeless. Let him guess whether I was bluffing. I knew one thing: there was no fear in them. I saved that for things that could actually hurt me, like the creatures milling about behind me. I had none left over for this pudgy Californian.

"I—"

"Move."

I let go of his shoulder then and he scampered back to his blanket. Without a word, he gathered his gear and scuttled away.

"Tommy?" Sandra called after him. Then to me, "What did you say to him?"

"Nothing," I shrugged. "Guess he didn't want to stick around."

"Goddammit." Her face got pinched, as if I'd taken hold of it and squeezed.

"Sandra, look. I felt real bad about what I said to you the other night." I grinned at her. "Right up until you punched me in the stomach." I flipped open my case and strapped on my guitar. Unpacked my sign and tape deck. "Now, I figure we're even. You can leave it at that, and we can get along till the Fringe is over and we go our separate ways." I strummed a G chord. Adjusted the tuning on my B string. "Or we can have a problem."

She just stared at me, openmouthed.

"Your choice," I said. "We going to have a problem?"

"Why do you have to be such an asshole?"

A good question. I gave it some serious thought before answering. Leaning in closer, so I would no longer have to shout over the din of both markets, I said, "Because I'm out of the game, and you're still in it. And nothing we say or do can change that."

I straightened back up and strummed the G chord again. All tuned up and ready to play.

"But what if I want out, too?" Her voice was thin and plaintive, barely audible, and I could tell how much it cost her to say those words to me.

"I can't help you."

I really was an asshole.

THE DAY PASSED slowly. Every song I sang was either a dirge or a slow air, and my customers were not pleased. Business slowed to a crawl before petering out altogether, and eventually I just sat cross-legged on the ground, picking random melodies while I watched the faeries.

After some time, I decided their color groupings were political. The coloring of surcoats, hats, cloaks, boots, patches, belts, ribbons—either green and white or black and gray—all seemed to indicate allegiance to one side or the other. Creatures wearing the same colors moved in groups and shopped together, avoiding those who wore a different color whenever possible. Yet, in such a confined space, confrontations were unavoidable, and occasionally two different groups came together. Insults and taunts were exchanged. But I never saw any of them come to blows. Which struck me as odd, considering the amount of animosity there seemed to be between them.

However, regardless of affiliation, the other faeries were unfailingly polite to the imperious elves. To their faces, anyway. When the elves of the other color's backs were turned, I saw creatures wearing the green and white sneering, or spitting surreptitiously on the ground, or making bizarre signs with their small hands, like the ones Grandma McLaren said were used to ward off the evil eye.

The signs the black and grays made were more universal and easier to interpret. One boggart in particular had a habit of bending over and farting loudly whenever an elf in green and white passed.

He apologized profusely, usually on bended knee, if caught in the act but never looked that contrite once his target had moved on.

I poked my guitar case with my foot. It barely clinked. I needed to shake off this malaise and get to work. The Fringe had less than two weeks left to it, and if I wanted to avoid playing in the cold this winter, I was going to have to stop wasting time moping, even if I did call it research.

Time to make the donuts, I thought. Heaving myself to my feet with a grunt and a sigh, I vowed to give the hard sell to the next person I saw.

That next person was Father Croser.

He was limping down the steps, a hand pressed to his side. His nose was bandaged, his left eye blackened and bruised, with more discoloration leaking out from behind the eyepatch over his right. Despite his obvious pain, he still had a broad grin on his peasant face as he reached the bottom of the stairs.

I wanted to shrink into my own skin and disappear. But the only thing to vanish was my formerly brimming confidence in the ability of my new wardrobe and hairdo to disguise my identity.

"Services tomorrow morning, folks," Father Croser said, sweeping his gaze right past me and on down the line of vendors. "I expect to see all of you there."

He hadn't recognized me. Passed me over without a second glance. I was home free. I bit my tongue to keep from grinning like an idiot.

"Yes, Father Croser," Sandra said. She was echoed by many of her fellow peddlers.

She knows his name?

Father Croser continued down the promenade, ostensibly chatting with the people gathered to buy or sell, but all the while keeping his magic eye on the market only he and I could see.

Faery watching, I thought. Then to Sandra, "You know him?"

Her spine couldn't have been stiffer if it had been nailed to a board. "You talking to me?"

No matter the situation, those four words would always trigger the same reaction from me. "*Taxi Driver*!" I shouted. "You talking to me? I don't see anyone else here. You must be talking to me."

Despite herself, Sandra smiled. "Fuck's sake, that's the worst DeNiro I've ever heard."

I shrugged. "You should hear my Clint Eastwood." I squinted and aimed two fingers in her direction, my thumb pointing straight up. "Do you feel lucky, punk?"

"Oh, God, no!" she squealed.

My hands were now back on my guitar, and I let them idle over the strings. I looked down at Sandra, picking out a tune at random. The melody struck me as familiar, but I couldn't place it for a second. Then it hit me.

Only bone remains . . .

It was the song I had written for her the other night. I grabbed control of my fingers and forced them into a difficult jig in D major.

That ought to keep the treacherous bastards occupied.

"So," I said, trying to keep my voice light, uninterested, just making idle conversation. "You know that priest?"

She nodded. "Oh, aye. He's got a church on the other side of the Mile. Stops by here a couple times a Fringe, trying to get us heathens to show up for Mass. He's a persistent bugger. Always seems easier to just agree with everything he says." She grinned. "And then sleep late on Sunday, anyway."

"Couple times a Fringe, eh?

Sandra nodded.

Wonder how many faeries he kills per festival? I mused. *What'd he say? Twenty-three? Twenty-four since '93? None of my business, I guess. If he doesn't recognize me, and I stop acting like an imbecile whenever a faery looks in my direction, it's clear sailing.*

"Douglas?" Sandra asked, knocking me out of my brief reverie. I noticed my fingers had stopped their jig and crept back into "Sandra's Theme." The bastards.

Sandra hadn't seemed to notice, however. "About before . . . ," she said.

I interrupted her with a shake of my head. "Let's drop it, Sandra." Her face suddenly turned bright red and I went on quickly, resisting the urge to raise my hands to a guard position. "No, no, not like that! I just don't want to talk about it anymore. I don't want to fight with you anymore. I just . . ." I tried to gather my thoughts. I might as well have been herding cats, so I just said the first thing that popped into my mind. "It's just that you may be my only friend in this whole country."

There it was. Despite my best efforts, my standoffish behavior, my supposedly monklike existence, I had made a friend.

And it had to be a junkie, didn't it?

"So we're friends, Douglas?"

"Yes. Maybe. I don't know. That's not even important." It was all coming out in a rush now. "Look, I know I'm an asshole at times. But I have to be. You have to be willing to cut yourself off from everyone and everything to get free. I've done it. And I won't go back. Not for anything." I stared hard into her eyes. They were brown. A deep brown, almost black, like freshly turned earth. *How come I'd never noticed her eyes before?* "Not for anyone. Talking about it won't help. It just makes things harder to handle. We can be friends. I want us to be friends. But there's some things we just can't talk about."

She met my gaze without flinching, looking sad but determined. "Sounds like a crippled kind of friendship, Douglas."

I gave one short nod. "It's all I can offer. Well, maybe not all."

She raised an eyebrow at me. "Not all?"

"I can write you a new song," I said. "I believe I still owe you one."

"Oh, aye, that you do." She smiled to soften her next words. "You asshole."

I grinned back at her. My fingers left "Sandra's Theme" behind and launched into a jaunty two-step.

"You, sir!" I called to a passing tourist. I shot Sandra a wink, then turned back to my intended mark. "Does your life need a soundtrack? Do you need a theme song?"

The tourist agreed that he might, and I launched into an extended spiel that netted me a few pounds and him a quick song. Three tunes and two tapes later, and I knew I was back in the flow. The rattle of coins was a jangling gypsy tambourine, the murmur of the crowd a rhythmic chant. Passing trains were a thumping backbeat and the skirling dissonance of distant pipers a twisted keyboard pad. The whole world was music. I picked people's melodies from the air, sang their songs from lyrics that seemed to march across their foreheads like ticker tape. I answered unasked questions in metered verse, playing songs for people before they told me anything about themselves, before they even spoke.

The faeries murmured and pointed at me, and the crowd of people stood around gape-mouthed, dropping coin after coin into my guitar case. Even Sandra shot me a curious look.

I don't know what they were all staring at; it was just me, doing what I always did: singing for my supper.

SANDRA DIDN'T SHOW up the next day. Still in the zone from the day before, I played practically nonstop until dark and didn't really notice she wasn't there. I was making too damn much money to see anything but the people passing by and the coins hitting my case. I went home with a sore throat, aching fingers, and a burning desire to get to work again in the morning. The next day was the same: lots of music, lots of money. No Sandra.

When she still hadn't put in an appearance the following morning, I started asking around. I figured she was off on a bender, but Ian at the incense booth said she'd taken ill and Catarina, one of the older henna girls who wore blue contacts at odds with her olive complexion, concurred, saying that she was bringing Sandra some soup that very night.

"I'll take her some tomorrow," I suggested. "If you give me directions to her place." I thought about my dubious cooking skills. "And make the soup."

Catarina chuckled. "All right. But what kind of person can't make soup?"

Half the men on the east side raised their hands. The rest must not have heard her. Catarina laughed again and jotted down the address of the flat Sandra stayed at during the Fringe, promising to bring more soup tomorrow.

But the next day, Sandra was back.

"You," I said when I saw her, "look like shit."

She tried a smile but it came out all crooked and lumpy. "Is that any way to talk to a girl?"

Her eyes perched precariously over dark cavernous circles. Her hair was tangled and greasy. She had lost several pounds she could ill afford, turning her already bony form into a veritable stick figure.

"Must have been a hell of a flu."

She gave me a look I couldn't interpret. Then nodded. "Oh, aye," she said. "A hell of a flu." She shook herself like a wet dog and started setting out her wares. "On the mend now, though. On the mend."

"Glad to hear it," I said. Then I was playing for another customer and didn't give Sandra or anything else another thought.

THE NEXT WEEK passed in a haze of music and money. I barely noticed the strangeness of the faery market, so intent was I on my work. The songwriting was effortless now, and on occasion I wondered if Aine's gift was responsible. But I didn't wonder too deeply or for very long. I was having too much fun; I was making too much money. And I wasn't going to examine the reasons behind it too closely, for fear that I would break the spell.

Father Croser came to the market twice more, sending my heart into my throat each time I spotted him stomping down the steps. But he never paused when he walked by; I was invisible to him in my button-down shirt and short brown hair.

Sandra got over her illness quickly. We fell into a pattern of companionable lunches around noon and brief platonic hugs at night before going our separate ways. I still had the scrap of paper with her address on it and I wondered if anything would happen if I stopped by some night, unannounced. For all my talk of friendship, I was still a young man. A young man with needs. Needs that hadn't been addressed in quite some time. And Sandra might be thin to breaking, especially after her brief infirmity, but she felt soft in all the right places when we embraced.

Let go of her, I told myself. *She's a junkie. She's poison.*

"Good night, Douglas," Sandra said, giving me an extra little squeeze. "See you tomorrow."

"Yeah," I croaked. I cleared my throat and tried again. "Yeah, see you tomorrow." *Smooth. Real smooth.*

I watched her as she flounced up the steps, peasant skirts swirling around her reedy ankles. She turned at the top and caught me looking. Flashing a knowing smile, she waved once more.

Poison, I thought. And headed for home.

I SHOT AWAKE at three that morning, sweating and shaking.

Jonesing, I thought. *Shit.*

And, "Shit," I said aloud. My voice was jarring in the quiet house. I levered myself out of bed and stumbled downstairs on quivering legs.

Sandra, I thought, filling a glass with tap water. *Thinking about her has got me thinking about junkies. And shooting up. And how I'd sure like a hit or two.*

I figured my body was just trying to keep up with my thought processes. I plopped down on the couch in front of the TV. It was time to shut my brain off and hope the rest of me followed suit. *The late-night garbage on the BBC should be perfectly suited to the task.*

"Dougie?" Grandma McLaren called from her bedroom. "What are you doing up?"

"I could ask you the same question, Grandma."

She didn't answer for a second, and though I couldn't see her, I could almost feel her shrugging.

"I'll put on some tea," she said.

As she came out of her room in a worn housecoat and slippers, it struck me how fragile she looked at this time of night. So unlike the vivacious senior I was accustomed to seeing during the day.

"No, Grandma. I'll make it."

I heaved myself off the couch and went to the kitchen. Filled the kettle with water. Kicked on the AGA.

"You haven't answered my question, Dougie," said Grandma McLaren, as she joined me in the kitchen.

I leaned against the counter and looked at my hands. I had a lot of reasons for not sleeping well. Not many I could mention, though.

"You didn't answer mine, either," I said.

"Which one was that? What am I doing up at this hour?" The lines around Grandma McLaren's eyes multiplied as she smiled. "I'm an old woman, Dougie. The creaking of my own bones wakes me."

The kettle started rumbling, going into its prewhistle routine.

"But what's a young man like you doing up at this hour?"

Grandma McLaren asked. "Aren't you kids supposed to sleep for twelve hours at a stretch?"

I grabbed three tea bags from the shelf and tossed them into a flower-print teapot before answering.

"I don't think I'm a kid anymore, Grandma."

"I know, Dougie." She patted my hand. Her skin was nearly translucent where it stretched over her knuckles. "I know."

"But as to the sleep," I said. "Women troubles, I guess."

"Och!" she said. "If you lose sleep over women, you'll never get a decent night's rest your whole life."

I mulled that over until the kettle started whistling. Grandma McLaren pulled it off the stove.

"I suppose you're right, Grandma."

"I usually am." And she patted my hand once more as she poured the water into the teapot. I watched the steam curl out of the spout. Smelled the brewing leaves. Felt the shakes in my legs fade, the sweat dry on the back of my neck.

"Thank you, Grandma."

She blinked up at me. "For what, Dougie?"

"For being you." I reached over her and pulled two teacups out of the cupboard. Plunked them down on the counter. "You probably saved my life by putting me up here. You've definitely kept me sane."

I waited for Grandma McLaren to pour the tea, but she just kept looking up at me.

"What?" I said. "I got something in my teeth?" I bared them at her.

"Pour the tea." Grandma McLaren smiled. "I've got something for you."

I raised a quizzical eyebrow at that, but she said nothing more as she went back to her room. I filled the teacups, listening to her rummage around. The sounds of closets and drawers and boxes being opened were accompanied by various "Hmms," and "Hrmphs," before a final triumphant "Aha!" floated down the short hall to me. I hooked the teacups and met Grandma McLaren in the living room.

"Douglas," she said. "I want you to have something."

"Um . . . OK, Grandma."

She looked stern, even in a ragged housecoat. Holding out her hand, she revealed a silver signet ring. "It was your grandfather's." She placed it solemnly in mine.

It was a good-sized ring—my grandfather was a large man, it seemed—and bore an image of St. Andrew holding his cross, and the Latin phrase NEMO ME IMPUNE LACESSIT on it.

"Isn't that the national motto of Scotland?"

"Yes," Grandma McLaren said. " 'No one harms me with impunity.' But it was also the motto of your grandfather's regiment." We both looked down at the ring in my palm. "He was a soldier to the core, was Donald. A true warrior." She chuckled. "No one harmed *him* with impunity. Me either, when I was with him. The scourge of the Glasgow pubs we were, before he shipped out."

" 'No one harms me with impunity.' I like it." *Might make a good tattoo,* I thought. *Run it down my forearm. Remind me not to take any shit from anybody, be they mortal or faery.*

Grandma McLaren's smile faded quickly. "No, Dougie. You're missing my point."

"What do you mean, Grandma?"

She stepped in close. Grabbed my arms and looked up at me. "No one harms me with impunity. It sounds good. It sounds tough." Her eyes shone. "But Donald died when he was twenty-four years old, and Scotland has been a subject nation for seven centuries." She plucked the ring out of my hand and held it out. "Now put it on."

I had nothing to say. The ring fit well over the index finger of my right hand.

No one harms me with impunity.

I still liked the sound of it.

THE SUN ROSE invisibly the next day, hidden behind a thick wall of clouds and fog. It wasn't raining, however; it didn't have to. The moisture hung in the air, and when I left for work, I felt as if I'd walked into a cold wet washcloth. Hidden by the mists, the faery market was indiscernible until I was practically on top of it, and I didn't realize anything was untoward until I was nearly to my spot. Then it hit me: half the booths were gone.

The leprechaun remained, still doing a brisk business, but the old witch and her head shop were nowhere to be seen. The troll looked like he was leaving any minute, stuffing rotting carcasses into a big cloth sack. Embroidered banners and glowing signs were being carefully folded or dispelled and put away, and elven girls boxed and labeled potions, philters, specimens. Everywhere were the signs of a market disassembling and closing for the season.

On the human side it was the same: those who weren't gone already had half their wares packed up. The whole promenade looked as if it were on wheels, ready to roll at a moment's notice.

I guessed the Fringe was over. For both sides.

"What happens now, Sandra?"

She looked up from the few pieces spread out on her folding table and pushed damp hair out of her eyes. "On to the next festival. What about you? Coming with us?" She swept her arm down the hazy line, encompassing the assorted gypsies, hippies, and artists who had shared the marketplace with us these last three weeks.

I fiddled with my new ring as I considered it. The invitation had a certain appeal: traveling the open road, guitar slung over my back, young Sandra on my arm, no faeries in sight.

I'd be shooting up before the week was out.

I shook my head. "I'm going to stay in town. Grandma McLaren needs me." *Like she needs an aneurism; it's me that needs her.*

Sandra tilted her head at me. "I guess this is it, then?"

"Yeah. Looks like."

Clichés suddenly flashed through my head: *in for a penny, in for a pound; nothing ventured, nothing gained; might as well be hung for a sheep as a lamb . . .*

"Hey," I said, knowing it was a mistake. "How about I take you out for a farewell dinner tonight?"

"Sounds great!"

Well, you've done it now, Douglas, I thought miserably. *Dinner and a show? Or you going to pick up some junk for an aperitif?*

"Tonight it is, then." And she smiled at me, full of hope and promise. It felt like a shot in the arm.

IN KEEPING WITH the bipolar nature of Scottish weather, the sun had burned off the fog and the day was turning quite warm by the time Sandra broke for our normal lunch. I told her, "I'm going to work straight through. Last chance at Fringe traffic."

"Not a bad plan," she replied. "But I could murder a cheese toastie." She rubbed her stomach and went on alone.

Said traffic was curtailed somewhat but still good, and I was in the middle of my fifth tape in a row when I noticed a hush come over what was left of the faery market. Work ceased, conversations sputtered and died, and even the bogies stopped tripping tourists and pinching babies, and fell quiet. The faeries turned their heads nearly as one and stared at the Playfair Steps.

I was too practiced in ignoring them by now to allow even such a drastic change to affect me, and I let the song I was singing end naturally before following the faeries' gazes.

Six burly elves were marching in formation down the stone stairs. Unlike their velvet-clad brethren, they were in full battle dress: hard leather armor, horned skull helmets that obscured their faces, and, strapped to their backs, longswords that appeared to be carved whole from the bone of some huge animal. Draped over their armor, the marchers wore hunter green surcoats, each emblazoned with a white hind rampant. In their midst walked a regal figure in a dress of the same striking green, her black hair tied back with a silver clasp, her sharp blue eyes looking in my direction.

Aine had returned to the market.

• • • seven • • •

Aine raised her hand when she reached the bottom of the stairs and one of the rear marchers called out. The guards halted with military precision. Aine came on alone. As she passed, the faeries began to bow and curtsey, a cresting wave of obeisances. The elves in black and gray merely nodded or bent stiffly at the waist. Those clad in green gave her great sweeping courtly affairs that ended with legs splayed and hands outstretched, or curtseys that went so low I thought they were going to lift their skirts clean over their heads. The smaller fey did their own variations on the theme, some flying or leaping or dancing a step or two before doing the bend-and-bow. One house brownie even threw herself to the ground and pawed and scraped till I thought she'd scratch a hole in the pavement with her long, cracked fingernails. Aine paid no attention to any of them, gliding past with her head held high, as if all the fawning adoration was her due. She stopped in front of me.

"Come to see him play, Your Majesty?" called a foppish elf, covered in green velvet and silver jewelry.

Your Majesty?

"He is quite accomplished," said another elf, this one in black and gray. "For a mortal."

She turned around deliberately and stared at each of the speakers in turn. All I could see was her back, rigidly straight, and I was certain that I wouldn't want to be the target of the looks she was shooting the two elves.

"Ah. Hrmm. Yes," said the first, bowing rapidly. "I suppose we could go about our business." He toadied away, the black and gray one right on his heels, escaping with only a touch more dignity.

The market ground slowly back into gear as the faeries returned to their buying or selling or packing up and very pointedly didn't look in our direction. There must have been more than a few ears still aimed at us, however, because when Aine spoke it was in a conspiratorial whisper.

"Singer," she said out of the corner of her mouth.

For all she knew, I had thrown the vial away and couldn't see her or the faery market. I ignored her.

"Singer!" she hissed.

I called to a passing tourist. Strummed a C major seven.

"Ah," she said. "Is that how it is to be?" She leaned her weight on one foot and tapped the other on the ground. Once. Twice. Then she seemed to come to a decision. "That is acceptable. Perhaps I will go talk to your girlfriend."

Go talk to my girlfriend? The hell does she mean by that?

"Sandra, is it?"

I tuned my low E down a whole step. Started fingerpicking something quick and Celtic.

"Oh, you are a cool one, Singer. Maybe I will give you another gift. Maybe I will give one to your girlfriend. The same gift I gave you, perhaps."

She's bluffing, I hoped. *Just trying to make me blink.*

"What is it you people say? Speak of the devil?" Aine gave a tiny nod toward the stairs. I didn't turn my head but I could easily see Sandra in my peripheral vision, skipping down the stairs, a cheese toastie in either hand.

She'd bought me one. Sweet of her.

"Do you think your girlfriend will survive her first view of us with the same grace you did, Singer?"

Grace, is it? I thought. *I'd have called it mad flight and dumb luck.*

Sandra stopped on the stairs to say something to a long-haired youth who was sketching the distant castle.

"I am not sure she would," continued Aine. "I do not think she could do what you are doing now. You are cold, Singer. Almost . . . inhuman?" She smiled, but it never reached her eyes. Hell, it barely reached her lips. "I think you are like me. I think she is like them." Aine indicated the last vestiges of Fringe traffic. "Sheep."

Sandra waved to the artist and slipped unknowingly between the six elven soldiers. She was five yards away and closing fast.

Maybe Aine was bluffing; maybe she wasn't. *Was I willing to bet Sandra's life on it?*

"She's not my girlfriend," I muttered.

Aine grinned, perfect teeth like pearls. But there was still no joy in it, only scorn. "Was that so hard, Singer? Maybe you are not so cold, after all."

Sandra skipped up to me and pressed a cheese toastie into my hand.

"Who's that?" she whispered. "She's pretty."

"Who's who?"

Sandra giggled. "Douglas! I'm not jealous. It's not like we're going out, right?" She turned and held her hand out to Aine. "Hi. I'm Sandra."

I thought for a brief second that Aine had made good on her threat to Sandra's sight before I realized what had happened.

I'm an idiot. She's visible. Aine had been laughing at me the entire time as I pretended not to see her.

"I am Aine," she said, though she didn't take her hand. "Very nice to meet you, Sandra. I think Douglas is angry with me at the moment. I was having a little fun at his expense while you were gone."

"Oh, aye." Sandra stared at her own hand for a second before shrugging and letting it drop to her side.

Probably noticed Aine's accent and decided that her customs must be different in whatever country she's from. Good luck guessing where that is, darling.

"He gets that way," Sandra continued. "I think he has an artistic temperament. Or temper."

"Is it an inherited trait to talk about men like they aren't there?" I asked, shaking my toastie at them. "Or do women learn it from their mothers?"

"Do you hear something, Aine?" Sandra said, laughing.

"Only a little buzzing, Sandra. As from a tiny insect." And she, too, laughed. It sounded forced to me, but Sandra didn't seem to notice.

"Is that so?" I said, unable to keep the anger from my voice.

"Calm yourself, Singer. I am merely amusing Sandra and myself. Besides, I have acquired the information I need and will be going now."

Information? What information? The only thing she learned is that I shot up her "gift." Why would she need to know that?

"Charmed to have met you, Sandra." Now it was Aine's turn to put her hand out, but palm down as if waiting for someone to kiss her ring. No one made a move toward it.

It's about need. If she needed to know whether or not I had done her vial, then she needs me to be able to see faeries. Or maybe I just need to see her.

"Wait a second, Aine." *It's about need.* "Maybe I need some information, too."

"Yes, I am sure you do," Aine said. "But I hardly see how that is my concern." And she turned to go.

She needs me. "Maybe I'll get my information elsewhere." I inclined my head toward the faery market. "Maybe across the street."

That stopped her. "You would not dare."

"Why not? I'm sure they'd be happy to help."

"You would not dare," she repeated.

Sandra looked as if she were watching a very confusing tennis match, her head jerking back and forth between Aine and me, a bewildered look plastered to her face.

I leaned toward Aine and said deliberately, "That hardly matters, does it, Aine? You need me for something and all I want in return is a little information. So let's go someplace quiet and talk."

Her eyes flashed and she pressed her lips together till they turned white. I thought she would call my bluff, just turn and march back up the stairs without another word. I couldn't stop her, and I certainly wasn't going to ask any of the murderous creatures across the way what this was all about. But whatever she wanted from me, it must have been big. Big enough to get her to say, through clenched teeth, "The Meadows. In an hour."

I nodded. *Gotcha!* "Okay. But leave your large friends here."

"What friends?" Sandra asked. "What are you two talking about?"

We had been talking quietly enough so those in the faery market couldn't hear us. But Sandra was too close.

"Just a little business I have to clear up with my old friend Aine," I said to Sandra. "I'll be back in a flash. We're still on for dinner, right?" She nodded and I turned back to Aine. "I'll leave in a half hour, you get yourself clear and follow." I winked and waggled my cheese toastie at her. "I'll bring the sandwiches."

She didn't smile.

"Douglas?" Sandra asked, as Aine stomped away. But I shook off her unasked questions and launched into a jangling blues number built around the fact that *Aine* rhymed with both *pain* and *insane.* I had a half hour. I could still make a little money before leaving.

I HAD NO intention of walking into a meeting with Aine unprepared. I left after a half hour as I'd said I would, but instead of going straight to the Meadows, I doubled and tripled back, stopping and looking into store windows or tying my shoes, trying to see if I was being followed. It's surprising how many people look like undercover operatives when you think you're being followed. Every man in a suit became James Bond; every bearded longhair Serpico. Swarming children were suddenly the Baker Street Irregulars, seeing everything and overhearing everyone. Tourists wielded sniper rifles cleverly disguised as cameras, snapping idle pictures as they waited for a clear line of sight for a good clean head shot. And since the things I imagined stalking me may have been supernatural, every bird, every insect, every piece of garbage lifted by the wind suddenly became a boggle or a boggart, a padfoot or a pooka, a mock-beggar, mumpoker, melch-dick, Meg-with-the-wads, or any number of insidious creatures I remembered from my readings, all bent on doing me harm. But even paranoia has its limits, and eventually I convinced myself that I was alone, and I stopped circling and pressed myself against the blackened stone of the Bedlam Theatre.

From this vantage point, I had an unobstructed view up George IV Bridge—more of an elevated street than a bridge—and the quickest route Aine could take from the market to the Meadows. If she didn't come that way, I could see down Candlemaker Row, as well. And I could twist and look back over my left shoulder to see the unicorn column she'd met me under the first time, in case she snuck around me altogether. Waiting here, I thought I could make sure that she, too, came alone. I wasn't certain what I would do if she had guards with her, or if she took a route I didn't have covered—but information, I was learning, was power. I might as well try to garner some.

The sun was shining hard enough for it to be hot, but the wind off the Firth brought a refreshing bite to the air along with its salt smell. I spent the wait thinking about where I would take Sandra for dinner that night. So far, our meals together had consisted almost exclusively of pub fare: cheese toasties, tuna potatoes, ploughman's lunches. I wanted to take her someplace nice, somewhere she wouldn't normally eat.

Maybe the Witchery, up near the castle, I thought. Expensive as hell, but I supposed I could afford one good meal. *I'd better make a reservation, though.*

I managed to make time pass like this, but slowly. At last, Aine came marching down George IV Bridge as the hour of our meeting approached. She managed a regal bearing even when moving quickly, and she was—as far as I could tell—alone. I tried to guess whether she was cloaked from normal humans' vision by watching the reactions of the men she walked by. None turned to check her out as she passed.

Must be invisible.

I suddenly realized that she was following the same path I had taken on my helter-skelter flight from the boar-man almost three weeks ago. I'd taken such a circuitous route to my present location, I hadn't put it all together till that very moment. But there was the church I had escaped into—and then out of—a couple hundred yards up on the left. I could just make out the window Father Croser had pulled the boar-man through. Something wriggled at the back of my mind. Something about the market, the Meadows, Father Croser . . .

Nothing came of it. I watched Aine walk and thought, *She's quite beautiful. Right up until she speaks.*

Then Father Croser burst from the door of his church and the thing at the back of my mind blossomed into a full thought: *Father Croser's church is on a direct line from the faery market to the Meadows.*

He had a thurible in his right hand and he let it swing back and forth on its three long steel chains like he was saying High Mass. But he was moving much faster than the slow march of a processional, and there was no incense smoke coming from the thurible's dish.

Father Croser's church is on a direct line from a big concentration of faeries to a location they seemed to favor for private meetings.

Aine saw the priest coming but paid him no mind; she didn't think he could see her. I knew better. He had his eyepatch on his right eye.

If I were a hunter of faeries, I might well call the route she'd taken a game trail.

I pushed myself off the wall and started running toward them. I didn't know what I planned to do, but it didn't matter; there was still plenty of street between us when Father Croser reached her.

He came out of the churchyard six feet behind her and spun the thurible once over his head. Aine finally realized something was wrong and turned to face the danger. Thrusting her hands out in front of her, she shouted something in a language I didn't recognize and blue lightning shot from her fingertips. It leapt toward Father Croser and I waited for him to disintegrate or explode or turn into a toad, but the electricity fizzled against the big iron cross around his neck and died. Then he took a graceful leap forward and swung the thurible at Aine's head.

He missed.

Or it looked like he had. The plate for the incense flew harmlessly past her head before whipping back on its three chains and wrapping neatly around her throat. Aine screeched as the steel burned her, wisps of smoke rising from her neck, and Father Croser worked the chains like a schoolgirl manning the jump ropes at double Dutch. He tossed three quick loops around her neck before turning a half-pirouette, putting himself and Aine back-to-back. Bending forward at the waist, he heaved on the chains with both hands so that her feet came off the ground. Then he shambled into the church while Aine hung from his back like a laundry sack, kicking at the air and scrabbling at the thurible's chains.

I skidded to a stop. Watched Father Croser toe the big wooden door closed behind him. Waited for my legs to start pumping again, for me to charge manfully into the church, slay the mad priest, rescue the elven princess.

It didn't happen.

Instead, I stood frozen in the middle of the street, thinking once again, *Damn, he's quick!*

He had worked those chains like Jackie Chan on meth. The whole snatch couldn't have taken more than fifteen seconds. I realized just how lucky I had been when we'd fought in the church. If Father Croser had been a little less confident in the drugs he'd given me, or if he hadn't slipped on the wet floor, I would have been gutted like a mackerel and had my eyes plucked out.

A taxi honked its annoyance at me, and I moved to the far side of the street before I got run down.

Glancing around, I thought, *Had anyone else seen the capture?*

The George IV Bridge was far enough off the Royal Mile for the Fringe traffic to thin out, but there were still plenty of people on the sidewalks. Right in front of me, three French tourists smoked Gauloises while reading a fold-out map. They took one step back so a gaggle of Scottish teenagers could get by, the girls stuffed into New World fashions and strutting like runway models. A workman in a dusty tee shirt dashed across the street, pushing through a temporary chain gate and into a small maze of scaffolding and drop cloths. I took a hesitant step forward as a pair of German bikers mounted twin BMWs, their Hein Gericke leathers creaking before the hum of the bikes' engines took over. No one stopped or commented or seemed in any way put out by the sight of a large priest leaping out of his church and swinging his incense burner around like a madman. Maybe the locals had seen the show before; maybe the tourists thought it was part of the Fringe. I tried to picture the scene in my mind, erasing Aine from it. It might not have looked that unnatural. Like a strange Catholic *kata,* a black belt priest exercising in the sunshine.

I walked past the church slowly, eyeing it, trying to talk myself into going in. There was no way. Father Croser was bigger, stronger, faster, and better armed. Probably had God on his side, too. I couldn't fight him by myself. Not without getting even luckier than last time. I supposed I could go in and try to talk him into letting her go. But I didn't see how that could end any other way than with me lying on the church floor, bleeding from empty eye sockets.

I shuddered. Whatever Aine had needed me for, it looked like she wasn't going to get it.

I kept walking, reviewing my options as I trudged up the George IV Bridge. I couldn't call the cops. Obviously. Or Grandma McLaren. And I couldn't tell the faeries that their . . .

Their what? Queen, I suppose.

I couldn't tell the faeries that their queen had been taken. I couldn't tell anyone anything.

Screw it. It's not like she was a friend. She nearly got me killed, threatened Sandra, screwed up my life in uncounted ways in the brief time I'd known her . . .

She'd had it coming.

But even I didn't buy that. This was different from when Father Croser had killed the boar-man, or when I had almost killed Father Croser. Both of them had been actively trying to hurt me. They deserved what they got.

Nemo me impune lacessit, motherfucker.

But I didn't know what Aine had wanted from me. It certainly hadn't seemed like it was going to be anything good, but I might have been wrong. No way of knowing now. And though I blamed her for giving me the sight, I couldn't deny that I had, in the end, given it to myself. She'd just provided the means; she hadn't stuck the needle in my arm.

I've been a stupid, arrogant coward for as long as I can remember. And someone has finally paid the ultimate price.

Of course, it wasn't me who'd had to pay, and part of me felt relieved by this. The rest of me felt guilty. I would have sworn to do better next time, but it seemed a feeble thing to promise. There wasn't going to be a next time.

My pace slowed as I berated myself, but I kept moving back toward the market. By the time I reached Bank Street, I decided to stop reproaching myself. It was a moot point anyway—Aine had probably been dead ten seconds after the door closed. Even if I had charged right in and by some miracle disarmed, subdued, or killed Father Croser, I couldn't have saved her.

And, I thought, being pragmatic, *half the people in the world who know I can see the faery world have just died.*

With Aine dead, I was sure I was much safer than I had been that morning when she was still alive.

What a relief.

I felt like puking.

"Where's the Scottish weather when you need it?" I thought, looking up at the afternoon sun that beat insolently down on my head. Darkness and rain would have better suited my mood. I reached the end of Bank Street and stomped down the long stone steps.

Sandra smiled a question at me when I reached my spot, but I just grunted and strapped on my guitar. I launched directly into an aggressive instrumental, pouring my cowardice and anger into discordant intervals and jarring augmented arpeggios. I thought it would be cathartic, but I just grew madder as I watched the unpleasant sounds rush people past me.

Last day of the Fringe and I'm driving my customers away. Brilliant.

I wasn't running everyone off, however. A group of black and gray clad bogies whirled and stomped in front of me in a punkish frenzy. They moshed, they skanked, they spilled more than a little of each other's blood with their sharp elbows and tiny fists. Seemed to enjoy themselves, though. The rest of the faeries paid me no mind, too involved in last-minute shopping or packing up. I looked for Aine's six bodyguards and spotted them standing at the far end of the market like six martial statues.

They've got a long wait ahead of them, I thought.

But they didn't hang around too long. With no discernible signal, they turned as one and marched the length of the market. Then with a syncopated clatter of bootheels, they disappeared up the Playfair Steps.

I brought my cacophonous symphony to a close and the miniature mosh pit cleared. One of the bogies shot me a giant raspberry as I began a jazz interpretation of "Ave Maria." I refrained myself from giving him the finger. But only just.

"Douglas? We still on for dinner?"

Sandra. "Yeah." *Might as well be. A normal dinner out. How was your day, Honey? Oh, fine. Got up, got dressed, got the Queen of Elfland killed. You know, the usual stuff.*

"OK." She tilted her head to the side. "What did you and Aine talk about?"

"Nothing." *Well, that was true.* "We won't see her again."

She waited for more. Nothing came. "Um. OK." She tried out a few different smiles but none seemed to fit on her face. I attempted a reassuring grin of my own but I imagine it looked more like a grimace. "Ave Maria" did its damnedest to fill in the awkward silence.

I left my fingers on autopilot and watched the faery market pack up. The troll, his sack finally full, lumbered off toward Princes Street. The leprechaun still banged away on his cobbler's stool, but his line of customers had diminished to a single galley-beggar who held his head under one arm, scratching it idly.

My view was suddenly obscured by a young mother—human, with the haggard expression all young mothers seem to wear pasted to her face—pushing her pram between Sandra and me.

"What can you do me on the price of these?" she asked, pointing to Sandra's few remaining necklaces.

The age-old dance of offer and counteroffer began, the mother looking to garner a clearance-type bargain while Sandra tried to hold firm to her original prices without losing the sale. I glanced inside the pram. An infant of indeterminate gender slept contentedly.

They really do look like Winston Churchill, I thought.

Not wanting to wake the baby, I kept my playing soft and lilting. I wasn't going to attract any customers that way, but I hadn't been in any danger of doing that for some time. "Ave Maria" became Miles Davis's "All Blues," and I alternated between picking the melody out on the harmonics and tapping it with my right hand, Stanley Jordan–style. I slipped into an improvisation in the relative minor and noticed that the bogie who had blown me a raspberry was approaching again.

Back to listen or to shoot me another rude gesture?

I was wrong on both counts. Ignoring my playing altogether, he slinked over and squeezed into the small space left between the pram and me. He was waist-high and skinny, mostly manlike in appearance, but with an extended jaw and upturned nose that made him look part rat. He wore a short jacket made of gray moleskin—I could see the little mole noses hanging off of it in places—and he carried a piece of wood half as long as himself in his left hand.

Maybe he wants to be better armed if the mosh pit starts up again.

Before I could discover if that was, in fact, the case, I was distracted by a loud hue and cry: Aine's bodyguards were charging back down the Playfair Steps.

They marched in double time, shoving faeries from their path, and formed a square in the middle of the promenade. The normal activity of the market once again ground to a halt. Faery heads swiveled in the guards' direction, asides were whispered, and fingers pointed. Finally, one of the faeries, a redheaded pixie in a short green dress, called out the question that must have been foremost on all of their minds:

"Where is Aine?"

Yes, I thought. *Where is Aine?* Only I knew. And I couldn't tell anyone. *Poor bastards.* I sighed. *Poor Aine.*

I ran it over in my mind, trying to change the memory into something heroic: me warning Aine, me killing Father Croser, Aine fainting into my arms in relief . . .

I shook my head. *Back to the real world, Douglas. Nothing you could have done.*

The bogie passed back in front of me, whistling happily. His piece of wood was gone. I looked in the pram. There was the wood. Then back at the bogie.

There was the baby.

Without thinking, I shot out with my right hand and grabbed the rat-faced bogie by the arm. He yelped in surprise as I yanked him right next to me.

"Put it back," I whispered and squeezed his arm. Hard.

"No problem, Guv'nor," squawked my prisoner, all Cockney obsequiousness. "We're all friends here."

The baby kept sleeping.

"Now." I squeezed his arm again.

"OK. OK." He lowered the baby gently back into the pram. "Now, tell me," he said, oil dripping from each syllable, "which eye do you see me with, young fellow?"

Great, I told myself. *You're a fucking hero now, Douglas. Hope you enjoy it for these last two minutes you're alive.*

I had to think. I had stepped in it hard this time and needed to weasel my way out somehow.

I looked at the market. None of the faeries were looking our way. They were all too busy eyeing one another suspiciously, putting their backs to creatures wearing the same color as themselves, fingering their weapons. It looked like the market was about to explode into open warfare.

Think! Can I kill him without anyone noticing? Can I kill him at all?

It seemed the only option. But I needed to buy some time, put my guitar down, get to one of my knives.

"You'll not blind me, little bogie," I said as confidently as I could. I was going to have to go for the ankle knife. I couldn't open the clasp knife one-handed. And if I let go of his arm, I didn't like my chances.

"And why not?" asked the bogie, the oil drying from his voice, his accent fading. "You think that hunk of metal will save you?" He pointed to the cross around my neck.

Actually, I'd had high hopes of that. Up until a second ago.

I had my guitar by the neck in my left hand now and lowered it into my case. It didn't have to share the space with too many coins.

"I saw a queen's spell break on something quite similar," I said. Leaving my guitar in its case, I let my hand edge toward my ankle and the knife hidden there.

"Interesting," said the bogie. I felt his arm tense slightly. "But I'm not much for spellcasting myself." And with his free hand, he whipped a razor-sharp piece of porcelain out of his jacket pocket and raked it across my knuckles.

I cried out and the bogie laughed and slipped out of my suddenly blood-slick grasp. He leapt and twirled away, stopping just out of my reach and slipping his weapon back into his coat. Then he pulled a foot-long hollow reed from a different pocket.

"You OK, Douglas?" asked Sandra, without looking away from her bargaining.

Not for long. The ankle knife was forgotten as I automatically pressed down on my bloody knuckles with my left hand, trying to stanch the blood flow. My reflexes were done with fight and now screamed for flight. But I was trapped by railing, bogie, pram, and Sandra. I gathered myself for a leap over the pram and a sprint toward Princes Street, but the bogie's next words stopped me cold.

"You won't make it three feet," he said. He had the tube in his mouth and was speaking around it. The words sounded half-hollow. "You ever hear of someone being 'elf-shot,' Douglas?"

I didn't reply.

"A tiny elven dart. You won't even feel it enter. But you'll be stone dead in seconds."

Can't run. Can't fight.

I heard a loud scraping as six large weapons came out of their scabbards. The bogie looked back over his shoulder to see what was happening in the market.

The bodyguards had their weapons drawn now and were backing their way up the stairs, a crowd of elves in green and white gathering around them. A bigger group of assorted creatures—dunters, goblins, bogies, and more—wearing black and gray snarled and hurled insults at their retreat. I noticed an elf wearing an intricate golden brocade and carrying a long thin sword of his own make eye contact with the biggest of Aine's bodyguard. A brief nod was exchanged and the whole group, bodyguards and other elves, stopped. Then they charged down the steps toward the mob.

The black-and-grays scattered like cockroaches when the kitchen lights come on. Aine's bodyguards strode forward in a phalanx, swinging their huge swords in unison, lopping heads and limbs off of anything that got too close. Elves in green and white darted back and forth, stabbing and thrusting with daggers and rapiers, or firing arrows from the middle of the bodyguards' formation and putting shafts through the backs of the fleeing black-and-grays. Unarmed brownies and hobs dove for cover while a urisk galloped in a tight circle, bleating in fear. A bodyguard at the rear of the formation stepped out and whacked him on the backside with the flat of his sword, sending him off toward High Street.

Humans got conflicting urges from the different faeries trying to clear space to run and they were buffeted and knocked down. Sandra and the young mother both stared wide-eyed at the pandemonium. I tried to envision what they saw.

A strong wind sweeps through the marketplace, knocking people to the ground. A whirlwind, perhaps. A freak occurrence, but nothing supernatural.

I dragged my attention back to my current predicament. The bogie was gone, disappeared when the fighting started.

Time to leave! But I never got a chance to. The bogie had slipped behind me somehow and now he leapt onto my back and wrapped a small hairy arm around my neck. And with his makeshift knife once again drawn and pressed up under the point of my chin, he said, "Tell me about this queen's spell you saw broken. While you still have your eyes." I felt a tiny prick as the knife barely broke the surface of my skin. "And don't lie to me. Trust me, I'll know if you lie."

Think!

With my knuckles bleeding freely and a supernatural creature a quarter-inch away from turning me into a human shish kebab, this was easier thought then done.

Aine disappears. Aine is a green-and-white. The black-and-grays get blamed. Looks like war. And if this fight is any indication of their skill, the black-and-grays won't last long.

This bogie is a black-and-gray. And he doesn't want a war. He wants to return Aine to the green-and-whites.

"I'll need a guarantee," I whispered. Hopefully this creature was as obsessed with fairness as Aine had seemed to be.

The knife pushed closer. "You'll need a mortician. Talk!"

I gulped. "Aine. I know where she is. And who took her."

"Show me."

I started to shake my head and nearly skewered myself. I spoke instead.

"No. Not without a guarantee."

"What kind of guarantee?"

I spoke as calmly as I could. "Promise not to take my eyes, and not to tell anyone that I can see you, and I'll show you where Aine is."

He didn't even hesitate. "Done." And the knife was gone. I began to let out a big breath I hadn't realized I was holding, but caught it short when the knife returned. But this time it was just there to cut the leather cord holding my cross. The big Celtic symbol clattered to the ground. "And the knives, too," the bogie said. "Carefully now."

I did as he said. I didn't see that I had any choice. Besides, I had his guarantee; I hoped it was good for something. I pulled the clasp knife from my pocket and then bowed awkwardly to get the *sgian dubh* from my sock. I thought about trying to fling him over my shoulder while I was bent over. The bogie must have sensed something, or maybe read my mind, because his knife was quickly back under my chin.

"Just put them all in your guitar case and close it up. We'll take it with us."

"Why?"

"Why? Because I wouldn't want to separate a musician from his instrument." As soon as I latched the case he left my back and skipped around in front of me. "I'm a musician, myself. I play a little pennywhistle," he said, and whipped his blowgun out again. "Of course, it's more of a ha'penny whistle when I play it." He mimicked playing a flute on the hollow reed. "I'm no master like yourself." And he bowed deeply without taking his eyes off of me.

"Let's get this over with."

The bogie's gaze darted toward the far end of the marketplace where the green-and-whites were clearing off a few last stragglers. "Yes, let's be away."

"Douglas? Douglas?"

Sandra.

I wondered how long she had been calling my name. I was getting confused with these multiple conversations. It was much easier when I could just ignore the faeries and talk to the humans.

"Douglas, are you okay? Did you see that crazy wind?"

I held up my bleeding hand. "Got cut. Going to go bandage it."

"Ow! Let me see. I have a kit here somewhere."

"Ooh," said the bogie. "She wants to play doctor! I think she fancies you."

"Nah, I have to run home anyway. Get changed for tonight." And to the bogie. "Shut up."

"So sensitive!" he replied.

Sandra called something after me but the bogie and I were halfway up the stairs, moving fast as he cleared the crowd from our path.

I TOOK ANOTHER circuitous route, trying to buy time, trying to think of some way to get the upper hand in this impossible situation. We went up the Playfair Steps but turned right to Mound Place and Ramsay Lane instead of left to Bank Street. Across Castlehill and down the other side, taking steep stairs and thin closes till we reached Grassmarket. With the bogie occasionally prodding me in the back with his porcelain knife, I felt like one of the condemned criminals that had been marched to the gallows here not so long ago. We turned right again over the more direct left, and circled far out of our way, past the Mountbatten Building, the College of Art, the Royal Infirmary.

By the time we reached the church, I had thought of several plans for doing in my adversary. Sadly, they all involved Father Croser. And besides the difficulty I envisioned getting the bogie into the church or getting the priest out of it, I couldn't figure out how to stop Father Croser from killing me, too.

I faced the street and sat down, putting my back to the low churchyard wall. Poking my thumb back over my shoulder, I said, "She's in there."

The bogie stood on his toes and peeked over the wall before sitting next to me.

"That so?"

I nodded.

"How did she end up in there? None of us would enter there voluntarily." I hesitated and he went on. "Come now, Douglas, the truth will set you free. Isn't that what you mortals always bleat?"

"I certainly hope it'll set me free. You gave your word."

"And not lightly, either. Let it never be said that Martes ever went back on his word."

That's it then. Do I believe him? Or do I try to get him into the church?

I didn't much like either option. So I chose the easier of the two.

"Okay, then—Martes, is it?"

"Aye, Martes. My calling name, not my true, though I don't suspect that'd mean anything to a dullard like you."

"Whatever," I said. Took a deep breath. "Here it is then, Martes. A big priest walked out of the church, wrapped Aine in chains, and dragged her inside." I stood. "And a deal's a deal. I'm off."

"One second, young fellow."

I gave him the finger over my shoulder and kept walking.

"You're going in after her, Douglas."

Wrong choice. He's breaking his promise.

I whipped my case to the ground and knelt beside it. Began flipping latches. I had two open and broke the last when I wrenched the case open in a fit of panicked strength. I had my hand on the *sgian dubh* but never got a chance to use it. Martes shot into the small of my back like a missile. He didn't weigh much, but he hit with enough force to knock me to the sidewalk and send the *sgian dubh* flying from my grasp. I rolled over in time for him to land on my chest. He put his little knife right up to my right eye. I couldn't even blink for fear of cutting my eyelid off.

"You're going in after her."

"The fuck I am!" I tried to shift my weight but he inched the knife closer. I swore I could feel it touching my eyeball. "And let it be said that Martes went back on his word," I said. My voice only broke a little. "Let it be shouted to the goddamn rooftops."

He grinned sharp yellow teeth at me. "I'll not break my word, Douglas. My kind never do." The knife moved from my eye down to my throat. "I won't take your eyes or tell anyone that you can see." The grin got wider and he shoved his rat face closer until I could feel his hot breath on my cheeks. It smelled of rotten fruit and stale beer, like a bar garbage can. "But I will kill you if you don't go fetch Aine for me."

And with a deft flick of his wrist, he cut a three-inch gash in my right cheek.

I screeched and tried to throw him off. He clung fast with his knees and rode me like a rodeo rider on a bucking bull. Grabbing me by the hair with his free hand, he slammed my head back down on the pavement. Then he slipped his legs to either side and stood on my arms, pinning me.

"I will kill you," he said.

Slash. Another cut right next to the first.

"I'll kill your little jeweler friend."

Slice. The left cheek this time.

"I'll even kill a couple guys who have the same name as you."

He pulled his hand back for another pass and I flinched away, screwing my eyes shut and anticipating the next blow. It never came. Instead, he patted my cheek. His palm came away bloody.

"Now quit screwing around and let's talk about how you're going to get Aine for me."

• • • Eight • • •

I lay on the sidewalk, the pain of the fresh gashes screaming at me, *Get up! Kill him!*

Trust me, I told the wounds. *There's nothing I'd like better.*

Martes leapt off of me and sheathed his knife. Mine was three feet away on the pavement. It might as well have been in Minneapolis; I'd never reach it. I sat up and scanned the street. Even though it was the end of the Fringe and people crowded the sidewalks, nobody was looking my way. Or if they were, it was just to make sure I wasn't getting near them: *Gotta stay away from the crazy guy with gashes all over, talking to himself and rolling around in the street.*

"I can't go in there," I told Martes. It came out in a high-pitched whine I hated myself for. "The priest will kill me."

"No, no, no," Martes said, twitching his little rat nose in time with his words. "The priest *might* kill you. Your chances with me are far worse than that."

He was probably right. But I still couldn't go inside if Father Croser was there. And I certainly wasn't going to do Martes a bunch of favors and then have him kill me when I was done. I was going to have to try to cut another deal. A better one this time.

But can the cat's-paw bargain with the monkey? Maybe. As long as I'm the only one who can enter the church, I suppose I have one card left to play.

I took one last look at my knives and then faced Martes. "Okay, say I go in there and get Aine out. What will you do for me?"

"You go get Aine and I won't kill you."

"Or any of my friends? Or people with my name?" I tried to sew up loopholes in this surreal argument. But I was tired and bleeding and enraged and I knew I wasn't thinking straight.

"Sure," Martes said. He said it far too quickly and much too smoothly. He must have seen another way out.

I sat on the pavement and bled. Got a hand towel that I kept in my guitar case to wipe the strings with. Held it to my cheeks, one after the other, direct pressure.

"Okay," I said, trying to think past the pain and the anger, tie up the loopholes Martes must have thought of.

It's like the genie and the three wishes. Whatever you wish for ends up fucking you in the end.

I had to think like a lawyer. A really good lawyer.

"If I do this," I said and stopped. Took a deep breath. Then went on in a rush. "I want you to promise not to harm me or mine. In any way, through action or inaction. In fact, I want you to promise to be my protector in all things faery-related. To perform, at all times, in my best interests and in the best interests of my family and friends. And that if there is *any* question about what the correct course of action should be, you will discuss it thoroughly with me before any action is undertaken."

Martes blinked. He twitched his upturned nose from side to side, looking more ratlike than ever.

"Do we have a deal?" I asked.

Martes stood stone-faced for a few seconds.

"I don't even understand what you just said, Douglas." His rodent face split in a wide grin. "But sure, I agree. You and yours. Faery-related. Blah, blah, blah." He turned serious. "Now go get her."

I shook my head. "We have to wait."

"Wait?"

"Yeah, wait. I can't barge in there and grab her when the priest is there. I told you: he'll kill me." I looked up at the sun and tried to gauge how much daylight we had left. "We have to wait for dark, wait for him to leave."

Martes chewed on a fingernail. It was a dirty fingernail, long and pointed. "I don't want to wait."

I shrugged. "I don't much care what you want."

"Is that so?" His nose twitched once, upward, and held there. His eyebrows came in and down to meet it as his brow furrowed in anger.

I scooted back to the wall. I tried to make the maneuver look nonchalant, like I was just making myself comfortable, settling in for a long wait. But I was pretty sure Martes saw right through my act.

"Remember your pledge," I told him. My voice didn't squeak too much.

Martes held his scowl trained on me for a moment more before finally shrugging and squatting down next to me.

"All right," he said.

"All right?"

He nodded. "We wait."

IT DIDN'T TAKE long. After ten minutes, I spotted Father Croser.

"Shit," I said.

Martes turned from his close watch of the front door and asked, "Shit?"

I still had my back to the wall, content to let Martes watch the door for me.

"There he is."

The big priest was coming down George IV Bridge, swinging a Tesco's shopping bag in one hand.

"Titania's tits, Douglas," Martes hissed. "You could have been in and out already."

I shrugged. I didn't want to speak. Father Croser was closing quickly. It would be a disaster if he saw me talking to a bogie.

Martes wouldn't shut up, however.

"In and out. No time at all. Like a teenage boy at a brothel. Now I'm going to have to sit here with you for hours." He eyed the approaching priest and twitched his nose. "Look, you're a fine musician, Douglas. But you're no conversationalist. You've been boring my pecker off, sitting there moping. I know, I know, 'Martes beat me! He cut me!' Get over it!"

"Shut up," I hissed, trying not to move my mouth.

"Now, now, no reason to get huffy."

"He can see you."

"What? Who?"

"Father Croser. The priest. He can see you. He can see all of you. How do you think he grabbed Aine?"

Martes stared at Father Croser, forty yards away and eating up the distance with his big strides.

"I suppose you're right," Martes said. "Though I doubt you warned me out of the goodness of your heart." He winked and dashed across the street, the mole noses on his coat waving at me as he ducked into a close and out of sight.

Run! my mind screamed at me. *Now's your chance. Get out of this nightmare for good.*

But I didn't run. I couldn't. I needed to go get Aine. Martes certainly wasn't far away, and if I didn't fulfill my part of our bargain,

I didn't see what would keep him from killing me. Or worse.

I flipped open my case and got my guitar out. Stared at the clasp knife in the compartment that held strings and picks. I let it lay; it had been worse than useless so far. Maybe I could return it. Get my money back.

"Good evening, son."

We were the only two people on the sidewalk, but it still sounded like he was playing to the back pews.

"Evening, Father." I tried to make my voice lower than usual. It was the first time I had spoken to him since being in his church. I poked my case with my foot. "Spare some change?"

He looked down at me. I couldn't read his expression. Disapproval? Pity? At least he didn't look like he recognized my voice.

"Don't ye usually play down near the National Gallery?"

Recognizes the face, though. Just from the market. I hope.

"Fallen on hard times, have ye?" He waggled his finger at the gashes on my cheeks.

I couldn't argue with his assessment. "I reckon I have, Father."

"Well, then, don't despair. It's all part of God's plan. God's will." He was looking through me now. All the way to Heaven, perhaps. "He tests the faithful, puts obstacles in our path to see if we are worthy of His kingdom."

I strummed a half-diminished chord. It sounded like it should resolve, but I couldn't decide to where.

"What if I'm not one of the faithful?" *What am I doing? I should be running away from this murderous freak. Not discussing theology with him.* "What if I don't believe in God?"

Father Croser scowled. "Then He is punishing you."

I grinned. "Fair enough, Father." *Up a half step to the major seven. Ah.* "Now, how about a song?"

Father Croser raised one eyebrow, staring down at me for a full ten seconds, before smiling and pushing back his cassock. He reached into a black trouser pocket and came out with a pound coin. Flipping it into my case with a satisfying thump, he said, "Do you know 'The Spanish Lady'?"

"Sure." *Common time, key of D. Irish.* "But I might not remember all the words. You'll have to sing along."

As I went out through Dublin City
At the hour of twelve at night . . .
Who do I see but a Spanish lady
Washing her feet by candlelight.

Father Croser's voice was unsurprisingly quite strong. *Basso cantante.*

First she washed them then she dried them,
Over a fire of amber coal.
In all my life I've never seen
A maid so sweet about the sole.

It was a cute song, and I couldn't help but smile when we roared out the meaningless chorus.

Whack for the tura lura laddie,
Whack for the tura lura lie.

But something changed in the third verse:

When she spied me quick she fled me
Lifting her petticoats over her knee.

I was suddenly hit with a vision of Father Croser wrapping his thurible's chains around Aine's neck. I could smell the charred skin where the steel had burned her. The whole song twisted in my mind. No longer the puff piece, it was now a dark nightmarish tune about stalking and slaying the Spanish lady. About Aine.

In all my life I'll never see
A maid so sweet as the Spanish lady.

Father Croser glanced down at me curiously as I stumbled over the easy open chords.

Christ, pull it together, Douglas.

I shook off the vision and skipped the last verse, breaking into a quick reel. I played it twice through while Father Croser shuffled his feet in an impromptu Highland fling.

He whooped as I ended, and shouted, "That's magic, lad. That really is."

"Thank you, Father."

He reached into his pockets again and flipped another pound coin into my case.

"God be with you, my son."

"You got an evening Mass tonight, Father?" I nodded my head toward the church.

"Och, no," he said. "Just have a wee bit of business to finish up, then I'm away home." He held up one hand as a good-bye and picked up his shopping bag. "Cheerio."

"Good night, Father Croser."

I watched him unlock the big wooden door and go inside.

"Crazy bastard," I muttered.

"Not a bad singer, though," Martes said, suddenly by my side once more. "Thought you said he was going to kill you."

"He would if he caught me trying to rescue Aine."

"[illegible]lla, he is." Martes scrunched his shoulders up, making his neck disappear. Flexed his little arms. "Probably tear your limbs clean off."

I shivered despite the summer temperatures. "Thanks, Martes. That's helpful."

Martes cackled. "We wait?"

"Yeah. We wait. Shouldn't be long."

"I hope not, for your sake. You don't get her soon, Douglas, I might just consider our contract null and void."

"I'll get her." *Her body, anyway. Hope that's not a deal breaker.* "I'll get her."

I settled back against the wall. Tucked my pick up under my pinky and travis-picked some country blues. Martes's eyes closed to slits as I played. He wasn't sleeping, however. His ears twitched to the beat and I could hear a low whistling from his rat lips, a counterpoint to the simple melody on the guitar's high strings. Without opening his eyes, he reached deep into the folds of his moleskin coat, pulling out a long thin flute and putting it to his lips.

Screw this.

I placed my right hand flat on the strings and the music stopped. I took the two coins out of my case, replaced them with the guitar. Flipped the case shut and shot two of the latches. Let the broken one flap in the breeze.

Martes opened one eye.

"Why'd you stop? I was enjoying that."

I winked at him. "Exactly." Then I closed both of my eyes and leaned back against the wall once more. "Wake me when Father Croser leaves."

Martes grumbled and sputtered but didn't end up saying anything. I kept my eyes closed. I was exhausted from fear and pain and blood loss, but I knew I'd never sleep: I had too much to think about.

First things first: Aine was dead. I was sure of that. The only uncertainty was what Martes was going to do when I came out carrying a body, not dragging a live Aine behind me. Would he stick to our bargain? After all, I'd be returning Aine—she just wouldn't be alive.

But what if there was no body?

That was a chilling thought. No body and there'd be no proof Aine was ever in there. No body and Martes was going to kill me as soon as I left the church.

There had to be a body.

Unless Father Croser was inside there right now, cutting up Aine's corpse and shoving it down a garbage disposal. Or stuffing it in an incinerator. Or maybe he had a herd of pigs in the basement. Pigs would eat anything. Anyone who grew up in the Midwest knew that.

Yeah, a herd of faery pigs to feed the faery bodies to.

I smiled to myself and shifted against the wall, getting a little more comfortable.

Pigs. Fey pigs.

Big pink bastards with tiny gossamer wings, hovering over a muddy sty. Father Croser throws Aine's naked body into their feed trough and they dive down to devour her, grunting and snorting and flapping their wings furiously.

Then he turns to me and says, "Och, that's magic, Doc. It really is."

It was then I realized I *had* actually fallen asleep.

And I couldn't breathe.

I came awake to Martes pinching my nostrils and holding my mouth closed. I swatted his hands away and drew in a huge wheezing breath.

"The priest comes." Martes scuttled back across the street and out of sight.

I rubbed my eyes and took a quick peek over my shoulder. Father Croser was locking the front door.

No going in the front then.

I got out my guitar. Tuning up, I tried to gauge what time it was by the position of the sun. Maybe another hour until dark. That's when I'd begin my burglary career.

"Still here, young man? You don't seem to be making much money." Father Croser pointed to my empty guitar case.

"Hope springs eternal, Father."

"Oh, aye. That it does."

Father Croser scanned the street, and I followed his gaze. A woman in a dark skirt and crisp white shirt marched past on the opposite side of the street, arms ending in bulging shopping bags held rigidly at her sides. A haggard couple rounded the National Museum with a sullen teenager and two noisy middle graders trailing behind them. Desultory traffic cruised by: a Peugeot, two Minis, a sleek Jaguar. There was no sign of Martes.

"Well, good night, Father."

He seemed to think for a moment, eyeing the traffic again. Then he gave an almost imperceptible shrug and said, "Aye. Good night it is." Then he turned south away from the George IV Bridge, and his long strides carried him quickly out of sight. Martes was back at my shoulder immediately.

"Go get her, Douglas."

I shook my head.

"Douglas," Martes sighed. "Do you *want* me to kill you?"

"We have to wait." I raised my hand. "Just a little longer!"

"Why?"

"For dark." I pointed to the window to Father Croser's office. "The front door is locked. I'm going to have to crawl through that window. And you can see it from the street. So we wait till dark."

Martes said nothing for a moment, looking at the small window then up at the sky. "All right," he said eventually. He sighed again, a big theatrical affair. "We wait."

• • • • • •

I WAS TOO nervous now not to play, so I didn't stop this time when Martes pulled his whistle out. I alternated between slow Irish airs to soothe my jagged nerves, and speedy rockabilly numbers I aimed at the sun, trying to push it faster toward the horizon. His claim of making his flute a ha-penny whistle notwithstanding, Martes kept pace easily; his playing was talented if uninspired, like someone who had read all the books, done all the practice, but never once let go and just let the music take him where it willed.

Maybe all faery musicians are like that: well-practiced technicians who could stand to trade in a few centuries of scales and exercises for one full night of drunken, free-for-all jamming.

The sun finally set in a horizon-long blaze over the Old Town, and the dim amber streetlights came on. The churchyard had no lights.

"It's time." I got to my feet. Martes stayed put. "You're going to help," I said.

"I told you," he said. "I can't go in there. If I could, you'd have been dead hours ago, Douglas."

I suppressed a shudder. Didn't want to give him the satisfaction. "You're not going in. But I need help getting up to the window."

"Oh. All right then."

Martes hopped to his feet and followed me the three steps to the low iron gate that led to the churchyard. I held it open, resisting the temptation to slam it on him as he came through, watch the metal burn him like the thurible had Aine. We picked our way through the gravestones until we were underneath the office window, hidden by the dark shadow of the church. I hoped Father Croser hadn't repaired the latch.

I peered up. The foundation was raised and the window was a few feet higher on the outside. And I couldn't leap as far as the boar-man had.

"Brace yourself against the wall, Martes." I put my guitar case down. "I'll climb up on your shoulders. See if I can reach."

He blinked once. "No. I don't think so, Douglas."

I held up my hands. "Then what do you suggest? I fly up there?"

"Of course!" With that, he pointed his finger at me and shouted, "Up horse and hattock!"

Hands, invisible even to me, grabbed me by my legs and the collar of my shirt.

"Martes?" I said and then I was shooting upward as the invisible hands dragged me into the air. I thought my shirt would rip. But the fabric held, and I came to an abrupt stop next to the window.

Well, I've seen stranger things these past few weeks. Shouldn't be shocked by this.

"Grab ahold of the window, Douglas. This isn't a sightseeing flight." I heard him cackle. "And I told you I'm not one for spell-casting."

I looked down. Bad move.

"One sec, let me—"

"That's about all I can hold ya for."

I reached out and caught the ledge one-handed. The hand holding my shirt resisted only a short second before letting me pull myself in. Peering inside did me no good; the window was dirty, the office dark. I held on with one hand and worked the fingers of the other under the edge of the ancient window. Relieved to discover the latch was still broken, I levered it outward with little trouble.

"I'm in."

No sooner did I utter these words, than the magic hands let go, leaving me holding on to the window with only one of mine. Flailing with the other only served to swing me out away from the wall and give me another look at the ground.

Where I would be in very short order if I didn't get both hands on the sill.

I got my flapping limb under control and twisted my body to face the wall. My free hand slapped down on the sill next to its mate. Digging my toes into the wall gave me just enough purchase to pull myself up and stick my head through the window. I couldn't see anything. Even with the window open, Father Croser's office was nearly pitch-black. I kept scrabbling with my feet and awkwardly pulled myself inside until I was balanced on my stomach on the sill. I took a few deep breaths and listened to my heart pound.

"No harm to me or mine, Martes," I hissed over my shoulder and down.

Sarcastic laughter drifted up to meet me. "Are you hurt? No? Then quit your whining."

Asshole.

Taking stock of my situation, I realized something. The window was small. Real small. This was a problem. If the window were bigger I could have just swung my legs in, sat up, turned around, and lowered myself until I had an easy drop to the floor, even in the darkness. But I didn't have enough room.

No problem. Roll over, grab the top of the window, pull myself through.

I tried to roll over but discovered the window wasn't even big enough for me to do that.

Crap.

"What's the holdup there, Douglas?"

I ignored him. Thought for a bit. I came up with only two options, both piss-poor. I could either sit here, torso in and ass out, till morning came and Father Croser killed me. Or I could reverse my grip, squirm forward, letting my upper body tilt down until it was flush with the inside wall, then swing my legs through, essentially turning a slow somersault, so I ended up hanging from the window by my hands, like a gymnast finishing his rings routine, a few short feet from the floor.

Okay, option two sounds marginally better than option one.

But I was no gymnast. I managed to get myself parallel to the wall easily enough, but from there things went bad. Real bad. I wriggled my butt in and was almost through when the back of my shoes hooked onto the top of the window.

Uh-oh.

I now formed a triangle against the wall, with my ass and feet as the two corners at the top and my head as the bottom point.

Oh, for crying out loud.

I tried to back out a little, free my feet, but I didn't have any leverage to move in that direction. I couldn't pull my legs down to sneak them through, either—they were held fast. The blood was rushing to my head, and it was getting hard to think. And my grip was weakening. As soon as it went, I would plummet to the ground face-first. I decided to try to use the wall to pull my shoes off. But in my panic, I gave it a little too much gusto. With a mighty heave, I popped my shoes clean off. My legs, freed so abruptly, shot in like they were fired from a slingshot, and my shoes fell outside.

I hope they hit Martes in the head.

Then the momentum of my legs made my precarious grip fail and I flew away from the wall. I felt like a cartoon character, hovering in the air, my arms flailing for balance, my legs straight out in front of me. It was strangely peaceful, hanging there in the dark, not touching anything, not seeing anything, no sensation of falling.

Until impact.

My back hit first. I thought my lungs would burst through my chest as my breath was forced out. Then my head whipped back, smashing into the floorboards, and the darkness flashed bright white for an instant. I didn't remember my feet landing, but I imagined the worthless bastards, after failing their job and letting most of my vital parts break the fall first, alighting with a feather touch.

I lay there, gulping like a fresh-caught walleye, till my lungs stopped spasming. But even when I could breathe normally, I didn't move. I was afraid to. If my spine was broken I didn't want to know. I counted ten breaths, then another five, before finally deciding that knowledge was better than ignorance. I started with my left hand, the most important part of a guitarist. Flexed my fingers. Ran a major scale in the air. Everything seemed in order. Then I checked my right hand.

So far, so good.

I wriggled my toes, twitched my legs, then bent at the waist and sat up. A quick exploration of the back of my head revealed a golf ball–sized lump. And it would probably get a fair bit bigger before I got to an ice pack.

Well, a lump won't kill me. May have to wear a bag like the Elephant Man if it gets much bigger, though.

I tried to remember if I'd blacked out for any length of time. I didn't know. Which made me think that maybe I *had* blacked out. Hopefully I didn't have a severe enough concussion to kill me in my sleep later that night.

I'll have Grandma McLaren wake me every two hours. That's all the doctors ever tell you to do, anyway.

I stood. I was a little shaky on my feet, but I attributed that more to nerves than the fall.

Time to find a damn light.

My eyes were beginning to adjust to the gloom, and I was starting to see shapes. I could just make out the big desk, and I tried to remember where it was in relation to the door to the church.

Against the back wall, I decided and turned around. *Yep. This way to the door. There's the bookshelf, the table . . .*

"Ouch."

A chair.

I pushed it away and kept creeping along until I reached the door. I ran my hands up and down the walls until I found a light switch and flicked it on. The office looked the same as when I'd last seen it, minus the mop, bucket, and unconscious priest. No faery princess, no faery pigs.

But I had an idea where to find them: the basement.

The iron-banded door was locked tight. I recalled Father Croser pulling the key to the door out of his desk, so I crossed the room to search it. The desk's surface was clean and tidy, being home to only a table lamp, a cordless phone, a nineteenth-century Bible, a leather-bound calendar, and a coffee cup bearing the phrase VENTIS SECUNDIS, TENE CURSUM that held a variety of pens and pencils. There was a dog-eared paperback Bible, more pens and pencils, a ruler, paper clips, and a small plastic pencil sharpener in the thin middle drawer; a dictionary that still looked brand-new sat atop stationery, envelopes, even more pens, a stamp with the church's address on it, and a large bag of rubber bands in the top right drawer. The left side of the desk looked like it held two drawers, but was actually a single drawer with two handles. It contained another Bible, this one with RONALD A. CROSER embossed in gold letters on the cover—*How many Bibles does one priest need?*—and a long black knife.

I stared down into the drawer. The knife was a true killing instrument, maybe a foot and a half in length, most of it blade. It had a serrated edge that ran halfway up the back and a subtle blood runnel down the side. If it was the same one that had done for the boar-man, then it was razor sharp, as well.

I picked it up. Swished it through the air a few times. The balance made it feel like an extension of my arm. I thought of the clasp knife in my guitar case, the *sgian dubh* lying in the street. They were peashooters; this was an M16.

Maybe with this, things will go a little different when I see Martes again.

I pictured myself half-crouched in the darkness, camouflage paint striping my face, waiting for my chance to leap up behind the bogie and slit his throat from ear to ear.

I sighed. *It's a poor craftsman who blames his tools.*

Martes was a vicious kidnapper and killer; I was a street musician with a drug habit and a talent for writing songs.

Give me a shotgun and a suit of armor and it's still no contest. I shook my head. *Be silly to just leave it in the drawer, though. Martes isn't my only problem.*

I tucked the big weapon through my belt at the small of my back and kept looking for the basement key.

I had one more drawer to search: the bottom right. It was locked. I pulled my new knife and worked it in next to the lock, tried to pry the drawer open. It looked like the knife would snap before the drawer would pop open.

Screw this, I thought, and heaved the desk over onto its side. Lamp, phone, Bible, calendar, coffee cup, and writing utensils all went flying. Then I kicked the desk completely over and the top drawer flew out, sending more crap skittering across the floorboards. I lifted my right foot as high as I could and stomped down hard on the bottom of the locked drawer. It gave way easily. Then I extricated my foot from the wreckage and dug around.

Bingo. One large antique key.

I grabbed it and went to the iron-banded door. The key fit and the door unlocked easily, leaving me staring at a set of stone steps, worn by age, that led down and down and down into a dark basement. I looked to my right, flipped on another light switch, and a bare bulb at the bottom of the stairs flickered on. As I started down, I thought I would be more frightened, but adrenaline had taken over like a hit of crystal, and all I felt was excitement. The air turned musty and dank as I went lower. The wall to my right opened up when I was halfway down and allowed me a view of the rest of the basement. Or rather, the wine cellar. The minute wine cellar. Dusty bottles in wooden racks lined two of the walls; the back wall was dominated by a life-sized oil painting of Jesus. It looked like it had been done by the same artist who'd painted the mural behind the altar. When I reached the bottom, I saw that the abbreviated wall underneath the stairs had a low door in it.

Aha! My heart was suddenly pounding hard. *There's the fear,* I thought, and pulled the knife. The solid cool weight of it calmed my nerves. A little. I took in a deep breath and held it. Then I whipped open the door.

It was a closet. Mop, broom, bucket, rags. Cleaning products. I looked closer at one orange squeeze bottle. FAIRY LIQUID, the label claimed. I laughed out loud.

I shut the closet door and looked around the room.

There must be more than this, I thought.

I spun slowly around, ignoring the contrary motion it started in my stomach.

Wine rack, stairs, closet, wine rack, painting.

I spun a little quicker.

Wine rack, stairs, closet, wine rack, painting. Repeat.

Faster still, getting a little panicky now, thinking, *No Aine tonight, no Dougie tomorrow.*

Rack, stairs, closet, rack, painting. Rack, stairs, closet, rack, painting. Painting.

I stopped. Stared at the painting. Jesus stared back, eyes full of compassion and pain. I gave him the finger.

What kind of asshole hangs a painting in his wine cellar?

I marched up to the painting and grabbed its left edge. Gave it a little tug. It came away from the wall with ease, swinging out on hinges hidden along its right side. Behind the painting was another door. Another locked door. But this was no thick iron-banded affair with a massive medieval locking mechanism; this was a cheap interior door, with a simple lock in the knob that was easily picked with a coat hanger. Not that I needed a coat hanger. The door was locked from this side, and all I had to do was turn the button on the knob to get in.

With my knuckles white around the pommel of my knife, I pulled the door open and peeked inside.

Anemic light from the bare bulb at the base of the stairs crept into the hidden room, illuminating just enough for me to guess at the room's purpose. My hand shook as I found another light switch.

Details sprang into view as the lights came up: crudely tiled floor, rusty drain in the middle of it; pegboard wall holding bolt cutters, jumper cables, handsaw, hedge trimmers, and assorted other tools useless for actually fixing anything; stained table with a car battery and work gloves lying atop it, several vises of different sizes clamped to its sides; metal shelf with cardboard file boxes on it, their hand-scrawled labels making my stomach flip: EARS, HANDS, CLAWS, NIPPLES . . .

Nipples? My stomach backed up to my throat and threatened to leap the rest of the way out. *Jesus Christ.*

Along the back wall, a half-dozen manacles were fastened to the stone wall with large concrete nails. Hanging from the rightmost pair was Aine.

Her legs were splayed at odd angles and bone poked through her left shin. One arm ended in a three-fingered hand, the other in a bloody stump, the manacle cinched high up over her elbow. Her tongue protruded from her mouth, swollen and gray. Her eyes were missing.

A cloying rotten stench hit my nose, and I staggered three steps into the room and threw up into the drain. Then, coughing and gagging, I stumbled out of the torture chamber and back to the closet in the other room. I grabbed a rag from the pile of cleaning supplies and wiped my mouth. Tied another around my face like a rustler's mask. Then I held my breath and went back in.

I grabbed the bolt cutters off the pegboard and put the stained blades around the manacle around her wrist. I strained and snipped until the metal gave way, then set to work on the one over her elbow. When I'd cut through that one, Aine's body fell to the tiles with a sick wet smack. I pressed my fist to my mouth and breathed shallowly while my stomach decided whether to void itself again.

Just get it over with.

I held my breath, bent down, and heaved the body over my shoulders in a fireman's carry. I gave a little shrug to settle the weight of it in and something shook loose and fell to the floor.

A shoe, I thought. *Her shoe must have fallen off.*

I ignored the little voice in my head that claimed she hadn't been wearing any shoes when she was chained to the wall.

I passed through the wine cellar and staggered up the stairs, the stench of her burning my nostrils. With every step, viscous fluids dripped onto my shoulders or drizzled down my neck and into my shirt. My vision swam as the knot at the back of my head began to throb in time with my heartbeat. I realized I was muttering, "Goddammit," over and over, and had been for some time. I clenched my jaw to try to stop, but the words kept spitting out through the gap in my front two teeth.

So I began humming. I had hoped for something lighthearted and cheerful, instead of the haunting melody that came out. But anything was an improvement over my chorus of goddammits.

And it helped. "Whistling past the graveyard," I'd heard Grandma McLaren call it. The weight on my shoulders lightened. The rotten stench faded into the background. I didn't even notice the dripping fluids anymore. In fact, they seemed to have stopped altogether. By the time I reached the top of the stairs, I was more concerned with what melody I was humming than my gruesome burden.

What is that song? I know I've heard it before. It's on the tip of my tongue.

It was in some sort of minor mode. *Dorian,* I decided. I looked up at the small window, hoping Martes would be there to fly us out. No sign of him. I was going to have to walk out the front door. Turning, I hummed the intro again, a long descending run.

God, I know I've heard it before! But where?

Then two steps from the door into the church proper, it hit me.

It's Aine's song.

My memory of the song and the day in the Meadows when I had first played it came back in a flash.

The melody.

The chords.

The *knowing.*

"Shit." My humming ceased as I swore. Remembering the *knowing* made the horror of the situation even worse. For one brief moment, I had been closer to Aine than I'd ever been to anyone. And now she was just a load of rotten meat, a grisly cargo to be hauled outside and dumped at Martes's feet. And I'd probably end up dumped right next to her.

"Singer," whispered a ragged voice right next to my ear. "Do not stop."

• • • Nine • • •

Shrieking like a ten-year-old girl, I flung Aine's body from my back. I turned to see who had spoken, but I knew already.

"Singer," Aine whispered. She raised herself up on one elbow from where she lay on the floor. "Do not stop." Her eyes were back, but they swam in milky fluids and blood still ran from the sockets. A new hand had grown, red and scabrous, where there had only been a stump a minute ago. "Singer . . ."

"Aine?" I asked stupidly. "Don't stop what?"

But she didn't speak again. Those four words had taken all her strength, and she slumped back to the ground. I knelt by her. I didn't know how to take a pulse; I had no mirror to check for breath.

Is she dead? Again?

I cupped my hand behind her neck and pulled her close.

"Aine?" I stared into her clouded, unblinking eyes. "Aine."

I kept staring until the rest of the room faded behind her, until all I could see were her lifeless eyes. They filled my vision, and I could suddenly hear a note in my head. A high E. Twelfth fret on the high E string if I was playing the guitar. Or I could hit the harmonic in the same spot. But I would play it on the B string, seventeenth fret. Because it was the beginning of a familiar descending Dorian run. The opening line to Aine's song. The song I'd been singing. The song that had revived her.

I hummed it.

No. That's wrong.

I tried again.

"No," I said aloud.

That's not it. I could hear the music in my head, see it before me, laid out in charts and tablature. It was all there. But it wasn't the right song. I hummed the line again. It wasn't the Aine's song I remembered.

"Goddammit."

It was all wrong. I stared at Aine again. Let her fill my vision. Sang the first line.

"Crap."

What had gone wrong? I sat, I stared, I sang. Just like in the park. Did I need an instrument? I didn't think so. I'd revived her with only my voice just a minute before . . .

Then it hit me. This new song was Aine *now.* Half or full dead—I wasn't sure which—but well and truly fucked up at the very least. I needed to sing the old Aine. The one from the park. The regal, beautiful, bitchy Aine who had given me the sight.

I hummed the line again. It was still wrong, but I didn't stop this time. I kept singing. Sang the new Aine, bleeding and broken. Sang the pain and torture, the terror and rage. I belted out rumbling low notes and screeching highs, till my voice scratched and tore. I sang vicious swooping runs and clipped atonal arpeggios till my chest ached and tiny capillaries burst in my bulging eyes. I sang on until I thought I would collapse next to Aine, sharing her life, her death. I sang her new song. Lived it. And committed it to memory.

Then I sang it again.

But this time I twisted it. Just a little at first. A note here, an inflection there. Minor third to major second. Major third to perfect fourth. Just half steps. But, like changing a word one letter at a time, soon I had a whole new meaning. It was a lighter song this time around, more lilting, more pleasant. More alive.

And then I sang it again. And again, changing it a little more each time.

Composing, I thought. *As opposed to . . .*

I shook that thought off. And kept singing. Soon I was close. Real close. Maybe a note or two away.

You're rushing, Douglas. That's hardly professional.

Wrenching the tempo back under control, I belted out the final song triumphantly, roaring the melody, sending sixteenth notes bouncing off the walls of the office. And then I did collapse next to Aine, utterly spent.

"Singer," she said, her voice tired but strong. "Thank you."

I opened my eyes and looked at her. Her eyes were clear but bloodshot, her limbs whole but hanging limp, the new hand and fingers tinged a raw new-skin red. Her face was crisscrossed with scars as if her ordeal had been years ago, not just that day.

I nodded, unable to speak for a moment. I struggled to my feet. "Can you walk?"

She sat up slowly. Winced. "I believe so. With assistance."

I crouched behind her and pulled her up under her arms. She hooked one arm over my shoulder and we made for the door out of the office. My legs gave way after only two steps, and I leaned hard against the doorjamb.

"Singer?"

My head swam as I shook it. "I'll be OK."

"Yes, you will. Eventually." We tried to prop each other up, like the first two pieces of a house of cards. Only not as sturdy. "But that was a considerable casting you just made. You will be weak for some time yet."

"No." I shook my head again. "I'll be all right in a second."

"I sure hope so," a new voice said from the window. Aine and I turned, still clinging to each other for balance. Nose twitching furiously, Martes floated outside the small portal.

I wonder how long he's been there.

"Because the priest comes," Martes said.

"Shit." I didn't think I could get us out the window in the shape we were in. "Can you—"

"No." Martes shook his head. "I have no power in there. Unlike you, apparently."

Shit. "Can we make it out the front door, Martes?"

"If you hurry."

Hurry? Great. But panic put a spring back in our step for the moment, and we lurched and stumbled through the church. We bounced off the pews and fell out the front door. No sign of Father Croser, but I assumed he would be coming up the street and entering the grounds any minute.

Going to have to go over the back wall. Can't let him see us if he's on the street. I grabbed Aine's hand. *Should be low enough to get over.*

I dragged her toward the back of the church, trying to avoid the tombstones and hedges between us and escape. When we reached the rear of the church, only a few scratches and bruises later, Martes was waiting there with my shoes and my guitar.

"Follow me," he said.

The run had taken the last of Aine's strength, and she clung to me, barely keeping herself upright. She whispered something.

"What?" I said, leaning down to better hear.

"No," she breathed. "We cannot go with him." She pointed at Martes. "Take me to Calton Hill, Singer."

"Let's go, Douglas," Martes said, hopping on one foot then the other. "The priest won't be happy that you've stolen his prize."

"One second." Then to Aine. "Calton Hill?"

"The hill with the folly."

I knew the spot. A high bluff just east of the city center, with a half-finished replica of the Acropolis on it. *Only in Scotland.*

"We'll never climb up that in the dark, in this condition. We need to rest. I'll drive you there later."

"Douglas," Martes said. "We have to move."

"I know. I know."

Aine thought for a second. "Then take me to your home," she whispered.

I nodded. Turned to Martes.

"Martes," I said, and drew the big iron knife from my waistband. "We're not going with you."

Martes looked at the knife and sighed. "Haven't we been through this already, Douglas?"

He might have said more, but Aine spoke first.

"Bogie," she said. She pushed herself upright, wobbling slightly, and blue fire danced around her fingertips. "Away with you."

Martes's eyes flicked from me to Aine and back again. He spoke hurriedly. "I promised to be your protector in all things faery-related, Douglas. You don't know what she's like. You go with her now and I can't—"

He squawked as a bolt of energy chewed up the dirt at his feet. Then he dropped shoes and guitar, and scuttled away.

"Singer," Aine said, and fainted.

I caught her without putting my knife through her kidney, but only just barely. She felt much lighter alive than she had dead. I tucked the knife away and scooped her up. Nothing fell off this time. I balanced her on one shoulder, managing to bend down and grab my guitar, then slip my feet back into my shoes. The low wall was a trial, but I succeeded in scooting over it without dropping any of my burdens. Then I staggered off, head swimming, shoulder aching, the weight of Aine and my guitar growing with every step. But I couldn't have been happier.

I felt like a fucking hero.

"GIE US A pound or two, mate."

I was beginning to see why nobody was giving me a second glance on my walk home: there was no shortage of other drunkards and crazies to stare at. Like the one standing before me, stoned and smelly, greasy hair standing straight up, dirty hand held out hopefully.

I was taking the long way home, avoiding the faery market entirely. Aine's friends would be indistinguishable from her enemies in the darkness, and if faery politics were anything like our own, there would be some in her own camp who wouldn't shed a tear if she never returned.

"I'm a musician, pal." I shook my guitar case at him. "I got nothing to spare."

After trying to focus his bleary eyes, he finally got a closer look at me: bloody and battered, my right arm hooked around an invisible burden. It dawned on him that I might actually be crazier than he was.

"Fair enough," he said, shuffling off. My eyes still watered from the whisky on his breath.

By the time I reached Grandma McLaren's my muscles burned and the smell of my own sweat nearly overpowered the gagging stench of blood and ichor still rising off my clothes. Nearly.

I hadn't thought of a way to explain my condition to Grandma McLaren, so I was relieved to see that the Peugeot wasn't in the driveway. She must have nipped off to catch one of the last Fringe events.

Just as well, I thought. *Aine can rest and I can shower. Maybe burn my clothes.*

I turned the lights off in my room and left Aine sleeping on the air mattress. I scrubbed myself under scalding water till my skin was beet red. Then I wrapped a towel round my waist and padded back to my room. Aine was still resting, but not comfortably. Her breathing seemed labored. I felt her forehead. Hot.

Maybe she's not out of the woods yet. Wonder if she needs another song. Or a better one.

I pulled my guitar from its case. Tuned it carefully. I wanted everything to be perfect. Perched cross-legged by the bed I thought, *What was the first chord? Oh, yeah. E minor 9.*

I strummed it. Played the Dorian run on the B string. I had to lean over close to see the frets in the moonlight. I sang along. Aine moaned softly in her sleep.

It really is a beautiful melody. Dark, though.

I played the song deliberately this time, without the nervous excitement that had messed with my tempo in Father Croser's church. I picked each note perfectly, sang every pitch clean. It was as flawless a performance as I could give. I meant to watch Aine to see if I could see the magic work, but I lost myself in the music partway through. I no longer had to look at the fingerboard; I played with my eyes squeezed shut while the melody and chords flowed through me like a river of wine, swift and sweet. When the song ended, I opened my eyes in surprise and saw that Aine was sitting up on the bed. All the scars had faded from her face except for a small crescent on her chin, as if from a childhood accident.

I frowned at the tiny imperfection. Strummed the opening chord again.

"That is enough, Singer." Aine said, placing one smooth hand over the guitar strings, muffling them. The fingertips of her other hand brushed my lips. "Enough."

I nodded. Put my guitar away. Looked at her sitting on my bed, still as one of the human statues on the Royal Mile. "What happened tonight, Aine? How was I able to bring you back to life?"

Aine arched an eyebrow. She got easily to her feet and took the two short steps to my bedroom window.

"Long has my line known the manner of their passing," she said. Moonlight crept in to light her face. It made her alabaster, a statue of an ancient goddess. "My predecessors often tried to escape their fate, but all their efforts were either useless or served only to bring about that which they tried to circumvent." She turned, shadow covering half her face. "Such is the nature of prophecy."

"You couldn't avoid your death, so you decided to come back from it?"

Aine held still for a moment, then gave a curt nod and turned back to the window. "I called you here, Singer."

"Called me?"

"Yes. Across continents and oceans. I called you here and gave you the gift of sight, the loan of power. And you have given me life."

"Called me here?" I sounded like a parrot. "But it was my idea to come to Scotland. It was The Plan!"

Aine turned back toward me. "Was it?"

"Of course it was! I . . ." Was it my idea? Or did someone plant the seed in my head when I was first here at thirteen years old, letting it germinate and grow and eventually draw me back? Since when did I ever think about Grandma McLaren, or Scotland, or anything but music and where my next fix was coming from? All of a sudden, my decision to come here seemed quite out of character. "You had no right," I said.

"I was dying, Singer."

Good point. "Still, you had no right."

"I was dying," Aine said again. Then she arched an eyebrow at me. "And perhaps you are better off now for coming here? Is this not true?"

It probably was. Sober, responsible, practically gainfully employed with all the money I'd made at the Fringe—all things I didn't recall being while in Minneapolis. I wouldn't give her the satisfaction of telling her that, though.

"So what happens now?"

"Now things go back to normal." Aine sighed. "In the morning I shall remove your fey vision. I will retrieve the memory of my true name. All will be as it was before. You can even go back to your homeland if you like."

"Back to my homeland?" I said. "I'd rather stay."

"That is your choice to make. But you shall not see me or my kind again after tonight."

I was strangely saddened by this news. Aine and the faeries had screwed up my life in countless ways, causing me no end of danger and discomfort. Yet, having been touched by magic, I didn't want to give it up.

"That's it? Don't I have a say?"

"You?" Aine snorted. "Of course not."

"And why not?"

Aine's voice softened. "I am sorry, Singer. But you are a pawn in this. You have done your piece. You have reached the end of the board and brought the queen back to life." She drifted away from the window, coming to rest before me. "And having done so, it is time for you to leave the game."

I stared at my feet, wondering if my sobriety had been just a function of her calling me here.

When her spell fades, will I go back to being a junkie?

I felt a hand on my face and saw that Aine crouched before me now. She lifted my chin with her fingertips.

"Do not sorrow for what was never yours, Singer." She stood. "And besides," she said. "There is still the small matter of payment." She pulled me to my feet.

"Payment?" It was my turn to snort. "Faery gold that'll turn into autumn leaves by morning, I suppose. I'll pass."

"Of course not, Singer." Aine sounded offended. "I would not deal with you in such a manner. You have given me a great gift. The gift of life." Aine looked me in the eyes for a long second and then smiled. For the first time since I had known her, it seemed to have real warmth and honest mirth to it. "And you know I hate to leave my accounts unbalanced."

I touched my eyes. Thought about the vial she'd given me in the park. "I've noticed."

"So, what to give in return." She tapped her cheek while she thought, pacing back to the window. "What to give, what to give." Her tone was playful, coquettish.

By God, I thought. *Is she flirting with me?*

I was suddenly acutely aware that I was wearing only a towel.

"I have it!" she exclaimed, spinning to face me. Her dress twirled around her ankles, and a few loose tendrils of hair brushed across her face. "You have given me life." She reached behind her neck to the fastening of her dress. "I will give you . . ." She twisted her fingers, releasing an unseen clasp. "Me."

The dress slipped off and she stood naked in the moonlight. A part of me noticed that she had no more scars besides the one on her chin, but it was only a very small part.

"Come, Singer," she said, smiling wryly. "I have unwrapped your gift, you must but accept it."

I crossed the room and pulled her to me. She smelled of gardenias, tasted of honeyed wine.

"My name is Douglas," I said throatily.

When our lips finally parted she answered, "And you know mine."

She was light, nothing to her, and I lifted her easily, dropping us both onto the bed when I reached it. My towel fell away and she was on me like a cat, guiding me inside and grinding into me like she wanted to finish in seconds. I had higher hopes than that. It was a wrestling match to switch positions, twisting and grappling until I was on top, holding her wrists over her head in one hand, exploring her slim body with the other. Our moans became nearly musical, and on a whim, I hummed the opening notes of her song into her ear. Aine gasped and arched her back, her hips thrusting hard into mine. Blue sparks suddenly shot from her fingertips, scorching the wall behind her head. I blinked at the black marks in the old paint and she ripped her arms free. Reaching around behind me, she began to spur me on with sharp fingernails and electric shocks, each accompanied by cries of encouragement and approval. I was bucking wildly now, but still humming her song, and she lifted her hips off the bed to meet me. I couldn't imagine what my back would look like in the morning, blackened and bleeding perhaps, but I didn't care, letting Aine climb on top once more so I could let go. She threw her arms wide as we finished, sending books and knickknacks flying with bolts of blue lightning, before collapsing on top of me, both of us drenched with sweat and gasping for air.

"Singer?" Aine asked some time later.

"Shhh," I answered, trailing one finger down neck, shoulder, breast, flank. I knew every inch of her—had known it before—and her song resonated in my mind, different notes pealing louder as I traced her form. Neck, shoulder, . . .

"Douglas?"

"Yes?"

"Are you ready for another performance, Singer?" She smiled at me, one eyebrow reaching skyward.

I looked down. "I believe I am." Chuckling. "I do believe I am."

And much later, just before dropping off into an exhausted slumber, a thought drifted through my head:

Some people say heroin is better than sex. They don't know what the hell they're talking about.

• • • Ten • • •

Douglas."

"Mrph."

"Douglas."

"Urgh. Sleeping."

"Time to wake, Loverboy."

A small fingernail flicked one of the still raw gashes on my cheek, and I shot awake. Martes crouched on my chest, porcelain knife pointed at my eyes.

"Ouch. Martes, you bastard!"

"Had to wake you somehow, stud." He hopped off my chest and made his little knife disappear. "We have to get you out of here."

"Why? Where's Aine?"

"Aine?" Martes snickered, showing sharp yellow teeth. "Long gone. Or did you think you were that good?" His voice shot up an octave. "Oh, Singer, you beast!"

"What have you done with her?"

"Done with her?" Martes was wide-eyed and his rat nose twitched with amusement. "Puck's sake, Douglas. You're even stupider than you look. Get up and get dressed. Before her guard arrives."

"Her guard? Aine's? Why would they come here?"

Martes started rummaging through drawers, throwing random clothes my way. "You know her true name, Douglas. You can't be allowed to live."

"But she said she would take that knowledge tomorrow." I sat up and swung my legs over the side of the bed. My back hurt. "And the faery sight too."

A pair of pants hit me in the face. I grabbed them before they fell to the floor.

"And she will," Martes said. "Take your life along with it."

I put one leg through. Stopped. "But she owes me . . ."

"Nothing. All accounts paid in full." Martes waggled a sock obscenely at me. "Isn't that right, Lothario?"

I put my other leg in the pants. Pulled them up and buttoned them.

"Why should I believe you?"

"You shouldn't." Martes threw me the sock and I slipped it on. "You should release me from my pledge and let me go about my business."

"Hardly a convincing argument."

Martes shrugged. "Stay here. Get your head lopped off." He glanced out the window. "Take a look, Douglas."

I stepped to the window. "What am I looking for?"

"You tell me."

Peering out the window, I realized that I hadn't slept for long; the moon was still bright in the sky, illuminating Grandma McLaren's sleepy neighborhood. I watched a Fiat creep down the road, its taillights springing to red life when a cat leapt across its path. A few leaves drifted past the window, early turners on a light breeze. A dog barked twice in the distance, then was silent.

And six burly elves, wearing green surcoats with a white hind rampant, marched up the hill toward the house.

"Ah," Martes said. "Your executioners come."

"Maybe they're coming to bring me to Aine."

"To live happily ever after in your lovely castle by the sea." His voice dripped with sugar-sweet sarcasm. "Oh, c'mon, Douglas! Wake up and smell the ball of crap life's dealt you. Look again. What do you see?"

I watched the guard come on. They marched in formation as usual, their weapons drawn.

Their weapons drawn. Nobody draws a weapon unless they intend to use it.

"Shit," I said.

"And you've stepped right in it." Martes grabbed my arm and pulled me toward the door. "C'mon now. Out the back window. I can't protect you here with nothing but a clay knife and a few crooked darts."

I nodded mutely and followed as far as the door.

"Wait a second." I went back in my room and rummaged around till I found the big knife. Made to tuck it into my pants again.

"Unless you've learned to fly by yourself I suggest you leave that," Martes said.

"Why?"

"We're going out a second-story window, Douglas. I can't help you if you carry that."

I looked at the knife longingly for a moment, then flipped it onto the bed.

"OK. Let's go."

We made it only to the bedroom door before I stopped again.

"Wait!" I said. "I can't leave. What about Grandma McLaren?" I jumped to the bed and grabbed the knife. "They'll kill her."

I held my weapon in front of me. Shook slightly as I imagined myself—shirtless and shoeless and carrying what suddenly seemed like a very small knife—facing six armored warriors.

"Why would they kill her?" Martes scoffed. "She's done nothing to them. It's you they're after." He tugged on my arm again. "She won't even see them."

I looked at the big knife. "I suppose she won't." Tossed it back on the bed.

"Let's go!" Martes's eyes and nose twitched in different directions, now toward me, now toward the door.

"Wait. Shoes."

"No time now." He nearly yanked me off my feet and dragged me out the door. We stumbled into the little upstairs bathroom, my knees banging on the edge of the tub. Martes flung open the window and then, "Up horse and hattock!" he cried, and out we flew. I thought I heard Grandma McLaren's door crash open as we alit behind the house, but I may have imagined it.

"Time to run, Douglas."

We ran. Despite my longer strides, Martes kept in front, calling out "Here!" and "This way!" taking us down twisting side roads and claustrophobic closes. It was late and what little foot traffic there was kept well away, wanting no part of the crazed sprinting freak I must have appeared. My shoeless feet slapped hard on concrete and cobblestone, and occasional patches of gravel sent sharp rocks into my unprotected heels. But I didn't ask Martes to stop or even slow down. I was in panicked flight once more and I'd keep running till Martes stopped or my lungs burst through my rib cage and splattered on the sidewalk.

Which at this pace, I told myself, wouldn't be long.

We burst from between parked cars and danced across a major thoroughfare to the grating sounds of screeching tires and honking horns. I was too tired to give anyone the finger. We were nearly back to the Old Town now, and after a few final twists and turns, Martes finally called a halt.

"That should lose 'em," he said, stopping and looking around.

I just panted. Judging by how far we were from Grandma McLaren's and how long our run had taken, I decided we might have broken a four-minute mile. Or a couple of them.

Should chase Olympians with swords. See how many records they break then.

"Don't stop, though, Douglas." Martes broke into a brisk walk. We were well east of the faery market and about to take a bridge over the train tracks near Holyrood Palace. "We still have a little more ground to cover."

I followed as best I could, gasping and wheezing and hopping on one foot after another to scrape loose stones off my socks.

"Where to?" I gulped.

"Someplace safe to hole up for the night. The fair's over by morning, and we'll all go home."

"Home?" As soon as I could breathe normally again, I swore I would put together a full sentence.

"Yes, home. Faeryland, I suppose you'd call it." Martes stopped and peered at me, giving me one slow twitch of his nose. "You didn't think we stayed in this pisshole year-round?"

"I—"

"It's just three weeks for the market in late summer." He turned and began walking again. "Then back to business as usual in the Land of the Ever Fair."

"Just three weeks, eh?" My mind was racing. If the faeries all left in the morning, it'd be clear sailing till next year. I could hole up till they were gone, maybe take a vacation during the Fringe each year.

"Well, most of us. Some stay throughout. A few house brownies, some loch spirits, maybe. But most of the affiliated fey, members of the Courts, will go back."

"The Courts?"

Martes gave an amazed snort. "You really don't know anything, do you, Douglas?" He shook his head and clucked his tongue. "You're dropped smack-dab in the middle of a millenia-old cold war, and you don't even know the players."

"Well, how about you enlighten me? I know Aine is the queen. But whose?"

"Aine is the Queen of the Blessed Ones. The Daoine Sidhe." He spit between his fingers. "The People of Peace."

"And what's your side called?"

"We are called by many names: The Damned Ones, The Sluagh, The Host. But I prefer . . ." He faced me and performed a sweeping bow. "The Guid Nichbouris."

"What does that mean?"

"The Good Neighbors."

"The Good Neighbors?" *Talk about your oxymorons.* "Is the Fachan a 'Good Neighbor'?"

"Yes. Why do you ask?"

"Because I don't think I'd like it if he moved into my neighborhood. Or you, for that matter."

Martes turned and sauntered off, his tiny chin in the air, his tone haughty. "It is of no account. Greater men than you have called us by the name."

I quickened my pace to keep up. "Who's your queen?"

"Queen? We have no need of royalty."

"Oh. You guys a democracy? Who's your leader?"

"Leader? We have no need of leaders."

"I'm sensing a theme here."

We reached the Royal Mile and turned west, back toward the center of the Old Town.

Strange to go this far out of our way just to head back to town.

"The Good Neighbors are kind of a . . ." Martes thought for a moment. "An autonomous collective."

"An autonomous collective, eh?" I tried on a broad English accent. "Come see the violence inherent in the system!"

Martes looked back over his shoulder. "What's wrong with you?"

"Nothing. Autonomous collective. Monty Python. Quest for the . . ." He stared at me blankly. "Oh, never mind. Go on."

"Yes. An autonomous collective. But not if you ask the Blessed Ones."

"What do they think of you as?"

"Not-so-loyal subjects."

I chuckled at that. "I'd guess that causes some friction."

"Friction is a good word for it. So is war." Martes looked nervously from side to side. "Okay, time for some quiet. We avoid the Daoine Sidhe for ten more minutes and we'll have you tucked safe away for the night."

I nodded, and we continued up the Royal Mile without further conversation. It couldn't have been too late at night, but the city seemed exhausted after three weeks of the Fringe and the mad press of people common during the festival had been reduced to a mere trickle of drunken revelers. We did nothing to avoid them, but Martes kept a sharp eye out for fey. At one point he saw something he didn't like and pressed me into a dark doorway.

"What's up?"

"Hush!"

He peeked out, while I stood with the doorknob poking me in the small of the back, breath and heartbeat quickening with anxiety.

What does he see? What's out there?

The mind invents what it cannot see. Standing there, unmoving, unable to tell what was happening, I decided that Aine's bodyguards had found us. That even now, they were marching toward our hiding place, their swords drawn. I could picture them swinging their big weapons, slashing, slicing, cutting Martes down. Then they came for me. And I had nothing to defend myself with. I cursed myself for leaving my knife at home. I could have thrown it out the window, picked it up once we landed. But I hadn't thought of it then, and it was far too late now.

I could almost feel the sharp edges of the bodyguards' weapons hewing through my ribs and flesh, muscle and bone, to pierce the organs beneath.

Move, Douglas! My own voice screamed in my head. *Run! Get out!*

But some small part of me knew that if I broke from my hiding place, it'd be the last thing I did. Martes had sworn to protect me, and I'd best help him in his job. I clamped down hard on my terror and stayed still. Shaky, but still.

After a short half a minute that felt like an eternity, Martes hopped back onto the sidewalk and waved me out. But now that he wanted me to move, I couldn't. I had begun to welcome the pain in my back from the doorknob, the stiffness in my knees and ankles, the rawness of my abused feet. I wanted to stay.

I shook my head. Martes waved again. I stood my ground. Shook my head again. Martes sighed heavily and walked back to me.

"Douglas?" he said, his voice dripping with kindness and concern.

I managed to squeak out one word. "Yes?"

"You're panicking, aren't you?"

I nodded. Tried to say "yes" again. Failed.

Martes sighed and stomped sharply on my foot.

I yipped like a Jack Russell terrier and hopped up on one foot. "Goddammit!"

In answer Martes slapped me in the face. I never saw it coming.

"Listen up, Douglas," he hissed, ducking out of reach as I swung a clumsy fist. "I take my pledge to be your protector quite seriously." His voice came from behind me now, and I spun to face him. "I have given it much thought, planned it carefully." He'd got behind me again somehow, and I turned just in time to receive another stinging blow to the cheek. "There is no question of the correct course of action: your one chance to stay alive is to follow me now." He was on the street now, scanning it for enemies. "Your one chance."

I put my hand to my cheek. Licked my finger. Salty. He'd opened up the cuts there. The cuts he'd given me.

Martes twitched his nose. "So, are you done panicking?"

Funny thing, I *was* done. Now, I was just angry.

I nodded to him. "I'm going to kill you."

"I doubt that very much." Martes grinned. "Let's move."

I pushed my anger and fear down into the pit of my stomach, where they belonged, and followed.

Canongate turned into High Street. I watched the side streets crawl past: St. Mary's, Blackfriars, Niddry. We were getting uncomfortably close to Bank Street and the steps down to the market.

Why are we going to the center of town instead of heading for the hills?

But there was no sense asking. I had followed Martes this far. I'd just have to trust him for a few hours more, much as that seemed like a bad idea. I probably couldn't get out of the city on my own now anyway. I was tired, it was dark, I was shirtless and shoeless, without money or a guitar, and a dozen faeries could sneak up behind me and tap me on the shoulder before I realized it.

We passed between North and South Bridge, slipped by Cockburn Street with its head shops and porn parlors, pulled even with the arches and pillars of the City Chambers.

I couldn't hold it anymore; we were too near the faery market.

"Martes, what the—"

"We're here," he said, ducking down a close that bore a plaque saying: WRITER'S COURT LEADING TO WARRISTON'S CLOSE.

We stopped short of an iron gate protecting a tiny courtyard that I assumed was Writer's Court. I saw no sign of Warriston's Close.

"Up horse and—" Martes called out, but I interrupted him.

"Hold on a second!"

The gate was made of spearlike rods. I didn't like the thought of him flying me over something that pointy. But to either side of the gate, the rods were set into a low concrete wall, giving me a foothold halfway up. Stepping on, I grabbed an iron bar in each hand, and swung myself over considerably more gracefully than when I had entered Father Croser's church.

Martes alit next to me moments later.

"I could have gotten you over," he said with a huffy twitch of his nose.

Six quick steps and we were at a set of modern double doors.

"Open them," Martes said.

I tried the handle. "They're locked."

"Are they?" And he waved a small hand at the doors. There was an audible click as the bolt snicked back. "Now open them, and be quick about it."

I swung the door open and we slipped inside. I heard the bolt slip back into place automatically when the door shut.

"Forward," Martes said, and we padded down a dark wood-paneled hall.

"What are we—"

"Right."

By the shelves full of tartan coffee cups, glossy booklets, and hand-crafted bric-a-brac, I guessed that this windowed room was a souvenir shop. We didn't get time to browse, however.

"Right."

Another lock came open, and we entered a tiny room with nothing but the words THE REAL MARY KING'S CLOSE in fancy white lettering on the wall and a worn stone staircase leading down into blackness.

"Down," Martes said.

I couldn't see the bottom. "Down?"

Martes nudged me in the back. "Down."

I shrugged and started down. Slowly. "What is this place?"

"Mary King's Close. Was a thriving little community till the plague hit."

"What happened then?"

"Depends who you ask. The old papers say the inhabitants were 'enclosed.' People figured that meant they walled 'em in and let 'em rot." Martes grabbed his throat and let loose with a choking death-rattle cough. In broad daylight, the sound would have been unsettling. Here, with the darkness closing in around us, it set my nerves twanging like a guitar string. "But now," Martes went on, "they say that 'enclosed' meant 'quarantined' back then, and that the folk here were well-fed and cared for."

"Oh yeah?" I counted eighteen steps, then we hit a landing. Feeling along the wall, I found more steps to the left. Still couldn't see bottom. "Which was it?"

"You know a little about human nature, don't you, Douglas?" Martes snickered. "Which do you think it was?"

I shuddered. Seven more steps. Another landing. More stairs. "You were there, weren't you?"

Martes didn't answer. I could hear him running a sharp fingernail deliberately across the stone wall. The scraping made my teeth ache.

"Friction," he said. "We were talking about friction."

Expecting another step, my knee jarred as I rammed my foot into a floor instead. It wasn't a landing this time. We were down.

"Friction," Martes said again and whipped his arm forward. A spark flew from his nail off the wall. Instead of flickering out, it slowed before us and grew to the size of a golf ball. It cast eerie shadows, dark caricatures that didn't seem to move quite in concert with us, their creators.

Despite our long trip downstairs, we now stood at the head of a thin cobblestoned street that ran steeply down and away. Laundry lines strung with flowing cotton shifts and puffy-sleeved sailor's shirts ran from building to building, and the windows hung open, as if housewives and serving girls would at any moment be leaning out to pull their washing in. I could picture children pouring out of the doorways to play in the street, could almost hear the chiming of workmen's hammers, smell the smoke and sewage of an active, if ancient, neighborhood. But it was quiet as the grave and two stories over our head, where a sliver of sky would once have been seen, the entire street had been covered over in stone.

"Enclosed," I breathed.

Martes held one hand out toward his magical light, as if recalling it toward us. With the other, he grasped my arm and pulled me off the street and through a door to our right. The light followed.

"The People of Peace hate us," Martes said. For a moment I thought he meant *us* as in Martes and me. Then I remembered the Good Neighbors. "They would like nothing more than to destroy us utterly. They might even be capable of it."

We were in a stone room, now, with a low vaulted ceiling. Martes beckoned me and I followed him through another door.

"Then why don't they?" I asked.

"Mostly because we provide certain services and products that they are unwilling or unable to procure for themselves."

We entered the next room and I jumped back in shock. In a fancy medieval chamber, complete with painted wooden panels, stained glass, and an ornate fireplace, two women in anachronistic dress bent over the body of a man, his crushed skull gushing blood into the floorboards. Coal tongs—the murder weapon, I assumed—lay on the ground next to the older woman, whose expression was torn between horror and satisfaction. Permanently torn. In fact, her expression wasn't changing at all.

Martes was chuckling. "Murder most foul," he intoned in a broad Scots accent.

It was a tableau. Three wax statues forever reenacting an ancient crime.

"Friend of yours?" I said, pointing to the prone figure, trying to keep my tone light.

"We weren't close." Eerie light glinted off his sharp teeth as he grinned. "Though he did owe me money."

I followed Martes out of the murder room and into a chamber with smooth wooden floors lightly covered with sawdust. Our feet slipped soundlessly across the boards. Sprawled across two beds, a family lay dying, plague buboes sprouting horrifically on their armpits and necks. A man in a grotesque bird mask bent over the father, preparing to cauterize one of his sores with a red hot iron. Wrapped in gray cloth, a corpse was stacked against the near wall. The people were all as motionless as the corpse.

"Nice," I said. "Real fucking nice."

Martes tittered once, his nose twitching happily. "As I was saying, we provide services the stuck-up bastards of the Daoine Sidhe would never do for themselves. My own humble talents, for example." He switched to an exaggerated posh-English-prep-school accent. "The Daoine Sidhe would never deign to procure labor for themselves, of course, but their whole society would fall apart without slaves to do the work." Dropping the accent, Martes put his hand to his chin. "I suppose it goes both ways, though. I've never met a Good Neighbor who could sew a decent shoe. That luchorpan's been making a killing off of us for centuries."

There were no horrific statues to view in the next room, just several scattered crates. Martes didn't immediately head for the exit at the far end, so I gladly sat down on one of the crates.

"So you all meet to hold the market?"

"Yes." Martes nodded, and his shadow head bobbed crazily on the wall behind him. "Once a year, on neutral ground. And your world, being a muddy reflection of our own, seems to have sprouted a festival of its own to match." Martes glanced around, as if confirming we were alone. "Now here's the important part, Douglas." His nose twitched once, then held remarkably still. "Not everyone is happy with the way things are. Some would like nothing more than open warfare with the Daoine Sidhe. They would rather go poor than sell their services. Rather steal than pay tariff to tyrants. Rather die as free fey than live as servants to the pompous People of Peace." Martes took a deep breath, his chest puffing out. "But as it stands, we don't have a chance. We have worthy individual warriors, but the Daoine Sidhe have armies, organization. The most we could hope for would be to make their victory a Pyhrric one. To make their casualties too great to populate the territory they would take from us." Martes fixed me with his stare, eyes glazed with revolutionary zeal. "If it comes to war, we would need an edge. Something big enough to turn the tide."

Martes must have been at the window of Father Croser's church longer than I'd thought. He'd seen me bring Aine back to life. And now he thought I had some power over her.

"Like, say, someone who knew the Queen's true name."

"Douglas," Martes beamed. "You're not as dumb as they say." He slapped me on the back as if we were old comrades. "With your knowledge and our power, we could crush them, send the bastards back to—"

"No fucking way, Martes. Why don't *you* do it? You obviously heard me sing her back to life."

"Hearing and *knowing* are very different things, Douglas."

"Well. Too bad for you, 'cause I'm not going to help."

"But, Douglas—"

"No," I said, leaning back against the wall. "There's no way I'm getting involved in this. I didn't do anything, anyway. Aine gave me her name. I didn't even remember it till just then in the church. Probably some sort of spell she cast so I didn't use her name for anything but bringing her back to life." I frowned, thinking about Aine telling me I was a pawn and it was time to leave the board. "I'll probably forget it by the morning, anyway. Faery gold. Autumn leaves." I yawned and closed my eyes. Folded my arms across my chest. *God, I'm tired.* "I'll wait out the night, then I'm gone. You can keep watch." I smiled, my eyes still closed. "As per your pledge and all."

"I was afraid you might feel that way," Martes sighed. "That's why I brought you here."

"What?" I shot forward and opened my eyes.

"He said, that is why he brought you here," a deep voice uttered from somewhere behind me.

Spinning to face the speaker, I saw a tall elf with a dark complexion just entering through the far door. He was dressed all in rich black velvet, with a sword hanging from either hip, their ornate silver guards clinking lightly against his belt as he walked.

"Martes . . ."

More creatures followed behind the tall elf, a nightmare assortment of "Good Neighbors." Limping, shuffling, slithering, hopping, they came into the chamber, all pausing to look at me and then at Martes as if to ask, "Is it him?" He nodded at each in turn.

Soon the room was stuffed full of monstrosities. If I hadn't seen most of them trying on shoes or shopping for vegetables at one time or another over the past few weeks, I might have fainted from horror. As it was, my skin crawled, and the terror I had pushed into the pit of my stomach earlier began crawling toward my brain, bruising my internal organs as it climbed.

"I know you think I betrayed you, Douglas," Martes said, his voice strangely comforting amongst the low murmur of the rest of the crowd. *The devil you know.* "But I promised to protect you. And I'd be failing my bond if I let you stay neutral in this. Aine's lot will kill you for sure." He grinned at me with pure, malicious pleasure. "The Good Neighbors will only kill you if you refuse."

"Fuck you," I said. But it came out more defeated than defiant.

"Take him away," said the elf who had entered first. "There is much to discuss."

A gigantic troll made his way through the crowd, tossing aside those of his brethren who didn't move out of his way quickly enough.

They may be an autonomous collective, I thought. *But that troll sure hops to it when the elf talks.*

I shoved my terror back down into my gut and leapt off my crate.

"Fuck this," I stated, and aimed a kick straight for where I thought the troll's nuts would be. The blow landed, a solid shot to the groin. My regret was instantaneous. It was like kicking a rock. Only harder.

I had just enough time for a short yelp of pain before the troll threw me over his shoulder as if I were a two-year-old having a temper tantrum. Bouncing upside down on his back as he lumbered out of the room, I was unable to track where we were going, sensing only that we'd passed through several rooms before the troll found a spot he liked: a six-by-six stone room, but with a dirt floor and one brick wall. And, most important, just the one door. Though it had probably once been the cramped living quarters of some poor tradesman in the Middle Ages, it looked like a jail cell to me. It appeared it was going to serve that purpose, as well. The troll tossed me in, then sat down in the doorway, forming an impassable barrier with his bulk. Jailor and jail door all in one immense, warty package.

Well, shit, I thought. *Drafted.*

I sat down in the corner. A bare bulb burned in the room beyond the troll, and light leaked in around him. Picking at my fingernails, I examined my options. They looked about as attractive as the troll did.

Let's see, I mused. *I can attack this gigantic mountain of troll.* I eyed my jailor's broad, muscular, wart-covered form. *And get killed. Or I can throw my lot in with the Good Neighbors and fight their war.* I snorted. *And then get killed.*

I had no illusions about the Good Neighbors keeping me alive after my usefulness had passed.

Leaning back against the one brick wall, I let my eyes unfocus. I'd lost track of time long ago, but I knew that it was late. I was hearing voices, I was so tired.

No, wait. I was *hearing voices.*

From through the bricks, I could just make out the discussion the Good Neighbors were having in the crate room. And it sounded like a heated one. I pressed my ear closer and strained to hear.

". . . the most powerful wizard of this age." That sounded like Martes.

"Can we use him?" That might have been the tall elf. "Can we convince him to side with us?"

"I say kill him!" I didn't recognize that voice. "We can't risk everything on one roll of the bones."

There was a muddle of raised voices then, presumably arguing for or against my demise. The tall elf's voice rose above them, shouting for silence. He waited for the din to settle and then asked, "What say you, Martes?

"I cannot tell you to kill him, because of the terms of our

bargain," Martes said, his voice so low that I nearly pushed my ear through the wall trying to hear. "But he resurrected Aine. And he did it here in mortal lands, where magic works poorly, if at all. It was a monstrous casting, one that would have drained the best of us. And not five minutes later, he was carrying Aine back home on his shoulders." There was a murmur of amazement. Martes spoke over it. "I say again: if allowed to live, he may grow into the most powerful wizard of this age. Too powerful, in my humble opinion, if he is not firmly on our side."

"You haven't had a *humble* opinion in six centuries, Martes!" called a new voice, watery and warbling. There was a burst of laughter. My racing thoughts drowned out any response Martes might have made.

"Most powerful wizard of this age"? "Too powerful to let live"? That didn't sound like me. Aine had given me her name, given me the power to use it. Hadn't she?

I couldn't wrap my mind around it: me, a wizard. It made no sense. I had no special powers. I was a street musician with a heroin problem, nothing more. Anything that had happened in the last few weeks was easily attributable to Aine and her skills.

Then why would these creatures argue for my death? If all I had was Aine's name, then they wouldn't hesitate to use me. But if I were dangerous . . .

I liked the idea of being dangerous, a man of consequence, someone to be reckoned with . . . but a quick glance at my surroundings dowsed my enthusiasm. I might eventually be the greatest wizard of this age, but for now I was a prisoner.

Okay. I brought Aine back to life. But how does that make me a wizard? If she gave me her name . . .

I blinked and sat up as a realization came to me.

Aine hadn't given me her name; I had taken it.

I stood. I wanted to pace and think. But the troll stood as I did and growled his disapproval at me.

"Whoa, big fella." I spoke to him as if soothing an angry dog. "Calm down, there. I'm going to sit back down."

He watched me carefully with infantile eyes as I sat on the straw. When I was immobile again he turned away, staring longingly toward where the grown-ups were discussing politics.

If I took her name, perhaps I can take another.

"Hey, big guy," I called. "Look over here."

He ignored me, so I stood again. That got his attention.

"That's right. Look at me."

I looked him dead in the eye, trying to remember if I had done anything special in the Meadows to bring out Aine's song.

Nope. Just sat and stared. Hope this works.

It took a minute, but soon I believed I could hear it: a deep plodding bass line as the troll's big eyes got bigger, filling my vision.

I suddenly thought of the ancient bards, considered magicians in their time. Weren't they supposed to be able to come up with songs at a moment's notice? Sing for their supper, writing instant songs about their hosts, whether those hosts were petty landowners or the king himself?

I could see nothing but the troll now, and his song filled my head.

Christ, I thought. *It's the songs. Taliesin, Thomas the Rhymer . . .*

I began singing, but softly, so as not to attract the attention of the other Good Neighbors. If I could hear them, then they could hear me. If they ever shut up for a second, that is. But even singing quietly, the low notes of the troll's simple melody rumbled in my chest cavity. The big creature watched curiously as I sang, but made no move to stop me. I finished the tune, noted absently that the bulk of the lyrics seemed to be, "I'm a troll, fol de rol rol," and launched into it again.

But this time, as I sang, I slowed it down. The notes were all the same, but the tempo dragged.

The troll's eyelids drooped.

I slowed the song some more. *Throwing out the sea anchor,* I thought.

The muscles in his face slackened.

I slowed. It. Down.

And the troll slumped against the doorjamb, fast asleep.

The song came to an end and I stood there, panting lightly.

"Holy shit," I whispered to no one in particular.

Time to leave, Douglas.

The troll blocked the doorway. Even asleep he was a formidable barrier. But I had to move. The Good Neighbors could come to a decision about my fate at any moment, and then I'd be faced with more than a dozen angry monsters instead of just one sleeping troll.

I was going to have to climb over him.

I put a hand out and touched him lightly, praying he didn't wake up. His skin was cool, like a stone in the shade. He stayed as still as one, too.

He's either faking or he's not, I thought. *There's only one way to find out.*

And I placed my left foot on one of his big thighs.

As soon as I did, the troll growled at me. It was a lion's roar that rose from his mountainous chest and exploded out of his jaws into my face, a fetid wind that smelled of things not long dead, but rotting quickly. I leapt backward, ducking instinctively to avoid the blow I was sure would follow. I scrabbled to the rear of the cell, catching my spine a jarring shot when I reached the wall. It was the only blow I received. The troll hadn't moved.

The most powerful wizard of this age, I thought. *Yeah, right.*

A troll takes a catnap while I'm singing and I start thinking I'm the second coming of Merlin.

The troll didn't do anything further after his one roar; he sat slumped in the doorway, breathing slowly.

It's still time to leave, Douglas.

I sat rubbing my back, gathering my courage, before finally raising myself into a crouch and sneaking forward, eyeing the troll. He growled again, but I was ready this time, and instead of leaping away, I watched him intently. His eyes never opened, and his chest expanded and contracted in a long, easy rhythm.

He wasn't growling; he was snoring.

I put my foot back on his thigh, reached up for a shoulder, and before I could think about it too long, heaved myself up and over. He gave a quiet snort as my full weight went on him, but nothing more. Then I was off the other side and into the room with the one bare light bulb. I picked my way through a forest of support beams propping up the crumbling ceiling, and hoped I was heading for the way out.

I wasn't. I stepped out onto another street, this one smaller than the first Martes had led me to, and I'd taken only two steps when I realized I was right next to the crate room. From behind the door, I could hear angry voices—most of them calling for my head, it seemed.

"We mussssst desssstroy him," hissed one creature.

"Yes, grind his bones to powder, boil his blood for soup," said another.

A guttural voice chanted simply, "Kill, kill, kill."

I ran.

But not for long. Almost immediately it became too dark to see, and I had to slow to a crawl, feeling my way along the wall. It was lucky I did, because it kept me from making "breakneck speed" more than just an expression when I hit another staircase. As it was, I barely managed to catch myself from falling when my foot suddenly met air where it expected floor.

"Shit," I whispered.

The stairs led down. I didn't know exactly where I was in relation to the exit, but I knew I was already far below street level. I didn't want to go farther down. But I sure didn't want to go anywhere near the room full of Good Neighbors.

You don't want to stand in the dark talking to yourself, either.

I padded down the stone stairs, only three of them. I was momentarily cheered by the thought that I wasn't going too far down. But it turned out to be a landing, and I felt my way to the next set of stairs, going down them, as well. It was cold and damp, and my socks made wet flapping noises on the stones. The stairs ended and I found a door. Pushing it open, I went on, moving faster now and damn me if I fell, needing to get away from the Good Neighbors. One hand in front of me, the other trailing along the wall, scraping my fingernails against the stone of it, wishing I could spark a magic glowing golf ball into life like Martes.

Well, why can't I then? I'm a wizard, right?

"Friction," I said, and flung my hand forward like he had.

I almost fell over. And it was still pitch black.

Didn't think my magic worked that way. Can't blame a guy for trying, though.

The echoes of my footfalls changed timbre, and I figured I'd entered a larger chamber, so I was ready when I reached the end of it, not flinching when my forward hand hit a wall. Left turn, then right through a doorway, and I was standing sideways, the floor suddenly sloping sharply up to my left. I knelt and ran my hand along the floor.

Cobblestones.

With any luck, this was the street I'd seen when I'd come in with

Martes. Sensing more than seeing ghostly white shapes overhead, I decided that they were the laundry strung across the street to dry, and that this *was* the street I'd seen earlier, and furthermore, I was due for some fucking luck, anyway. I pointed my feet uphill and started marching.

I must have been passing by an open window, one that led to where the Good Neighbors were still deep in conversation, because I could hear their voices again, from off to my left and overhead, this time.

"If we let him live," a deep graveled voice said, "we'll need something to control him with."

"Yes." *Martes.* "Something. Or someone."

Then I was at the end of the street, and up the twisting stairs I'd hoped were there, through the gift shop, and back out into the chill Edinburgh night.

• • • Eleven • • •

The air was far cooler than when I'd entered Mary King's Close, and for a moment I feared I had come out years later, like in the tales of people who went "under the hill." But a quick glance at the dates on the Fringe brochures still littering the streets confirmed that I'd been underground for only a few hours, no more.

Two drunken youths in Celtic jerseys stumbled past, arms around each other, their breath clouding rhythmically into the air as they sang. A car zipped past, something vaguely avian drafting it to save itself the trouble of flapping.

Vaguely avian, but definitely fey.

I ducked back into the shadows of the City Chambers doorway before I was spotted. I needed to get off the street, find a place to hide, somewhere to spend the rest of the night. But I couldn't go back to Grandma McLaren's—it was the first place they'd look. They'd probably stake out the train station, too. The bus depot, the airport. And I'd have a tough time getting a cab at this time of night in the condition I was in. I could maybe walk out of town, but who knew what was waiting in the darkness at the edge of the city lights. I needed shelter, but the only other person I really knew in town was—

Oh shit, I thought. *Sandra. Our date.*

I had stood her up. I rubbed my stomach where she had punched me the last time I'd made her mad. I hoped she could find it in her heart to forgive me this time. Because I was about to show up on her doorstep. It was all I could think of.

But what if Aine knows where she lives?

I thought about that as I dug for my wallet with numb fingers, feeling lucky I had left it in my pants. It was far from Minnesota-chilly, but I still wasn't wearing shirt or shoes, and it seemed like summer was suddenly over and autumn was eager to end before dawn. I fumbled Sandra's address out and deciphered Catarina's chicken scratches under a dim streetlight. It was a bit of a haul, but I knew the area. It wasn't a good one.

It'd be ironic, I thought, *if I avoided the two massed armies of Faery, only to get rolled like a drunk in the street by some human ne'er-do-well.*

I was going to have to risk it. If Aine knew where Sandra lived, then I was in trouble. But I was in just as much danger if I stood out in the open.

At least I thought I was. I waffled for a moment before thinking, *Fuck it. I'd rather die someplace warm anyway.*

I made one try at flagging down a black city cab, examining its wake for fey drafters first, but the driver took one look at me and sped off. Feeling sorry for myself, I started shuffling toward Sandra's flat. I was cold, tired, and hungry. My feet hurt from walking, the bump on my head throbbed, my back ached, the scabs on my face itched. My attention wandered and I had to keep jerking myself back to the present before I stumbled into buildings or bus stops or oncoming traffic. If any of the Daoine Sidhe had spotted me, they could have snuck up behind me and stabbed me a dozen times before my weary nerves would have sent a single message to my brain. But the luck I felt I was due for must have held, because I was still alive when the first false dawn lightened the sky and found me leaning hard on the buzzer to Sandra's flat.

Considering the hour, it took less time for someone to answer through the tinny speaker than I thought it would.

"The fuck you want?" *A man speaking. Lovely.*

"Sandra there?"

"Douglas?" It was Sandra, her voice faint with distance from the microphone. And something else.

"Yeah, it's me, Sandra," I said. "Listen, sorry about tonight. Last night. Tonight. Whatever night. Can I—"

"Fuck off," said the man's voice and the speaker went dead.

I leaned on the buzzer again.

"Look, mate," said the man's voice. "Lay off before I come down there and kick yer cunt in."

I hit it again, this time just to be an asshole. Because it sure didn't look like I was getting in.

Time for Plan B, I decided. *Whatever that is.*

But the door suddenly let out an obnoxious buzz and unlocked. I leapt to it and pushed through before whoever had buzzed me in changed their mind. I tromped up three garbage-strewn flights of stairs and, after a short search of sagging or missing door numbers, found Sandra's flat. I made to knock but the door opened before I had a chance to, leaving me standing in the doorway, fist half-raised like an uncertain revolutionary.

"Douglas, isn't it?" It was the man from the intercom, but polite now for some reason. He was big, nearly as tall as me, but probably a hundred pounds heavier. I had more teeth than he did, though. A lot more. "C'mon in, then."

He stepped aside and waved me into a smoky room filled with hard-used furniture. Another man, this one with more tattoos than the first had teeth, lay with his boots up on a torn couch. He turned his head to examine me as I entered, but his eyes remained flat, lifeless.

"Douglas!" Sandra called sleepily from across the room. "You stood me up."

She was perched on a folding chair in the tiny kitchen, looking at me across a rickety card table covered with cans of Tennent's Lager, overflowing ashtrays, and the detritus of a night spent chasing the dragon: tin foil, cotton balls, a Zippo.

She was wasted.

"Sandra, look at me." I held my arms out, showing off my lack of key pieces of clothing. "It was a rough night. Let me tell you what happened."

"No!" she shouted, and a shower of ash blew up from an ashtray in front of her. "I've heard enough of your stories." She stood shakily and stumbled toward me, tripping over her own feet and almost falling. No one made a move to help her—the man who let me in still stood behind me; the zombie on the couch had yet to show any kind of human reaction. She leaned against the wall, waiting for equilibrium. "I quit for you, Douglas," she said quietly. "And you didn't even fucking notice."

She quit for me? What does she mean by that?

But then I knew: the sickness, the weight loss, the missed days at the market. She'd been trying to get clean. And I hadn't noticed.

"You didn't even notice!" she screamed.

I wanted to tell her that you couldn't quit for someone else, but I'd missed my chance by days. She was long past listening, now.

This is bad, I thought. *But I just have to stay a few hours. Wait till dawn. Till the faeries have gone home.*

"Sandra, let's sit down. Talk about this a little." For the second time that night I was using the dog voice, soothing, patronizing. It didn't work this time, either. The Sandra I knew had gone far away for the night and left this maniacal changeling in her place. "Sandra . . ."

She interrupted me with a string of profanities that almost made me blush. They even provoked a reaction from the dead-eyed man on the couch.

"Och," he said, his voice a hoarse, diseased whisper. "She disnae like you much, laddie."

"I can see that." I turned away from Sandra's slurred tirade. I couldn't stay here. The situation was only going to get worse, and someone was going to get hurt. Most likely, me. I viewed my escape options. I was on the third floor, and there was no fire escape. The windows were out, then. And the man who had let me in was leaning against the only door, massive arms crossed across his chest. *Going to have to talk my way out.* "Sandra?" I tried on a smile. "If you're so pissed off, why'd you let me up here?"

Sandra's graphic description of my mother's pornographic escapades came to an abrupt halt.

"'Cause we're broke, like," she said. "Skint, Douglas." I sensed more than saw the dead-eyed man on the couch unfold himself and stand. He was as tall as the man at the door, but lankier. "And now we've got the mores, Douglas. You remember them, don't you?"

I sure did. The mores. When you want more. Need more. When you'd do anything or anyone to g[illegible]ttle bit more. I remembered them. But I didn't answer her. The way she was acting, I didn't think I could talk my way out. I was going to have to use my new powers. I kept my eyes on the man on the door, staring hard into his eyes, waiting for them to fill my vision, for the room to fade.

"Aye, we've got the mores," Sandra went on. "And I watched people pour buckets of clink into your case every day of the Fringe." She had apparently gotten her balance back and was approaching me now, her voice getting louder. I kept staring at the man at the door, waiting to hear his song. I thought I could sense it teetering at the edge of my imagination.

These bastards do not know who they're fucking with.

"Clink, Douglas. Cash. Buckets of it." She was right behind me, now, breathing into my ear. "And where is it?"

I looked at the man at the door, stared hard. Concentrated with my eyes, my ears, my heart.

"The fuck are ye lookin' at me like that for?" he said.

Nothing happened.

"Have any on you?" Sandra asked, reaching around me and patting my pockets till she found my wallet. She flipped it over, exposing its pitiful contents: Minnesota driver's license, Zack's business card, scrap of paper with her address scrawled on it. "No? Where's the money, Douglas?"

I held the doorman's gaze, but felt nothing.

"Do you fancy me?" he said.

No song, no power, no magic.

"Do you fucking fancy me?"

Nothing.

I finally broke his gaze and looked down at my feet. "Excuse me?"

"I said, do you fancy me?"

What had happened? Where was my power?

"I don't know what you mean," I said slowly, trying to keep the choking panic out of my voice. Why didn't the magic work?

"Do you fancy me?" the man said again. "Do you want to fuck me, lookin' at me like that?" He shook his head, then glanced over my shoulder. "He's a fucking poof, Sandy. That's why he never went for ye."

"Poof," whispered the dead-eyed man from right beside me. When he said it, it wasn't an insult. It was merely the sound of things disappearing.

I turned to look at him and he rammed his forehead into the bridge of my nose. The crack of my nose breaking sounded thunderous in my head and the world went white. My vision cleared a split second later, but I was already on the ground. I saw a boot coming too late, and it caught me in the temple before I could raise my hands. When I tried to cover my head, a sharp toe to my midsection sent the breath out of me. I grabbed for a boot, attempted to stand, tried to strike back, but it was like they had six feet each. The kicks came too fast, too hard; I couldn't stop them. I went fetal, guarding my balls, my face, the back of my neck. Tried to wriggle my back against a wall.

They've done this before, I thought.

I tried not to shift my guard around, figuring I had the vital bits covered. But when the shots to the back of my legs or forehead got too painful, my hands would shift to the hot spots of their own accord and immediately one of my attackers would kick something important. Teeth loosened, ribs cracked, blood filled my mouth. I hoped they didn't break any fingers.

"Stop it!" Sandra screamed. "Leave him alone!"

And as suddenly as it had begun, the beating was over.

I peeked up and saw Sandra pulling the man from the door away. He was smiling. The dead-eyed man, eyes showing the tiniest spark of enjoyment now, feinted a kick at my face. I flinched, covering up again. The doorman cackled, then the couch creaked as Deadeye sat back down. When I looked up again, he already had a cigarette lit and dangling from his lips, his eyes lifeless once more.

Sandra knelt next to me and stroked my hair. It hurt.

"Douglas, darling," she said. "Where's the money?"

Fuck you. "At my house."

"Take us there, honey?"

Fuck you. "Listen, Sandra." I was whispering to her, talking fast.

I didn't want to take these psychopaths to Grandma McLaren's; I didn't want to get kicked again. "I know you got it bad, and you'd do anything to get back to right." My voice had developed a strange sibilance. *I think I lost a tooth.* "Just let me out of here. I'll go get you some money. Hell, I'll score for you. Just—"

She put her finger to my lips. "Shh."

"Sandra," I whispered around her finger. "You're going to hate yourself in the morning."

She pulled her finger away. Blinked at the blood on it. "It *is* the morning, Douglas."

She was right. What I had thought was the false dawn had turned real, and anemic light now crept in through the stained window shades.

Well, I made it through the night, just like I wanted to. Fat lot of good it's going to do me.

"Are you going to take us to the money?" Sandra asked. "Or do the Craic brothers give you another kicking?"

When I didn't speak for a second, the doorman gave a theatrical sigh, and Deadeye stood from the couch. I hated myself more for the fear that I knew showed in my eyes than for giving Sandra a panicky nod.

"I'll take you," I said.

"Good boy, Douglas."

The Craic brothers pulled me to my feet. I made a feeble effort to shake them off, but they ignored me and dragged me by my arms to the door. When we got to the top of the stairs, I tried to throw Deadeye down them, but he kept his balance easily and stared at me blankly as his bigger brother stopped any more efforts at escape with a sharp punch to my kidney. I threw up, spattering the wall and stairs. It didn't look like it was the first time someone had done that.

"Oh, Douglas," Sandra said, her voice dripping with false sympathy. "We won't make you suffer. When we score we'll give ye a taste." She stroked my hair again. "Won't that be nice?"

It did sound nice. I was in bad shape: missing tooth, broken nose, maybe some ribs, at least two concussions, assorted gashes, bruises, ragged tears in my skin. But a hit . . . that'd fix me right up. No more pain, no more fear. Pure bliss.

A wave of gratitude washed over me. It made me sicker than the shot to my kidney.

You going to thank the strung-out bitch? Give the Craic brothers each a big kiss? Wake up, Douglas!

I leaned against the wall, tasting the bile in my mouth, feeling each and every cut and contusion. I spit on the floor. Silently called myself worse things than Sandra had minutes before. But I didn't stay mad at myself long. There were far better targets standing right next to me.

I'm going to kill the whole lot of t[illegible] resolved.

When we got to Grandma McLar[illegible]s, I would kill them all. I'd lead them to my room. To where the big black knife lay unsheathed on my bed.

Fuck magic. I'll do this the old-fashioned way.

They wouldn't see the knife when they came in. I'd shield it with my body.

"Douglas?" Sandra said. "Won't a taste be nice?"

I'd pretend to fall. They'd make to pick me up again. And I'd bury that knife to the hilt in Deadeye's chest.

The big fella goes next. Gut him like a pike. Then . . .

I suddenly had a vision of Sandra traipsing up the Playfair Steps, peasant skirts swirling. Turning at the top. Flashing me a flirtatious smile.

"Yeah," I croaked. "A taste would be nice."

Then Sandra gets hers.

I collapsed against the wall, and the Craic brothers had to carry me downstairs. I was hurt, sure, but even more I was playing possum, conserving my strength. When it came time to move, I was going to need every bit of it.

THE RIDE TO Grandma McLaren's was almost as painful as the beating had been. The Craic brothers' car was an unidentifiable piece of crap that must have worn away whatever shock absorbers it had come off the lot with years ago. I sat in the back, sandwiched between Tweedledum and Tweedle-Deadeye, while Sandra drove, swerving frequently to ensure that she didn't miss any potholes between her flat and Grandma McLaren's. When she asked for the address, I thought for a moment about leading them on a wild goose chase, waste some time, maybe let Sandra sober up, give me a chance to recover some. But I wasn't recovering; I was stiffening up. I feared that if it took too long to reach Grandma McLaren's, I wouldn't be able to move by the time we arrived. I was going to need to move. So I gave Sandra clear instructions on how to get there and then searched in vain for a comfortable position to sit in.

As we went along, I tried to watch out the window for faeries, but the buildings flashing by made my head swim and put me in danger of puking again. Much as I would have liked to throw up all over the Craic brothers, I didn't want to weaken myself with the effort. They also might have taken offense and spent the rest of the ride using my head as a speed bag. I kept my eyes on my own feet, only looking up to get my bearings when Sandra called for further directions from the front.

"Left here," I told her. "Now right. Third driveway in. The one with the flowers."

The sun was up, but just barely clear of the hills, and by my best guess it was still brutally early. Grandma McLaren's neighborhood was fast asleep. I hoped she was, too.

"This the spot, Douglas?" Sandra asked, her voice quavering. She was in bad shape now, shaking and sweating. Probably regretting what she'd done, too. But it was too late; the die was already out of the shooter's hand and tumbling down the felt, most likely to come up craps again. And no matter what Sandra was feeling, the Craic brothers didn't look like they were going to change their minds and walk away from free money any time soon.

We marched up the drive like Napoleon's army returning from Russia. I should have been screaming my head off. The cops would probably have shown up quickly for a disturbance in Grandma McLaren's sleepy little 'burb. But no one in our addled crew was thinking straight, least of all me. I had my mind set on a course of action, and I was going to follow it through. These people had beaten me, battered me, taken my dignity.

I was going to kill the whole fucking lot of them.

No one harms me with impunity.

But first I had to get inside. I suddenly realized that I had no keys on me. They were still sitting on a shelf in my room.

"Sandra, I—"

"Shut it," said Deadeye.

"Got no keys," I said.

"Disnae matter."

"Why's that?"

Deadeye pointed at the door. " 'Cause it's open."

He was right. As we approached the front door, I could see that it was slightly ajar. This was so unlike Grandma McLaren that I stopped dead in the driveway.

Had Aine's bodyguards stuck around? Waiting for whoever came back? Martes had said that they wouldn't . . .

Martes. Hardly a reliable source of information.

The last words I'd heard in the underground came back to me.

"*We'll need something to control him with.*"

"Yes. Something. Or someone."

Deadeye's brother slapped me hard on the back of the head, and I stumbled forward like a drunkard.

No, I thought.

I began running toward the front door.

"Wait, you fuck!"

The Craic brothers should have caught me easily, but fear gave me wings. Not of them, but of what I would find in the house.

I led the faeries here, both sides. And left Grandma McLaren alone to deal with them. Oh God, please let her be OK.

My only hope was that they had taken her and would keep her alive to control me. If they had, I would do whatever they said. I'd join whichever side they wanted, kill untold thousands if they wished. Just so long as they didn't hurt my grandma.

I burst through the door, banging already tortured limbs painfully on the frame. I lost my footing immediately, skidding in something slick, and sat down hard. The Craic brothers followed close behind but stopped in the doorway.

"Jesus," Deadeye breathed.

Sandra squeezed her way between the two big men. "What the fuck is—" Then she stopped talking to vomit onto their shoes.

Martes had talked about "elf-shot," tiny magical darts used by his kind to kill unnoticed. Whoever had been here had elected to use a very different method. Blood, like giant Rorschach blots, marked the walls, the stairway, the TV screen. Puddles of it—more than I thought one body could contain—congealed on the floor. Unidentifiable pieces of flesh and bone, which had once added up to something living, were strewn about like party favors.

And on the stairs, eyes unblinking, mouth open as if to utter a greeting to her early morning visitors, was Grandma McLaren's head.

• • • Twelve • • •

Sandra and the Craic brothers might have spoken. They might have touched me, hit me, kicked me. I had no way of knowing. My mind had shut off. I sat for a minute or a second or an hour. I might have cried. Might have screamed. Might have torn the last few patches of my own undamaged skin with my fingernails.

Eventually, I stood up. Saw that I was alone. My fellow junkies must have left. I wouldn't have wanted to stick around if I were them, either.

Gently, I picked up Grandma McLaren's head and placed it on the old comfortable couch. I gathered up whatever parts I could recognize and put them with her head. I tried to fashion them into some semblance of a human form, something I could recognize and point to and say, "That was once a human being. That was once my grandmother." But she was an old jigsaw puzzle now, with too many pieces missing. When I had her mostly together, I went upstairs and got my guitar. I pulled the coffee table next to the couch and sat down on it. Tuned my guitar. Stared hard at what was once my grandmother. I fiddled with different melodies, keys, time signatures, doodling idly as I looked into her opaque eyes. When nothing happened, I retuned my guitar to open G and tried again.

Nothing.

I tried every alternate tuning I could think of before muting my strings and starting to sing. Random descants, jazzy scats, gospel melodies, operatic arias.

Nothing.

I sat perfectly still. Stared at her. For a long time.

For as long as it fucking takes.

I stopped staring when I could no longer see her corpse through the stinging tears flooding my eyes. I wept like a child, rocking back and forth, hugging my guitar to my knees. My cracked ribs screamed in protest as I shook with huge wracking sobs. Fat tears joined with the blood and mucus that ran freely from my broken nose, waterfalling off my face to join the blood that coated me and my guitar. Grandma McLaren's blood. My blood.

When I gained control again, I dried my eyes. Carefully wiped my nose on the back of my arm. Tuned my guitar. And tried again.

I played with my eyes closed, remembering everything I could about Grandma McLaren, searching for a defining theme, a melody that spoke of her, a harmony that echoed the lives she touched, a chordal structure that was the world she moved through.

It was hopeless. Apparently, my magic was only good on faeries.

Which makes it no good at all. I stopped playing and stood. *Unless I can find some faeries to use it on.*

I placed my guitar on the coffee table in mute parallel to what was left of Grandma McLaren. Shuffled upstairs. I stripped off the few clothes I was wearing and got in the shower. The water was torture, like getting kicked again wherever it hit gash, bruise, or broken bone. I dried off painfully. Bandaged whatever bled, wrapped whatever ached, limped into my bedroom.

The knife still lay on the bed where I'd tossed it. I left it there for the moment and went to the closet. I dug until I found my old black jeans, my bloodstained boots. Struggled into them. I grabbed the knife and used it to saw the sleeves off of one of my nice black shirts. I put that on, too. I went to my guitar case to fetch the Celtic cross Martes had cut off of me. Retied the leather cord. Hung it around my neck. Bent painfully to retrieve the clasp knife and the *sgian dubh.* Tucked them into a pocket and a sock, respectively. I put on my old leather jacket, settling the now unfamiliar weight of it onto my bruised shoulders. And lastly, I slipped my grandfather's regimental ring onto my index finger.

No one harms me with impunity.

The black knife I kept in hand.

I carried my guitar case downstairs, wiped the blood off my guitar, and tucked it into the case. I ignored the corpse, telling myself that Grandma McLaren was gone and the mess on the couch had as much to do with her now as fingernail clippings or shorn hair. The spare Peugeot keys hung in the kitchen. I flipped them in my knife hand as I walked to the car. There was no one on the street.

The car started and I sat waiting for the world to get a little less blurry. The hum and vibration put me to sleep in seconds. When I started awake, the sun was a foot and a half higher in the sky. I dropped the car into gear and stomped on the gas before I drifted off again.

I rolled down the window and hung my head out like a dog, letting the chill rouse me. The wind hurt my nose. That gave me an idea, and when my eyes started to droop again, I took my fingertip and flicked myself right on the tip of my broken nose. I screamed and my eyes teared up so bad that I had to pull over. But I was wide awake.

I drove to the market. It was a mundane pedestrian thruway now, the booths and tables that had lined both sides for weeks replaced in one night by empty pavement. I saw no faeries. Not many humans to speak of, either: a lone piper setting up, a few men in suits scampering off to early meetings, an old man in a wrinkled overcoat shuffling toward the gardens. The city seemed hung over from the Fringe, and I suspected it would take quite some time today before it got up to speed.

I took the car to the City Chambers. Parked it and got out, tucking the big knife up my wide jacket sleeve. Needn't have bothered. The only person I saw—a businessman with a crooked tie and an overflowing briefcase—never looked in my direction. I ducked down the close and looked through the iron gate at the doors beyond. I couldn't climb the fence with these ribs, and even if I could, I'd never get through the locked doors. I stalked around the outside, looking for another way in, listening for voices, watching for faeries.

I found none, heard nothing, saw no one.

Back to the car, then, and down to the Meadows. I stopped by Father Croser's on the way, thinking he might have other faeries chained in his basement. Maybe I could pump them for information. But as I lurched up the walk, I realized it had only been last night that I had been down there, and it was unlikely that he had grabbed any others since then. Or if he had, he'd probably be down there with them right now. I thought of Father Croser in his basement, cutting the nipples off of a sprite or pixie.

Could Father Croser have killed Grandma McLaren? Had he driven up to her house to find me and, failing that, killed her instead?

He was certainly crazy enough. But I was sure he hadn't recognized me in my straight clothes. And if he didn't know who I was, he'd have no reason to chase me down. No reason to show up at my house.

It was all moot, anyway, as I couldn't get in the window without Martes's help.

I went back to the car. Swerved around mail trucks and buses and taxicabs like black boxes on wheels on my way to the Meadows. The park was wide and clean and I thought I could collapse in the grass, forget about Aine, Martes, Father Croser, Grandma McLaren . . .

The thought of my dead grandmother snapped me back to myself, and I stalked the field, examining every rock, every tree, every drunk sleeping off the last night of the Fringe, for signs of being fey. They were all animal, vegetable, or mineral, as far as I could tell. I limped back to the car.

They've gone, I thought. *The goddamned faeries are gone and they won't be back till next year. And I'll either be on the run or in jail by then.*

I didn't see how an old woman's junkie grandson, living in the country illegally, *couldn't* be blamed for her murder. And I certainly didn't have an alibi I could use.

Getting into the car, I slammed the door and pounded on the steering wheel till my hand ached. I had nowhere else to look. It was time to start thinking about escape.

"Grandma," I said. "I'm sorry." My eyes stung. "But I have to run now."

I engaged in a brief fantasy: me, lying shirtless on a beach somewhere in the Caribbean, a drink in my hand, tattoos fading in the sun.

I shook my head, ignoring the sharp pain of my nose, the nausea from my concussions.

Screw that. I'm not going to run. I'm going to find who's responsible. And I'm going to make them pay.

Nemo me impune lacessit.

But first I had to find someone. Anyone. As long as they were fey.

The Market, the Meadows, the Underground. Where else would they be?

Then I remembered Aine telling me to bring her to Calton Hill.

One last place to check in the city. Then I'll have to start haunting remote lochs looking for the few faeries Martes said didn't return to Faeryland for the rest of the year. If I don't find any of them, I'll have to stay hidden, come back next year . . .

But first, Calton Hill. The one with the half-finished Acropolis on it.

My right leg had stiffened up while I'd been thinking. I managed to get my numb foot on the gas by the simple expedient of lifting my thigh with my hands. Then I stomped down on the pedal, and the Peugeot jumped east. It, at least, was in fine condition.

A traffic light on Princes Street stopped me adjacent to the market. I stared hard across the now-open space.

Nothing.

A cab behind me tapped their horn, a reminder that a flashing yellow meant I could go. I hung one finger out the window and took another look at the market.

Nothing.

The light turned full green and I drove on. Past the looming Balmoral Hotel, and Princes Street became Waterloo Place and then Regent Road. I turned into a gap in a tall iron fence that must have once held a gate. Broken steel barriers were piled to one side, and a sleepy guard in reflective clothing gave me a half wave. I slowed and rolled down my window, but he told me, "I'm just here for the buses, mate," and motioned me through.

Steering the car between a gorse-covered hillside and the long iron fence, I followed the road up and around. As I rounded the final bend, bizarre monuments began springing into view. First, the abortive Acropolis, large and stark, a dozen pillars stuck into a thick stone foundation. Next, the Nelson monument, like the Leaning Tower of Pisa straightened and stuck on top of a birthday cake. Then a collection of smaller buildings as I pulled into the car park: squat domes and tall urns, crenelated towers and old stone walls, and everywhere pillars, pillars, pillars.

Long shadows from the Acropolis's columns formed bars on the ground that seemed to jail me as I stepped out of the car. I could see Edinburgh Castle at eye level across town, and the volcanic crags of Arthur's Seat seemed a mere step away, though they were still miles distant. The monument park was abandoned: no faeries, and no humans, either, at this time of day.

But I could feel something. I couldn't put my finger on it, wouldn't have been able to name it if someone had asked, but I definitely felt *something*. Though this spot appeared as empty as the others I had searched, there was something here.

Something fey.

I scanned the buildings, the grass. There wasn't much else to see. I followed the path around the back of the Acropolis, pain forgotten for the moment, trying to open my eyes, my heart, my mind. Trying to concentrate as I had when I'd learned Aine's true name, or when I'd put the troll to sleep, I stared at each structure in turn.

No, I thought. *It's not them. It's something different. Somewhere different. It's . . .*

There was a shimmer in the air near the Acropolis, probably right where the middle of the structure would have been if it had ever been finished.

There!

The shimmer only lasted an instant, less than a split second, and at any other time my mind would have explained it away. I would have thought it a heat signature despite the morning chill, a dust mote reflecting oddly in the slanting sunlight, a hallucination brought on by too little sleep and too much pain.

But I'd seen too much in the last few weeks to believe my mind's rationalizations. I kept my eyes on the spot where the shimmer had been, and moved toward it to investigate.

As I got closer, I felt a tingle in my inner ear. Not a note or a pitch—not even quite a sound yet—just something that tickled my mind, hinting at the beginning of an idea of a melody. I reached for it with a thought, trying to coax it into life, fan it into flame. But every time I got close, got so I could almost hear it, almost hum it, the notes would scatter, fleeing my inner ear and seeking shelter in the recesses of my brain—or, worse, on the tip of my tongue. It could take days for a thought to come back from there.

I tried a different tack, forcing myself to think about other things, idle things—the view, the weather, the sounds of the waking city drifting up the hillside. This old trick, that had ensnared hundreds of half-remembered names and song titles, failed entirely. The mysterious melody refused to jump into my head unbidden.

I tried singing a few random notes, to see if I could trigger something through actual audible sound. Some pitches seemed to strengthen the thought, some to make it disappear altogether, but I was not able to sense a pattern.

Of course, I thought. *I'm a better guitar player than I am a singer.*

I limped back to the car as quickly as I could and pulled out my guitar. Strapped it on. Checked the tuning quickly, then marched back to the Acropolis. I decided to use a scientific method to figure out the first note of the sound I was almost hearing. From the open low E string, I began a chromatic scale, following it up the neck and across the strings, hitting every possible note along the way, eventually sticking on the high E and running my fingers all the way up until I ran out of frets.

Nothing.

Apparently, scientific was not the way to go. I thought of Aine's song and let loose a flurry of notes in E Dorian. It didn't trip the melody off the tip of my tongue, but I felt something.

Just play, I told myself.

I stared off into the space where the mysterious light had flickered and let myself improvise. I started in E Dorian but soon drifted into B natural minor, fingerpicking a melody over a meandering bass line. Then E again, but Phrygian mode this time, raising the third after a few bars for a flamenco feel. Softening the sound by sticking on an F, I shifted to Lydian mode, which led me into the simple key of C major.

It was in C that something finally happened.

I was in seventh position. I picked the first three notes of a C major seven arpeggio, accent on the downbeat, and a light flashed in the air where the first shimmer had been, like a tiny star flaring to life then burning out a second later. Something clicked in my mind, like a combination lock's tumbler falling into place, and the notes merged with the melody hidden on the tip of my tongue and burned in my mind.

Yes!

I played it again. Same result. Bright light, burning notes in my mind.

Eighth fret E string, seventh fret same, eighth fret on the B.

I played the phrase over and over, keeping the light burning for as long as possible. But nothing else happened. Just a tiny light, burning in the air at eye level, smack-dab in the middle of an unfinished building.

That's it? All that work for the world's lamest light show?

There had to be more.

I stopped playing, letting the light fade. Examined the three notes burning in my mind. Compared them with the ghost melody sitting on the tip of my tongue.

There is more, I realized.

The three notes were just the beginning of a sequence, a jumping-off point. I began playing again, starting with the three notes. I completed the arpeggio, but the rest of the notes did nothing. Turned the arpeggio into a descending scale in C. Still nothing. Alternated notes in seconds, thirds, fourths.

Nothing.

Those are exercises, stupid. Not music. I shrugged my bruised shoulders, trying to release a little tension. *Just play.*

I cleared my mind as best I could.

And played.

I started out hitting the three burning notes as often as possible, but quickly decided that I wouldn't find the next notes in the sequence unless they came naturally, organically, not following the normal rules of composition and theory. And when I gave myself over to the music, losing myself completely in it, thinking about nothing, not melody or harmony, not tempo or pitch—not thinking at all, just playing—then the next step in the sequence came to me. I slid down to fifth position, trilling from the E to the F sharp—*F sharp? In the key of C?*—and then slid back up to the G.

Another light sparked into existence, six feet to the right of the first.

Magic, I thought. But hard work, too. I was sweating, even though a chill wind was blowing across the hill, and the salt water of my own perspiration stung my wounds. *Who knew magic would be manual labor? You'd think it would be all, "Up horse and hattock!"*

I was improvising madly now, incorporating the new notes into my theme and moving on. I discovered the next step moments later: a half-diminished chord that jarred a third light into existence. With this success something clicked, and I tumbled into an extended run that ascended and descended in equal measure, changing pitches and meter with no regard for the not-so-rigid-anyway laws of music. New lights flashed into existence. They were lining up in an oval shape roughly twice my height, but with its bottom quarter hidden underground.

A giant egg? I'd seen stranger things this month.

I thought I was maybe one or two notes away now, but from what I didn't know. I tried to think of what key I might possibly be in, but the notes seemed to have no logical order except their effect on the lights and the burning in my mind.

Then it hit me: These notes weren't *in* a key—they *were* a key.

I found the last phrase, a seemingly random collection of strings and fingers that produced a dissonant sound, at once pleasing and disturbing, that somehow managed to pull all the discordant notes of the long sequence together into one triumphant, defining chord.

The lights all flared as one, then faded quickly, leaving in their place a set of weathered double doors rounded into a half oval and roughly twice my height, black knotholes standing out against ancient gray wood, giant stag's horns forming handles at the center. No, not one set of doors, but a multitude of them. Smaller portals were cut into the wood in a variety of shapes and sizes: a man-sized rectangle with a plain wooden knob; a broad circle at eye height with thornbush hinges; a three-foot square, low to the ground with no visible means of opening. And more. There was even a tiny door carved into the bottom edge, no bigger than my palm, with what looked like mouse bones for hinges and handle. I could feel invisible energy leaking around the edges and through the keyholes, filling my mind with visions, my ear with melodies. Exotic, savory scents teased my nostrils, and my mouth watered as I imagined the foods that would create such aromas.

It's no wonder the buildings up here are so bizarre.

I couldn't imagine an architect working so close to this place and not coming up with the strangest of ideas, grand sweeping visions, Escher-esque fantasies of illogical structures that were doomed to fail, falter, fall. And the doors were right in the middle of the unfinished Acropolis.

I suppose Aine wouldn't have let this monument in particular be finished. It would have covered up the door.

"Well, you've done it now."

Martes!

I turned and saw him just yards away, sitting on one of the Acropolis's short walls, leaning insolently against a pillar.

"Even a back door to Faery has wards on it, Douglas," Martes said, picking at a nail with his little knife. "Alarms, safeguards, systems of warning. You've practically sent an engraved invitation for Aine and the People of Peace to come slaughter you."

"Martes." I could barely speak. Finally, a target for my rage. "My grandmother is dead."

"Sorry to hear it. Tragic, I'm sure." He hopped down off the monument and made his knife disappear.

"You broke your pledge, Martes." My voice shook with anger.

"I did no such thing!" He managed to look down his twitching nose at me—quite a feat for someone so short. "How dare you accuse me of breaking my word!"

"Me and mine, Martes. You promised to watch over me and mine."

He squinted at me. "You're saying her death was faery-related?" He didn't wait for me to answer, but waved his hand in the air as if shooing a fly. "No matter. I can't protect what I'm not near, and I've spent the entire night chasing after you."

My hand edged toward the big black knife at the small of my back.

No. I have a better idea.

"But I'm more concerned about your safety," Martes continued. "The Council has decided they want you alive."

"I'm sure you argued vehemently on my behalf."

Martes grinned. "Sure." He twitched his nose toward the big doors. "Now, we have to get you out of here. It's not just the People of Peace I came to warn you about."

I stood my ground, staring at Martes. With the power leaking into me from the doors, it only took a second. I *knew* him. And knowing him, I knew exactly what he would do next.

"C'mon, Douglas, don't make me hurt you."

"You can't hurt me, Martes," I said.

"Oh yeah. My pledge." He sighed and pulled out his hollow reed. "I hate to carry a big oaf like you, but . . ."

He put the reed to his lips, pointing the end at me. But I already knew what he was going to do. Knew it before he did, even. He puffed his cheeks briefly and blew a tiny dart out of the reed—not a killing dart, just one to make me slumber—but I was already two feet away and the dart flew harmlessly past.

"It's not the pledge, Martes," I stated. "You just can't hurt me. Not anymore."

For the first time since I'd met him, I saw a spark of uncertainty in his beady eyes. It didn't slow him, however, and he went to fire another dart, thinking to lead me a little more this time. But before he could exhale and send the projectile my way, I sang the first note of his song, backing it on the guitar with a chord of my own devising. He froze. His grip on the reed slackened and it slipped to the grass.

"But *I* can hurt *you*," I said through clenched teeth. "And I'm going to, Martes. Do you understand? I'm going to hurt you now."

It must have taken a Herculean act of will, but he managed to speak.

"Don't. Do. This. The priest . . ."

But I wasn't interested in anything he had to say. I just wanted him to hurt. Strumming another chord, I began to sing. I twisted Martes as I sang, putting dissonance into his harmonic structure. I gave him a hunched back, a cleft palate, a clubfoot. I blinded one eye, made the other laze around in the socket, grew his tiny rat nose to obscene proportions. I gave him nagging aches, constant itching, seeping stigmatas. When I grew tired of physical changes, I went deeper, giving him a conscience where there'd been none, causing him to feel the guilt of a thousand children stolen, the pain of a thousand families ruined. I gave him feelings he hadn't ever known before: remorse, sadness, regret.

I found where he kept his word. It was a tricky little piece, allowing him to sell me out to the Good Neighbors but still making him track me up this hilltop to try to save my life. I blew it out of proportion—no more white lies, no more friendly exaggerations, no more wriggling around the facts. He would now tell the truth at all times, regardless of the consequences. And act accordingly.

From far behind me, a car approached. I could hear the stutter of its engine, the mechanical whine of the power steering as the driver turned the wheel too far. Calton Hill was a tourist spot, I remembered. More and more people would be showing up as the day went on. I didn't have much more time.

I let the song wind down.

"Martes?"

He nodded mutely, his one good eye looking first at me, then drifting off over my shoulder. The car's engine sputtered to a stop and I heard its door open and close. Then footsteps.

"I'm going to ask you some questions now."

I had only moments, but it was all I would need. He couldn't lie to me anymore. If he knew who had killed Grandma McLaren, then I would know within seconds.

And once I knew, I would make whoever it was pay.

But I never got to ask Martes anything. There was suddenly a sharp pain in my lower back and my legs buckled. Martes squawked in fear and scuttled away, moving quickly despite his newly crippled legs. Suddenly weak as a newborn, I crumpled to the ground, sliding forward off the long knife in my liver. I landed on my guitar, hearing its jangling scream as it shattered and died. I tried to roll over, to crawl away, to put up some sort of defense. But I had almost nothing left; this last grievous injury was a hammer blow to an already overloaded camel's back. Grinding my teeth together, I gave one last massive effort, managing to lift my face out of the dewy grass and raise my torso an entire inch off the ground.

Then Father Croser sawed through the tendons at the backs of my knees, and I collapsed back on top of my ruined guitar, my legs flopping uselessly behind me on just cartilage and skin.

Thirteen

"Dinnae die on me yet, my son."

I must have passed out for a minute, because I came to with Father Croser crouched over me, slapping me hard in the face. It should have been painful, what with my broken nose and all, but I didn't feel anything anymore. I had moved beyond agony, beyond fear, my body's own endorphins giving me a heroinlike rush I hadn't experienced in far too long. I imagined when I died—which would be shortly, I was sure—I would go happy.

"Have ye opened yer own portal to Hell then, laddie?"

Father Croser must have searched me when I was unconscious; I could see my clasp knife and *sgian dubh* lying on the grass a short distance away. My cross was there, too.

I guess he didn't like me wearing a symbol of his God.

"Are ye going hame?" He slapped me again. I smiled. "How did ye escape me? How did ye enter my church?" He was slapping me in rhythm with his questions. "What kind of creature are ye, that I can see ye through both eyes?"

Lights flashed when he struck me, white lights, colored lights, dancing, flashing. I thought I could hear music.

"Ye think I can't hurt ye more? Ye think yer kind is immune to pain?" He stopped slapping me and drew two black knives from the folds of his cassock. One still dripped with my blood, the other I recognized. It had been tucked into my waistband just minutes before. "I've learned a few things over the years, laddie. The most important is this: everybody hurts. Ye just have to figure out where."

I had a feeling I knew where this was going, but I was outside myself, watching from a great height, thinking, *Look at that poor bastard*. I watched as Father Croser stuck the knives into the dirt on opposite sides of where my left hand lay outstretched, blades pointed in. Watched him flip the hand over and stretch the pinky out. Watched when, with a quick scissoring motion, he snipped the pinky clean off.

That brought me back. I snapped into my body with a tortured scream. I tried to grab one of the knives out of the dirt with my mangled hand. Tried to grab it and stab the priest through the heart, the eyes, the stomach. But the only finger I laid on the knife was the one he'd snipped off. Quick as a six-foot-eight jungle cat he snatched the two knives out of the ground and swung a big thigh over me.

"That's it, boy. That's it." His weight made my cracked ribs scream. I aimed blows at him, blood spraying from my left hand as I flailed it at him, but they had no power and he shrugged them off his tree-trunk torso. Then he tucked the knives away once more and grabbed my hands. Leaning forward, until his face was next to mine and my hands were pinned above my head, he whispered, "Don't think it's over, laddie. I've learned things. I am learned. I can keep you alive for days, weeks. Months if need be. The pain will never stop."

He's bluffing, I thought as my head lolled to the side. I could see my pathetic pile of weaponry and, a few feet beyond them, the door to Faerie. *I'll be dead within the hour.*

The thought was hardly comforting.

"But it doesn't have to be that way, my son." Father Croser crossed my wrists together so he could hold them in one hand. He patted me gently on the cheek with the other.

The endorphins were starting up again, and I welcomed the buzz, the relief from the pain, welcomed the lights that started dancing again. Welcomed the darkness they promised when the time came for them to fade.

"Just tell me," the priest continued. "What are you?"

From far away, I answered, "A musician."

The lights were changing, forming into a pattern, an oval roughly twice my height.

"A musician?"

They weren't a hallucination; it was some strange illumination seeping onto the hilltop from around the edges of the door. The light grew brighter, like it was getting closer. Then a sound accompanied it. Rhythmic but not musical, soft now, but growing steadily louder.

Thunder from an incoming storm?

"A musician?" Father Croser repeated. He sounded unamused by my response.

Then I had it. Hoofbeats. There were riders approaching. Lots of them.

The hoofbeats became thunderous, rumbling toward us like an incoming train. Father Croser finally heard them and dragged his attention away from me to look for the source of the noise. With a crash barely heard over the thunder of hooves, the double doors flew open. Bright rays of light, like those bursting from storm clouds in a Christian postcard, erupted from the open doorway.

Riders, bathed in heavenly light and clad in shining silver chain mail and green surcoats bearing a white hind rampant, streamed onto the hilltop on flawless ivory horses. They parted around Father Croser and me as if we were boulders in a swift running stream. I recognized the rider at their head, long black hair streaming out from under a high helmet in the shape of a hawk, her bearing regal even when sitting a horse at full gallop.

Aine.

Father Croser didn't wait to see what the elves had planned, but sprang into action at once.

" 'The Lord is my light and my salvation!' " he shouted, and in a swirl of black robes, leapt far off the ground, hooked a rider around the throat in midair, and dragged him from his mount. A black knife went between the seam of helmet and chain, and the elf was dead before the two of them tumbled to the ground.

" 'Whom shall I fear?' " cried Father Croser as he rose up immediately. The riders were forming a ragged semicircle, with Father Croser and me at the open end, our backs to the double doors. " 'Though a host should encamp against me, my heart shall not fear.' " He straddled me like a lion protecting its kill, holding the bloody knife at guard in one hand, and thrusting his big iron cross out in front of him with the other. " 'Though war should rise against me, of this will I be confident.' "

Aine reined in her horse and the entire troop came to a stop. They turned inward as one, horses taking slow measured steps until row upon row of elaborate helmets and faceplates pointed straight at us. A solitary car horn drifted up the hill; one of the horses snorted in reply.

"What're ye waiting for?" Father Croser said. " 'When the wicked, even mine enemies and my foes, came upon me to eat up my flesh . . .' " He pointed his knife at the elf he had just killed. " 'They stumbled and fell.' "

Aine's horse took a prancing step forward, separating her slightly from the rest of the elves. She pulled her helmet off and shook out her long black hair. I remembered that hair fanned out on my pillow, those eyes closed tight, fists clenched, back arched . . .

Then I remembered Grandma McLaren's head on the staircase.

"Look upon me, Priest of the Dead God," Aine called out. "I am your fate. I am your death."

Father Croser peered at her, then shrugged. "As I was yours." He beckoned her with the knife. "Come. Come upon me. I'll kill ye again."

Aine smiled. Pure scorn. "I think not."

She raised her right hand and the other riders whipped long wooden bows from their backs. Father Croser's eyes widened. Perhaps he'd been expecting her to offer him single combat. Whatever he'd been expecting, he didn't hesitate when things looked to be going differently, and he made to throw his knife at Aine. After tossing it, maybe he would leap for the double doors, escape through them. Or maybe mount the riderless horse of the elf he'd killed, hang off one side as he rode down the gorse-covered hillside, using the animal's body to protect him.

He never had a chance. Aine's hand plunged down, and the elves notched arrows and let fly all in an instant, causing a swarm of shafts to suddenly sprout in the middle of his chest. He looked down at them. Then farther down at me, his eyes unblinking.

"I was . . . ," he managed, before stumbling backward a half step and falling to his knees. The knife dropped from his hand, forgotten. He let go of the cross, too, its chain tangling in the flights of the arrows. It looked as if he would pitch forward and die then, but even with two dozen arrows in him, Father Croser struggled to stand. He didn't struggle long. Aine shouted a single syllable, and bolts of energy arced from her outstretched hands.

His head exploded like a watermelon hit with a bat, and I was showered with skull fragments and gore.

Aine turned to me. "And you, Singer," she said. "What brings you to the gates of Faerie?"

I watched as Father Croser's headless body toppled over backward.

Do something, Douglas! I screamed silently. But all I could think to do was squeeze the base of my missing finger. Try to stanch the flow of blood.

She's the one who killed Grandma McLaren.

I tried to *know* her, tried to get her under my control, but I couldn't concentrate. I was in too much pain, my mind wandering away from Aine and back to my pierced liver, my useless legs, my missing finger.

The elves reached over their shoulders to their quivers, put hands to arrow shafts. Aine made no move to stop them.

I tried again to *know* her. The effort left me gasping. The power that I had wielded so easily on Martes seemed to be leaking out the wound in my back and grounding out in the bloodstained grass.

"Aine," I croaked.

She arched an eyebrow. "Yes, Singer?"

I found I had nothing else to say. I'd thought to buy some time, keep the elves from turning me into a pincushion like Father Croser. But it didn't matter: they could shoot me now or just wait ten minutes—I'd be dead either way.

I wish I hadn't broken the Gibson. I've been real tough on my instruments lately.

The endorphins were kicking in again, relaxing me, sending me floating out of my body once more. But before I detached, before I moved on, a little tune tickled the back of my head.

Aine's song.

Of course, it does me no good, I thought. *That's the Aine of days ago.*

"Singer?" Aine called, singsong. "Are you dead?"

Not yet. I ran the song through my head, enjoying the dark beauty of it. *Well, it can't hurt to try.*

And I sang the opening run.

It was a ragged performance, my voice rough with pain. But it certainly got everyone's attention. The elves stood with their arrows notched and turned to Aine. Her expression looked frozen, like it was painted onto a block of ice.

"If I go," I bluffed, "you go, too."

She didn't answer, but tilted her head back a little, like an antelope sniffing the air for predators.

"Aine." *God, it hurt to talk.* "Tell them to drop their weapons."

She paused, then nodded to her soldiers. Arrows went back into quivers, bows were slung. Then they dismounted, putting them a step closer to me.

"Singer," she finally said. "Did I not just save you from that . . ." She pointed at Father Croser's corpse. "That . . ." She failed to come up with a word vile enough to describe him.

"You had your own reasons to kill him."

"True enough." She lifted her chin. "But it does not change the fact that I have just saved your life."

"Hah!" I scoffed. Or tried to. My sharp exhalation turned into a death rattle of a cough that had me gargling blood for a moment. The elven soldiers were a step closer when I got it under control. I sang the opening run again and they stopped. "You haven't saved it for long."

"But I could." She dismounted. Took a step forward. "Singer," she said, taking another. "Douglas."

Too close. "You tried to have me killed, Aine."

She stopped. Stared down at me where I lay dying.

Probably gauging whether she could lie to me or not.

Then she gave a curt nod, barely a movement at all.

You bitch!

"But that was before you came into your powers," she said. "Before you knew what you could become. It is different now, Douglas. Let me touch you. Let me heal you. Let us go into Faerie. You can be my Consort. My Prince. My—"

"You killed my grandmother."

Aine looked aghast. "I did no such thing. She was an innocent, uninvolved. I would never—"

"Bullshit, Aine."

"Douglas! You know me. Sing my song. *Know* me. Tell me if I would kill the mother of your mother." She folded her arms. "I will wait."

And she was right. She couldn't have done it. I didn't need to sing the song; it was laid out in my head already. Aine was capable of a lot of things in the name of self-preservation, but the killing of innocents wasn't in her.

"It must have been the Sluagh, Singer. Your bogie friend, perhaps? My guard returned to me after failing to find you. They reported nothing else. They did nothing else."

Maybe I was wrong. Maybe it was Martes. Or one of his "collective."

"If you wish to kill me, Singer," Aine went on, "then do it for the right reasons. I tried to have you killed. This is true. But I did nothing to your grandmother."

"Wait—"

"Come, Singer. I made a mistake. Forgive me and let me heal you."

I can't think with her talking. Are the elves closer now?

"Singer?"

"I need a promise."

"Certainly."

One of the elves was definitely closer now. I tried to sit up. "Hold it. Everyone hold still."

"Yes, everyone hold still." Aine's tone was soothing. "No one is moving, Douglas. What is this promise you require?"

What had I made Martes promise?

"I need . . ."

It had seemed so ironclad, I thought. *But the little bastard still found a way around it, anyway.*

"Yes, Singer?"

Well, it didn't matter. I can tell by her song that she's no weasel like Martes. A simple promise should suffice. Look at her there. She's beautiful. Quite an improvement from when I found her in Father Croser's basement. Not a mark on her.

Not a mark on her.

"Singer?"

Hadn't she been left with a scar? I tried to think back to when I'd sung her in my bedroom. It was a different Douglas who had healed her, held her, made love to her. I had fractured since then, broken into pieces the moment I saw Grandma McLaren's head on the stairs. But . . .

Yeah, I remembered. *A little scar, right on her chin.*

But there was nothing on her face now, not a single blemish. She was beautiful, though her was nose was still a little too hawkish to be called perfect.

But what does it mean? Why is the scar gone? Did she get it fixed when she was in Faerie? And why didn't it heal when I had sung her?

"A promise," I said. "Yeah, I need a . . ."

Maybe it was because my knowledge of her wasn't complete. When I first sang her, maybe I hadn't been strong enough yet. Maybe I hadn't known enough yet. Maybe I didn't know her as well as I thought. What if she had held back something, some part of her being that she didn't want me to see? Something she didn't want me to know.

And why do these elves keep creeping closer?

"Enough, Singer. I am coming to heal you." And she marched swiftly toward me, the others close behind.

Well, she's called my bluff. I thought. *And I've got nothing left. If she's going to kill me, there's nothing I can do to stop her. Not here anyway, where, as Martes had said, "Magic works poorly, if at all."*

I looked at the open doors to Faerie. Felt the power still emanating from them.

Not here.

I glanced back at Aine. At her flawless, unscarred face.

Then I twisted my tortured frame, throwing myself into a painful barrel roll that would carry me the two yards to the double doors into Faerie.

Aine screeched and leapt forward. The ring of elven soldiers followed suit, all of them trying to reach me before I got through the doors.

I'm not going to make it!

"Up horse and hattock!"

Martes flew out from behind a pillar, throwing himself into Aine's path and lashing out with his clubbed foot. She tripped over the crippled bogie, tumbling to the grass, and lightning from her fingertips sent sod flying over and around me.

"You and yours!" Martes yelled.

Me and mine, I thought in reply. But I didn't say it out loud. It was taking all my energy to keep moving.

"Go!" Martes urged me on, and I went, rolling over the low threshold just ahead of the soldiers' outstretched hands. My wounds screamed in protest and I must have left a blood trail three feet wide. But I was through the doors.

I was in Faerie.

• • • Fourteen • • •

I had a brief impression of low, rolling hills covered with odd, iridescent flowers and a red river winding its way along the horizon, before pure raw power flooded into me like a speedball into virgin veins. I reveled in the wild rush that filled me, raising me up. Suddenly I was standing, then spinning, my wounds forgotten, though blood sprayed in thick droplets around me.

The first elf broke the plane of the doorway in pursuit. I heard him as much as saw him. He was a song construct, a creature built of melody and pitch as much as flesh and bone. I *knew* him without effort, without thought.

It's so easy here!

The elf raised some sort of sword high over his head and charged. I barely needed to breathe the notes to take him and change him into something harmless. Another elf appeared, bobbing and weaving, thrusting at me with his weapon, before losing interest and hopping away in search of flies.

The open doorway looked like a wall of water from this side, and I could see Aine's distorted form exhorting her soldiers to charge and take me. They obeyed and more elves streamed through. I sang them in bunches, slowing some till they slept, one or two just ending abruptly. But suddenly I could feel my wounds again. The power that had so recently filled me was pouring out of the wounds in my body like water spouting from a cracked vase.

Oh, I forgot. I'm dying.

It became harder to control the elves, and one of them almost reached me before suddenly developing two left feet and falling to the ground.

It's too bad, I thought, singing him to stone. *I could learn to enjoy this.*

But I was dying, and I didn't think I could stop it.

I'm sure going to try, though.

I shut the double doors with a low note and barred them with a chord. Then I began a song of myself, searching deep inside for my defining theme. It seemed I was made of different stuff than the elves, at once simpler and more complicated, stronger in some parts, much weaker in others.

The differences are fascinating. Not really where I would have guessed. But forget about that. The question is whether I can heal myself. And if I can do it in time. How about . . . here!

And the pain in my nose disappeared, the cartilage shifting back into place.

And there!

My ribs smoothed over and I could breathe easily again.

Hrmm. How about this?

The ligaments at the back of my legs knitted themselves back together.

Now for something a little more complicated.

I sang myself a new finger, watching in fascination as it sprouted raw and red.

And the big one.

My liver resumed its normal function as the gaping hole in it closed.

The doors crashed inward, their hinges shattering, and Aine finally entered the portal. She shone with power; elemental, electric power, nothing like my own. She came through crackling and sparking, shooting bolts of energy in my direction. She was stronger than the other elves, her namesong echoing off the hills of her homelands and resonating with centuries of rule, millennia of hereditary dominance. And she held Martes, my former tormentor, and at present my only ally, before her like a rat-faced shield.

I bent her easily to my will.

Hello, Aine.

Examining the new song of her, I found it subtly different from the one I had learned in the Meadows. Darker, harder, colder. She had a moral code much like Martes's, requiring only that she owe no one, and that no one owe her. Caring solely for herself and her own kind, she had dealt with humans only when it seemed the only way to avoid her own death. When that fate had been overcome, she had settled her accounts and then sent her guards to Grandma McLaren's to kill all who were there, erasing any memory of her true namesong from the world of men.

Quaking with fury, I thought, *I will make her regret that decision. I will make her pay. With every bit of my power, every inch of my being, I will make her pay.*

I looked down at my grandfather's ring. The letters of the inscription seemed to glow at me, and the translation rang in my mind.

No one harms me with impunity.

For a moment I could almost hear Grandma McLaren's voice telling me, "It sounds good. It sounds tough. But Donald died when he was twenty-four years old, and Scotland has been a subject nation for seven centuries."

But it was you Aine harmed, Grandma. Not me. And I'm going to make her sorry she ever came back to life.

I began to sing her again. It wasn't pleasant to hear. What I'd done to Martes would seem kind compared to what I had planned for her. I wanted to torture her, make her suffer, make her bleed. I wanted to see her head on the ground like Grandma McLaren's.

She's going to wish she was back in the basement with Father Croser before I'm finished.

I intended to wrack her, wreck her, destroy her piece by piece. Tear her down to nothing. Then restore her. Only to do it all over again. And when I was done, when there was nothing left of her but blood and pain, I would finally snuff her out. She'd probably be relieved to die by then.

But suddenly I stopped, remembering something important. Aine had already foreseen her own death once.

Was there another Douglas waiting in the wings to revive her? Would killing her actually release her to come after me again?

I didn't want to be too hasty. I had spent too long stumbling in the darkness, letting events rule me. It was time for me to take charge. Time to think, time to plan, time to make these creatures dance to my tune, instead of the other way around. To do this, however, I would need to change some fundamental things about my character.

I took Aine's ability to move away for the moment, all but her eyes.

Let her watch.

Then I sang the song of me again.

I changed a few things on the fly, superficial stuff, just improvising, really. I gave myself jet black hair and irises to match—no need for dye jobs or colored contacts. Sick of being junkie-thin, I put a few pounds on my frame, distributing them evenly. Then I snaked a Celtic knotwork tattoo up my new pinky.

Time to go deeper. I'm dealing with near immortal creatures. My aging is going to be a real nuisance.

I turned my song into a round, making my life loop in on itself instead of running its natural course.

Easy enough.

Human frailty? I strengthened my harmonies, bulked up my chords. My skin was leather now, my bones steel. In doing so, I discovered a circle of fourths underlying my main theme, each chord leading to the next in a sickening yet satisfying downward spiral. It infused every part of my song, wrenching the melody around and about, affecting my chordal structure in strange ways. It was parasitic, as if trying to make my life its own.

My addiction.

A simple matter to eliminate it, resolving a note here, a chord there, snapping the cycle off before its inevitable end.

I was cured.

I did the same for all my needs, eliminating the necessity for food, drink, sex, love.

What about resolve? Will I eventually forgive Aine for what she did?

I didn't think so. But one could never be too sure. I brutally stripped away any pleasing notes in my moral code. Forgiveness, love, guilt, remorse. All gone. Anything that might weaken my resolve I tore out, leaving myself nothing but a burning desire to revenge myself on Aine and her kind for what they had done to Grandma McLaren.

There was one I didn't think I'd punish any further, though.

"Douglas?" Martes said, as I pulled him to his feet.

"Yes?"

"What . . ." He paused, looking around at the dead, the sleeping, the twisted and deformed bodies of the elven soldiers. He twitched his now large rat nose. "What have you done?"

Yes, what had I done? A tiny note of uncertainty I hadn't managed to eradicate crept into my thoughts. *I've turned myself into a monster, a creature without—*

I shook my head and hummed the first notes of my new theme. *Resolve!*

The tune calmed me and a smile crept onto my features.

"I've decided to become king of this place, Martes."

Martes said nothing. I could feel Aine's eyes boring into my back. Could sense her testing the bonds I had laid on her.

You'll not break them, Aine. I put the words directly into her mind. *You'll not get free.*

She struggled then, as well as she could without the ability to move. I turned to face her, watching her intently. She concentrated every bit of strength she had, every ounce of will, every piece of power she had built up since birth, and she sent it in my direction, trying to burn me down to my big black boots.

One tiny spark dropped from her index finger and fizzled on the ground.

You'll never get free.

I turned back to Martes. "Well?"

"Em . . ." He sputtered. "Er . . . What can I do for you?" he asked, his voice positively quavering. I raised one eyebrow and beckoned for just a little more. "Um . . . Sire?"

My smile broke fully open into a long slow grin. "You can go, Martes," I said. "Go and prepare my kingdom for me."

"Yes, my lord," he said, bowing repeatedly as he backed away. He turned and broke into a speedy limp after a few yards, and then shouted the now familiar, "Up horse and hattock!" Rising into the air like a misshapen helium balloon breaking free of its child, he soared toward the nearest hill. Reaching the top, he hovered there for a second, then turned and came screaming back.

I sighed and hummed the first note of his song, wondering if I should just kill him and be done with it.

Tough to get good help these days. But if he can't follow the simplest of directions . . .

"Boss, wait!" he screamed. "We've got company."

"Oh, do we?" I watched the horizon. I didn't have to wait long.

A hundred horses trampled iridescent flowers into mud as a troop of elven cavalry crested the hill that Martes had just fled. Rows of elven archers followed behind, the strings of their slung bows cutting crosswise across the white hind rampant on their chests. Two elephantine creatures, like the Pictish beasties carved into standing stones, flanked the archers on either side, the large baskets cinched to their backs holding more elves armed with halberds and spears. Then a mass of lower-caste faeries came whooping and hollering over the hilltop, swinging and waving a variety of weaponry.

"You and yours, Douglas," Martes said. "I am pledged to advise you in all things faery-related."

A ballista creaked into view, like a giant crossbow on wheels. It appeared to be manned by humans. Changelings, captured as infants and raised for slave labor.

Possibly caught by Martes himself, I thought.

Glancing at Aine, I could see her eyes were smiling, though the rest of her couldn't budge.

No, I put in her mind again. *You'll not get free.*

But she still looked happy.

No one man can face down an army. She didn't have to put the words in my mind; it's what she would have said.

"And after much thought," Martes continued, "I advise you to run."

I turned back to the advancing army, trying to count them, but only for a moment. There were too many.

"No," I said. "I don't think I'll run."

And I walked forward to meet them.

One of the mounted elves shouted an order, and the mob of foot soldiers charged down the hill, still shouting at the top of their lungs. The cavalry split into two groups and streamed around the flanks, slowly lowering their long spears till the points faced forward. Toward me. I heard whips crack and the two beasties began lumbering up to speed. The archers notched arrows and aimed high, waiting for the order to send an arcing volley in support, and a member of the ballista team poised over the trigger mechanism, preparing to skewer me with a ten-foot bolt.

I blew them all apart with a single note.

"Poof," I said, and turned to look at Aine. Watched the hope die in her eyes.

And as a blood mist settled to the ground, I smiled. Apparently I had missed one nonessential emotion in my purge: the satisfaction of a job well done.

No matter. I shall keep it.

I took one last look at the carnage surrounding me, before facing downhill, toward the red river that snaked across the horizon and the kingdom that lay beyond. My kingdom, now. Then I marched into Faerie, with Martes by my side and Aine, like a dog at heel, two paces behind.

• • • Epilogue • • •

Time moves strangely in Faerie, sometimes rushing forward like a horse at canter, sometimes pacing off the hours with torturous precision. On occasion, I thought I could feel it stop altogether. Or move backward.

The Battle for Calton Hill may have been yesterday or centuries past. I didn't know. Or much care.

"There are grumblings in your kingdom, my lord." Martes's grotesque nose twitched, a habit even I couldn't seem to break him of. "Prophecies and portents, omens and—"

I hummed his mouth closed. "Enough." Shut his nose, too, for good measure. "I've heard it all before. If they become worrisome, I'll sing them away." I waved my hand, and an elven girl scampered forward with a bottle of wine. As she poured, I noticed that she looked a bit like Aine. Well, like Aine had when I'd first met her. In fact, most of my servants ran to type: slim, raven-haired beauties with blue eyes and—

Hrmm. May have to sing myself again. Cure myself of some of these hidden sentimentalities.

I whistled two notes and Martes's mouth popped open. As he gasped for breath, I asked, "Do you have any real news?"

"I do." He rubbed his hand over his mouth, as if checking to see if his lips were still there. "It's Aine."

"What about her?" *She couldn't have escaped. Or died. I'd made sure of that.*

"She's pregnant."

"What?" I must have roared, for Martes flinched, twitching his nose frantically, and the servant girl dropped the wine bottle to shatter on the floor.

"Pregnant. A boy."

"What?"

"I said she's pregnant." Then the old Martes resurfaced for a second as he added: "Bugger a brownie, boss, deafness going to be a problem for you? Being a musician and all?"

Might have to re-sing him, *too.* I watched the wine pooling on the flagstones. *Or not. His oath keeps him as loyal as any spell. And honestly, it'd be pretty boring without him around.*

"Who got her pregnant? No, wait." I sighed. "It has to have been me."

Martes gave a leering grin. It was an amazingly ugly expression on his twisted face. "Once you had her, *jefe,* you ruined her for anyone else."

I didn't smile. "I guess I'll have to sing her again. Get rid of the baby."

Martes's smirk faded. "I suppose so, my Lord."

Not wishing to risk another bottle on the terrified slave, I stood and walked to the wine rack myself. I chose a thousand-year red, and popped the cork with my hands. "Or . . ." I took a long pull straight from the bottle. "Maybe I'll let her have the little bastard."

"Whatever you say, my lord."

"Yeah. Maybe I will." The wine was thick as blood and sweet like cherries, with a pepper note that livened the tongue. "Wonder which one of us he'll look like?"